TERMINAL PULSE

A Codi Sanders Thriller

BRENT LADD

ARCHWAY
PUBLISHING

Archway Publishing books may be ordered through booksellers or by contacting:

Archway Publishing
1663 Liberty Drive
Bloomington, IN 47403
www.archwaypublishing.com
1 (888) 242-5904

ISBN: 978-1-4808-6418-4 (sc)
ISBN: 978-1-4808-6417-7 (hc)
ISBN: 978-1-4808-6419-1 (e)

Library of Congress Control Number: 2018907151

Print information available on the last page.

Archway Publishing rev. date: 07/10/2018

CHAPTER ONE

JANUARY 1945

Dust blew past Axel's face as he peered down at the old barn from his high vantage point. He spit out a mouthful of the coppery earth and blinked several times to clear his vision. He checked the black-and-white map for the tenth time and then gave his compass one last furtive glance. He was sure this was the wrong location. But all the information up to this point that Oberfuhrer Hans Kaufman of the German High Command had given him had been spot on.

Military intelligence in 1945 was a delicate recipe. An intercepted communiqué or even boots on the ground still didn't guarantee accuracy or success. More than once Axel had been blindsided by incomplete or outright false information. At age thirty, he was one of Germany's most experienced field agents.

Axel had spent the last three days on a highway to nowhere. It seemed equal to the entire breadth of Germany without a single turn. This cursed country was just too big and spread out. The desert, though at times beautiful, was not to his liking. And the never-ending sameness could easily lull the senses, or worse, get you lost.

His objective was an old barn in northern Arizona. He'd almost laughed out loud the first time he heard the name; it was such a funny word—Arizona. The weathered green building looked about as threatening to the war effort as Hitler's dog. The wind had picked up in the last few minutes and the sand it carried pelted him without mercy. Axel pulled his collar up around his neck and covered the side of his face with his left arm. He wondered how this could possibly help Germany win the war.

So far, he'd been very successful and if he could find and terminate his next two targets, he would have accomplished what no other agent in the history of the war had. Axel smiled at the thought as he raised his binoculars for one more look. Yep, he was definitely in the wrong place.

Ten days ago, he had slipped ashore onto Cat Island, a five-mile-long, T-shaped spit of dirt seven miles from the Gulf Coast of Mississippi. The U-boat had found a deep channel on the backside to make his egress relatively simple. It had taken only seven minutes once the conning tower of the submarine surfaced until it was back under for Hauptmann Rittmeister Axel Gunther and all his gear to evac. He then swam to shore through the warm current, pulling a rope attached to his wax-coated US Army musette gear bag. The bag was a donation from a captured US Army POW.

The backside of Cat Island was layered. It started with a soft sandy beach that gave way to saw grass and finally to a clogged forest of trees and swamp. It was void of all life except for mosquitoes and water moccasins. Snakes didn't bother Axel, but mosquitoes, that was another story. The annoying buzz around your ears, the sneak attacks that left you scratching for days. The little blood suckers were undoubtedly the worst of God's creations and they were copious on Cat Island.

The far side of the island hosted the US Army's secret war dog reception and training center. And every now and then he could hear a distant bark carried on the light sea breeze. Axel smirked as he recalled reading the details of the facility. The sole purpose of the center was to train dogs to detect and attack Japanese soldiers based on their unique scent. The army had grabbed twenty-five Japanese Americans and conscripted them to act as bait for the attack dogs. *What a waste of war funds,* he thought. *Surely the Americans were doomed to lose this war.*

Axel's footprints left a trail in the soft sand as he pushed past the beach and through the saw grass. He picked his way through the forest of pine and water oaks, trying in vain to keep the mosquitoes at bay. The underbrush was thick and impassable. He glanced back out at the ocean one last time. There was no sign of the U-boat that had brought him, just the sliver of a waning moon dancing off the silvery reflection of the water.

There was no turning back. His country was counting on him and Axel would do everything in his power to succeed. At five-foot-ten, Axel had a lean, muscular torso that read like a history book of previous missions: two scarred-over bullet holes and a C-shaped scar as a result of a knife fight he had nearly lost in Norway. Currently he was sporting a full beard and wild, matted brown hair.

It took nearly an hour of scrabbling through the tangled growth to go the half mile to the other side of the island. Twice he had to swim and crawl through fetid pools. Axel paused to catch his breath. He dropped his burdensome gear bag in the sand. The air was pungent with salt and rotten vegetation and the subtle warm breeze did little to cool his sweat-drenched face. But the sight of twinkling lights in the distance sent a small quiver down his spine. *America.*

He quickly got to work inflating a small Army Air Corp life raft that had been acquired for this mission. Nothing was left to chance. Even his clothes matched those of an American airman, just in case he was discovered. Axel felt the prick of a bite on the back of his neck and swatted it. This was going to be a long night.

He quickly launched the raft into the calm water and began his long trip to the mainland. He estimated it would take four to five hours to reach the marina he had in mind. He set a pace that would allow him to maintain a consistent three knots. At least he was saying goodbye to the mosquitoes.

The first inklings of light strafed the sky and started the perpetual morning transition from black to purple. Axel used his Rohm SS dagger to quickly deflate the raft and a loose cleat from the dock to help send it to the bottom of the marina. The dagger was his one ode to the fatherland that he had brought with him. He would never forget the moment Oberfuhrer Hans Kaufman had given it to him.

Hans was the closest thing to a father Axel had left in the world. It was Hans who pushed him to get involved with the Nazi Party and ultimately the SS, where his skills helped make him one of the most successful operatives in Germany. Axel was given the knife after completing a difficult mission three months prior in Liverpool.

Walter Gerlach, a leading German physicist involved in Germany's atomic development, had been captured by the British while on a train to Dusseldorf. He was then secreted out of the country. Walter Gerlach knew too much and the thought of the allies interrogating him was untenable at any level by the German high command. Posing as a Canadian colonel, Axel had gotten close enough to slip an ice pick into the right ear canal of the physicist. The act had caused such an intense manhunt that Axel had to abandon his planned escape route. It took two weeks and a lot of clever duplicity before he made his way back onto German soil.

Axel slipped the venerated knife back into a hidden sleeve just inside his coat. He crouched behind a battered crate at the end of a wooden pier and took in his surroundings. Thirty boats lay moored in the quaint harbor, some sailboats but mostly shrimpers. Single-masted diesel power boats with an open deck around a central cabin; each with a steep prow. The waterfront had its unique odor of diesel and rotted shrimp. The air was still and all was tranquil except for the normal clanking of cables and stays against their masts.

Axel's eyes finally fell upon a boat that would fit his needs. He grabbed his musette bag and silently moved towards her. The boat was named *Tiger Shark*, but nothing about her looks matched the moniker. The hull was painted a light blue that was mostly covered in rust, though how an old wooden hull had rusted was a mystery to him. A faded red cabin sat up by the bow and a single rigged mast followed behind with a flat deck work area behind it. He silently placed his gear bag over the transom on the aft deck and boarded.

Axel stepped past a mound of nets and carefully maneuvered around the detritus littering the deck. He reached for the tarnished bronze latch on the cabin door and then froze at the sound of movement inside. The owner was aboard and awake.

He pulled out his 9mm British Welrod silenced pistol. It had been confiscated from a dead spy in Norway and Axel had to agree it was perfect for this mission. The pistol was designed at the Inter-Services Research Bureau for use by irregular forces. It had a 1.25-inch-diameter cylinder that was twelve inches long. It used a ported barrel and multiple baffles to diffuse sound and, at the same time, slow the bullet down to subsonic speed. The knurled knob at the rear served as the bolt handle. The in-grip magazine held eight bullets. The Welrod could be fired as fast as you could recycle the bolt and in close range was as deadly as it was quiet.

Axel slid through the hatch door to the cabin and without hesitation shot the boat's owner. One to the torso and the one to the head. The owner barely had time to register the intrusion.

One down, many to go.

CHAPTER TWO

Cruising up the Mississippi River was new for Axel. The muddy water held her secrets and the wall of vegetation on her banks made it difficult to see the river from land. Only the occasional shoreline town broke the monotony. But the *Tiger Shark's* 13R Grey one-lung diesel engine held steady and strong with its distinctive *chug, chug* sound as it pushed north upriver.

It had been six months since D-Day and the Americans were proving to be a real problem for Germany. Axel held high hopes that this mission would make a difference. He had adopted some of the boat owner's clothes and together with his wild hair and beard that he had grown out during his Atlantic crossing, he fit the part perfectly—just another wild fisherman plying the local waters in search of a living.

As the breeze off the water cooled his face, he allowed himself time to reflect. This was what he had trained for. This was for his father and his country. If he kept his wits, everything would work out. After all, America was at war, so everyone was preoccupied. No one would take notice of a man who seemed to fit right in.

Private Andrew Rollins stood stock straight at attention. Even though it was night he could feel the heat radiating off the tarmac. The recent rain did nothing to quell the humidity or the temperature. But Andrew was used to the heat. He had been raised in a wooden shanty fifty miles from here. His daddy had spent almost every waking hour working the cotton fields for a nearby plantation. His momma was a strong woman who had literally beaten him into manhood, so at the first chance Andrew got, he ran off. His plan was to join the Coast Guard or the Army.

The Army said yes, but just barely. What he didn't know was that they had very little use for an uneducated black private.

Twelve weeks of boot camp was simple compared to how things were back home. Private Rollins distinguished himself in the physical components, but his lack of education made the mental part a struggle. The fact that he was a quick learner however, saved him in the end. Following boot camp, Private Andrew Rollins was loaded into a transport truck along with twenty-five of his fellow soldiers and dropped off here. Wherever here was, was anybody's guess.

"Ten-hut!" The new sergeant in charge approached. The enlisted men scrambled to assemble themselves, each one of them eager to serve his country. Private Andrew Rollins quickly filed in and stood ramrod straight at attention. His new uniform was the nicest set of clothes he'd ever owned. He would repay the army with only his best effort.

The sergeant walked up and down the line. Each man held his eyes forward, no one daring to make eye contact. The only sound was distant crickets sounding off in the night. "Riding herd over a bunch of Negroes is not my idea of a good time," the sergeant said. "But when the Army assigned you bunch to me, they said you were special. Is that right? Are you special?"

He was met with silence.

"I can't hear you!"

"Sir, no, sir!"

"I didn't think so. You there, step forward." The sergeant was clearly pointing at Private Rollins.

Rollins did a double-take and then stepped forward, blinking the sweat from his eyes. He tried to exhibit the best at attention ever displayed.

"I want *you*, Private…?" The sergeant looked at Rollins in anticipation of an answer.

"Private Rollins, sir!"

"…Private Rollins to make sure that all you 'volunteers' report to building F-12. Is that clear?"

He said *volunteers* in his most belittling way, but Rollins wasn't going to take the bait. "Yes, sir," He said with a false bravado. "Sir, where is building F-12?" He instantly regretted the question.

The sergeant walked right up to Rollins and stood nose-to-nose. Rollins could smell the collard greens and grits on the tyrant's breath. "Am I gonna have trouble with you?"

"No sir. Just a bit lost, sir."

The sergeant held his gaze and then started a slow nod. "Building F-12 is one hundred yards due east." He pointed. "You'll recognize it by the F-12 printed on the door. You know what an F is?"

Rollins nodded eagerly.

The sergeant continued to stare down the private. Rollins smartly dipped his head in defeat.

"Dismissed." The sergeant spun on his heels and walked off.

Rollins took a moment to collect himself. One of his friends from boot camp put his hand on his shoulder and they shared a silent, *that was close*. Private Andrew Rollins then gathered the men and the all-African American squad marched to building F-12.

Major Lou Grubbs watched as his team double-checked their equipment. He was proud of his work and knew that one day he would be personally responsible for helping end the war. At fifty-five, Grubbs was no figure of health. His obsessive personality, combined with a poor diet and zero exercise, had his blood pressure and his body fat high.

Fletcher Army Airfield, outside of Clarksdale, Mississippi, was well off the beaten path. The Major's little collection of "F" buildings weren't on any map. In fact, the top-secret classification kept his project very isolated from the well-publicized pilot training that the rest of the base was engaged in. Other than an additional security fence, it was all on a need-to-know basis.

"All set to go, sir," his corporal said.

"Good. Make sure the men get in and situated."

"Will do, sir."

Building F-12 was one of six wooden structures arranged in a U pattern. They were painted Army green and had grey asphalt-shingled roofs. In a word—unremarkable. The corporal unlocked and opened the door to building F-12. Private Rollins led his squad inside where there were three rows of wooden benches mounted to a forward slanting concrete floor. Two bare bulbs hung from the rafters and tried to illuminate the room. A large reflective glass panel was built into the front wall and four eight-inch drain grates ran along the floor in front of it. Baby poop-colored brown paint covered everything.

Private Rollins felt a sense of pride that he had been asked to lead the squad and was now delivering on the sergeant's orders. He couldn't wait to write his folks back home in Haynesville and tell 'em all about it. A special mission and *he* was in charge. Well, one of the leaders, anyway. That would set momma straight.

He waited until his squad was seated and then joined them, sitting on the edge of the front bench. The corporal moved to the front of the room and got everyone's attention. "The Army would like to thank you for your participation today." He moved as he talked and didn't look anyone in the eye. "Make yourself comfortable. I'll be back in a few minutes."

Axel stayed low as he serpentined across the empty field. Breaching the boundary of the base had required some stealth, but here inside the second perimeter fence there were no guards, just a collection of wooden buildings, each marked with the letter F followed by a number. He found a stack of five-gallon gas cans beside one of the buildings. One thing the US had in the 1940's was plenty of gas for its military. He quickly modified his plan and went to work.

Rollins beamed as the corporal exited and closed the door behind him. But his smile froze when the door made the sound of being locked from the outside. A speaker that hung from one of the rafters squawked and came to life. An emotionless voice cut in. "Hello. I want to thank you for being part of this test group. Your service to this country is much appreciated." From inside the control room Major Grubbs spoke into the microphone while he watched the soldiers through the one-way mirror.

"We will be running a few simple tests. If at any time you feel uncomfortable, please raise your hand and we will stop the exercise. Once again, thank you for volunteering. Your efforts today will help save thousands of allied lives."

Grubbs turned off the microphone and glanced at his corporal. "It's time," he said. "Batch 1023 first run, twenty-five subjects."

The corporal then twisted three levers and returned to the one-way mirror with a clipboard and pencil in hand. He casually wrote down the batch number and subject count.

Inside building F-12, a yellowish-grey smoke began to waft through the air. Concern turned to murmuring and then commotion, but everyone held their seats.

Private Rollins stared, disbelieving, as the smoke spread its way through the room. "What the hell?"

Someone in the back screamed like he'd been burned or maybe stung and immediately hands started to rise. Soon everyone was raising their arms and shaking them to make sure they were seen.

Then the second scream let loose. Whatever this gas was, it was literally melting their skin. Two men from the back row jumped up and ran for the exit door. When it wouldn't open, complete chaos ensued. The soldiers fought to break out of the room. Rollins stood back trying to put meaning to the moment. Some of the men had fallen to the ground, their faces unrecognizable. Their bodies twitched and convulsed with pain.

Inside the control room, Major Grubbs looked at the mayhem in a detached way. "Forty-five seconds to complete loss of control," the corporal said more to himself than to anyone in particular.

"Excellent," Grubbs said. "Looks like we have a viable solution. Let's get another group in here right away to confirm the results."

Private Rollins ran to the glass and pounded it with his fists as hard as he could, each impact leaving more and more of his flesh on the mirror. His lips and half of his face had already sagged to the floor. His mind now completely gone mad with pain, he managed one last thought before he collapsed—Momma was right. Never trust whitey.

Grubbs turned from the glass and sat down at his desk. He went through and double-checked his notes. The corporal turned off the gas valves and then flicked the switch to the exhaust fans. He watched as the smoke in F-12 was carried away, revealing a visage of carnage few would ever see.

Major Grubbs smelled it first. Smoke. "Shut down the exhaust! Something is burning." He grabbed the gas mask off a post and put it on. His lab assistants followed suit and moved for the exit. But it wouldn't open. Something was blocking the door. Flames were starting to break through. "What's happening here?"

"The building's on fire, sir."

Grubbs ran to the water valve that controlled ceiling sprinklers for just this event. He spun it to the open position—but nothing happened. The flames were now all around him and he quickly realized the hopelessness of it all. Sabotage.

He started grabbing all of his notes and files. He must save the research at any cost. Flaming pieces started falling from the ceiling, starting more fires. An assistant triggered the one fire extinguisher they had and fire-retardant foam shot out to delay the inevitable. Another flaming chunk of roof dropped and hit Grubbs. His hair went up in flames. Desperate, he started smacking his head with his lab notes to put out the flames and they caught fire too.

Building F-12 suddenly erupted in an enormous fireball. The three cans of gasoline that had been strategically placed had finally over-heated. It consumed what was left of the twenty-five-man squad, the observation lab and the two bordering structures. Major Grubbs' body was transformed into charred ash along with everything he had been working on. This was the kind of blaze that consumed wooden struc-tures with ease. And before it could be contained, there would be noth-ing left but six building-sized piles of ash and a blackened perimeter security fence.

Axel scooted across the road, back to the boundary fence from where he had come. Glancing back, he allowed himself a brief moment of satisfaction. This was a proud moment for Germany. He hoped his dad was watching. He took the time to repair the hole he'd made in the fence and to remove any trace of his infiltration before disappearing into the night.

CHAPTER THREE

Lieutenant Colonel James Whitsole sat in a booth in his favorite café. Louise's had two things going for it: the food was all-American and it was close to one of the largest military bases in Kansas, Strother Army Airfield. Plus, it had one of the first Wurlitzer model 1015's in the state. *Rum and Coca-Cola* by the Andrews Sisters played on what would become known as a jukebox. James sipped his coffee while he absently pushed around his remaining hash browns. A thought popped into his head and he pulled his ubiquitous notebook and a pencil from his pocket and jotted down something. Across the room at a booth sat two MP's who kept a wary eye on him. Sign of the times, James thought.

James, also known as The Professor, wore a white collared shirt with khaki pants. As far as he was concerned, his military rank was their idea, not his. He may be working for the Army Air Corps but he didn't have to advertise. After all, he was a distinguished scientist who'd proven his worth both in academia and in the practical world as well. He glanced at his waitress. She was a touch over forty and clinging to her fading good looks. Her sizeable rack strained just enough against her uniform to get attention.

He tried to remember her name, but that wasn't his thing.

"Professor, can I get you anything else?"

It snapped him out of his reverie and he slyly glanced at her nametag. "No thanks, Rita, I'm good. Just the check, please."

She smiled and set the check on the gingham tablecloth next to him.

As James headed out to his car, the two MP's followed. "I really wish you two would wait for me at the base," he said.

"Those aren't our orders, sir," one replied.

"What's gonna happen to me in the middle of Kansas? Better watch out 'cause Rita's serving extra spicy sausage."

The two MP's shared a frustrated glance. They couldn't agree more. The war was not here. They needed to dump this asshole and get into the real action overseas. But orders were orders.

Axel, now clean-shaven with his hair cut high and tight, lowered his binoculars from across the street in his stolen '37 Buick coupe, a two-tone cream-and-black hardtop. Its signature blade-like nose and bullet headlights helped conceal the powerful valve-in-head straight-eight-cylinder engine.

It had belonged to a couple traveling out of Chicago who had been kind enough to give him a lift. He had left their bodies in a small ravine two counties back.

The best part of the vehicle was attached to the inside of the Buick's windshield, an X gas-rationing sticker. Unlike the common A or B stickers which were limited to four or eight gallons per week, the X sticker allowed for unlimited fill-ups.

Axel breathed in the sweet pungent odor of the unfiltered American cigarette. Using his thumb and ring finger, he grabbed and flicked off a speck of tobacco from his tongue. Finally his patience had paid off.

He watched as the professor and his two bodyguards exited the café, got into a jeep and drove off. Axel was dressed in clothes that mirrored the professor's, a white collared shirt and khakis he had purchased at the local Woolworths. He had washed the clothes along with a half-cup of coffee to give them a lived-in look, the look that just about everyone in America had right now.

Axel strode with confidence over to Louise's Café, while whistling

Yankee Doodle. He gestured and smiled to a young couple leaving the diner. She was wearing a polka-dot skirt and a white round-collar blouse. He was wearing a leather bomber jacket and crutches. The man pulled out a cigarette and checked his pockets for a match. Without hesitation, Axel pulled out his lighter, saying, "Allow me."

The tip glowed red and the man thanked Axel as he and the woman left the diner.

Axel chose a booth in the back with a full view of the diner. He waited as Rita came over. "Howdy, little lady," he said in perfect English. "Coffee and two eggs over easy with bacon."

Rita smiled and took the order.

Axel had spent seven years of his youth in Detroit. His father, whom he idolized, was one of the top engineers for Opel Auto Manufacturing. In a business arrangement with the Dodge brothers, Opel was co-developing a new line of trucks that could haul loads over virtually any landscape.

During his time in Detroit, Axel's mother helped him learn all things American. His English became faultless and his ability to fit in uncanny. He even played baseball and ate apple pie.

German Military Intelligence had later seized upon these skills and thus began his intensive training program. Learning to shoot and kill was important, but he quickly found that his natural ability to fit in and disarm people with a smile or a phrase was priceless. He could beguile even the most cautious person.

When Axel's father was killed during an American bombing raid on the Opel truck plant in Russelsheim, something changed in Axel. What had always seemed like a game to him was suddenly something very real. He became obsessed with beating the Americans at all costs, blaming them for the loss of his father and making Axel the perfect choice for this deep-cover complex operation.

Before Axel left the docks in Hamburg, his surrogate father, Hans, came to see him off. They shared a coffee and a bratwurst at a *gasthaus* café. The sun made a rare appearance for that time of year and Axel took that as a good omen. Hans looked him in the eye and said, "Four targets are a lot for anyone. Take your time, don't get in a hurry and savor each kill." Axel smiled at the advice; he knew Hans was right. "Your father would be so proud of the man you've become."

Axel dipped his head for a second and then looked Hans in the eye. "Thank you for seeing me off," he said. He stood, saluted and left for America.

During the weeks it took to deliver him to the gulf coast, Axel spent his time going over every detail of his mission and committing them to memory, as it would be impossible to explain his way out of having these types of documents in his possession. He listened to wax recordings of popular American music and was given a few radio broadcasts from the Chicago ABC affiliate. He committed everything to memory so he could whistle a popular tune or talk about the latest anything-American to anyone he met.

Four targets in four weeks and then he was to be picked up off the shore of a little cove north of San Diego. Every detail and contingency had been thought of, but Axel knew plans rarely survived first contact with the enemy. And as a German spy on American soil, he was the enemy.

So far, however, his raid on the clandestine weaponized gases testing base in Mississippi had gone off with out any issues. He had watched in the distance as the fires he set had taken out the entire facility. By the time fire crews arrived, the wooden structures were all ablaze. Now he was on to his next operation, the assassination of one of the greatest avionics masterminds in America.

Professor James Whitsole, a man known for keeping his research to himself until it was fully developed, was currently working on a long-range radar system small enough to fit on a plane. He had an idea for a reduced power source using low-power gas tubes filled with argon rather than nitrogen gas. The initial tests were very promising.

Axel watched as Rita brought his breakfast over to him. "Here you go," she said. "Can I refill your coffee?"

"Sure. Wasn't that Professor Whitsole that was just in here?"

Rita braced at the stranger's question. "Yeah, why?"

"Oh, I'm Fred and I'm being transferred here to Strother. I'm supposed to be working with him starting tomorrow."

Rita's posture relaxed "Sorry. You know what they say, 'loose lips sink ships.'"

"Exactly."

"He's a great man, comes in here every morning and eats the same thing. He likes his routines, I guess. Always writing in that notebook of his. Plus, he always remembers my name."

"Is that so? Maybe tomorrow you can introduce me so I can get a leg up on my new job?"

Rita tugged at the red scarf in her chestnut hair. "Okay. But it'll cost you."

Axel looked up at her with a big smile and all the flirt he had in him. "Deal. As soon as I get settled, how 'bout dinner tomorrow night?"

Trying not to sound too anxious, Rita said, "That'd be lovely." She couldn't contain her smile as she walked off to serve another customer. Axel's eyes lingered on Rita's slim waist and ran down to her still-firm ass. Just maybe this job would have a few perks, he thought.

The moon hid behind a wall of clouds making their trek across the plains. Strother Army Airfield had something very important going on. Axel looked out at the lights and the guards stationed every couple-hundred feet. He was parked on a small dirt turnout several hundred yards away. The constant stream of aircraft coming and going made for good distractions, but the guards paid little heed, keeping their focus on the perimeter. Plus, there was no cover for at least a hundred yards out from the fence in every direction, leaving no easy way in.

Sunrise and sunset in Kansas look identical. The never-ending flat horizon has a mirroring effect. Axel awoke to his internal alarm as the first rays of orange spread across the sky. He was shaved, dressed and inside Louise's diner just before the jeep with two bodyguards and Professor Whitsole arrived. He was anxious to finish this assignment and move to the next, but Han's advice echoed back at him. Patience.

The coffee was just how Axel liked it, hot and black. He sipped with a relaxed exterior pose, while on the inside he was on full alert. He held no illusions of what would happen should he be caught.

Rita's good mood effervesced. She carried her emotions on her sleeve, excited about her date with the handsome new scientist that night. Her constant doting was getting to Axel, but he played along.

Eventually the place started filling up and she had to attend to other customers. Professor Whitsole ate his usual breakfast at his usual table, with his two bodyguards sitting at the bar keeping watch—truly a man of routine. As the check was brought over to the professor, Axel could see Rita whisper something in his ear. The professor looked Axel straight in the eyes. Axel did his best to look casual and smiled with a little wave. The professor paused to consider things and then eventually smiled back and nodded.

Axel pulled out the ring he had brought with him and slipped it onto his finger. It was made of burnished gold and looked like a class ring with an engraved eagle surrounded by a bezel of oak leaves with two crossed swords at the bottom. But this was not your average ring, because when the bezel was rotated, a small pin-like spike emerged between the eagle's claws. The spike was coated with a specialized chemical developed by his friends back at the medical division of the Schutzstaffel, commonly referred to as the SS. All Axel had to do was break the skin with the spike and the chemical would do the rest.

Axel rotated the ring so that the spike was facing outward from his palm. He had to be careful not to graze his own hand on the sharp spike. He looked up as the professor walked towards him. Axel stood up.

Immediately sensing something was amiss, the two bodyguards got up and moved in. The professor waved them off with a frustrated look and walked up to Axel and said, "So you're part of the new group?"

"I am."

"What's your specialty?"

"Now, Professor, you know I can't talk about that here."

"Of course, all these stupid rules. After you get checked in, come by my lab so I can see what you'll be good for."

"I look forward to it." Axel reached out and shook the professor's hand.

"Ouch!" The professor jerked his hand back reflexively.

"Oh, I'm so sorry," Axel said. "This stupid old ring."

The professor rubbed his hand. "Quite all right," he said, not meaning it. "I'll see you later." He stormed off in a huff with his bodyguards in tow.

Rita came bounding up as Axel rotated the bezel of his ring to cover the spike and then spun it back around his finger. She handed him a scrap of paper with her address. He acted as if nothing else mattered other than her. "Great. Pick you up at, say, seven?"

"That would be perfect."

He glanced at her large breasts packed into her uniform and felt almost disappointed he would miss the foray.

Just then, out of the corner of his eye he saw the professor drop to the ground outside by his jeep. Axel tried to look astounded as people from the diner moved to see what was happening. But he knew the professor wasn't long for this world. The two bodyguards were in a panic as their charge lay jerking on the ground. They quickly loaded him into the jeep and sped off to the base.

Rita spun around, saying, "Did you see—"

Axel was nowhere to be found.

CHAPTER FOUR

The binoculars revealed a weathered green barn that looked like it was built directly against a sandstone cliff. The barn was the classic style, two-story with a hayloft up top and a pitched roof. On the main level were two small windows on either side of a large rolling door. A small light glowed from the galvanized fixture outside, painting the front wall with an inverted V-shaped glow and illuminating a collection of unused farm equipment outside. A 1938 Ford flatbed pickup truck was just recognizable in the shadows haphazardly parked nearby. The darkness made its paint color unidentifiable.

This was definitely the wrong place. But until he had officially checked it off his list he had to take a quick look inside. Axel looked at the moonless sky covered in black clouds. There would never be a better time to make his move, so he did.

Years of training instantly kicked in as he dropped down off the slight berm he had been hiding on and quickly covered the distance across the field to the farm equipment outside the barn. He crouched beside an old disc plow that had more rust on it than an unpainted iron rivet in a sea wall.

Axel strained his hearing for anything out of the ordinary. There was nothing but the occasional cricket. This was definitely the wrong place. He considered moving to his next target, which he felt was the most important of them all, a physicist by the name of Robert Oppenheimer who was just to the south of where he was, working in secret at a laboratory in Los Alamos, New Mexico. Axel had something very special planned for him.

After listening to nothing but crickets for three more minutes Axel stood and casually walked towards the barn doors, just to be sure. Then he heard a loud clank and instinct took over. He was flat against the barn door in a flash. He waited a second and then slipped inside.

In an instant, Axel knew he was in the right place. The barn was built up against a large sandstone cavern that easily went back a hundred yards. Evenly spaced work lights illuminated four large radio-style towers in the center of the cavern. Beyond that was a large concentration of equipment that looked electrical in nature. The air smelled of ozone and he noticed that the hairs on his arms were standing on end.

He pulled the Welrod from its holster and cycled the rear bolt. He could hear some sort of tinkering in the distance over by an electrical apparatus. *Jingle Jangle Jingle* by Kay Kyser played on a static-filled radio in the background. Axel carefully made his way to the back of the barn. Wooden barn beams and unused apparatus gave way to a concrete floor with sandstone walls and ceiling. This place was not guarded because it was so well disguised. He wondered how his superiors had known of its existence.

A worker in a lab coat stepped out in front of Axel from behind a large metal console and for a brief second both men recoiled in surprise, but Axel wasted no time putting a bullet in the young man's forehead before he could call out.

Axel quickly cycled the slide-knob on the back of his weapon, ducked behind a coil of wire and tried to re-establish his surroundings. He could just make out another figure in the distance who was singing along with the song. "I got spurs that jingle jangle jingle." Spotting through the glowing fluorescent-painted sights on his weapon, Axel tried to get an accurate site, but equipment blocked the singing man. He moved into the space between the radio towers to get a better shot, but the subject again moved out of view. Axel slowly started creeping forward.

The man yelled, "Jackson, Test number 237 coming up. You ready?"

Axel put on his best American accent from the southwest and said, "Yep!"

The two radio towers started to hum. Then an ethereal glow started to emanate from the tops of the towers. Axel was mesmerized by the display, but soon realized he was not in a good location. He quickly moved for cover, but before he could go two steps, a giant ball of lightning formed between the towers and fired straight at him.

The last thing Axel thought before it hit him was, how he had let his father down and would never see his beloved motherland again. The ball pulsed once and then was gone. The only thing left behind was the Welrod silenced pistol and the Rohm SS Dagger he had carried in his boot.

Hauptmann Rittmeister Axel Gunther had vanished.

Chapter Five

Current Day

Codi sat with a definitive plop. She placed her hands behind her head and interlocked her fingers. Her shoulder-length brown hair swayed behind her. The frayed government issued black chair squeaked from lack of use but managed to allow a slight recline. She looked from her half-empty coffee cup over to the stack of boxes labeled with her name. Lieutenant Colette Sanders was printed in a very generic font on the worn cardboard boxes that had been delivered and stacked in no particular order. Codi flicked away a crop of stray hairs that had fallen in her face and paused a moment to take in her new surroundings.

The ten-by-twelve beige office with no windows and one door had the distinct smell of bleach and old carpet. That's when it hit her how far from her life's goals she had fallen. The normally unbending will that helped define and push her surrendered to emotion. It started to overwhelm her. First a burning in her chest and then excess water in the eyes. But this was not the time or place. She exhaled hard several times and let the sensation dwindle. *Get ahold of yourself.*

It was day one of her new job. Codi flicked the moisture from her eyes with her middle finger and gathered herself. She reached for the now cold cup of coffee and twisted at the bitter taste. It seemed every federal agency had bad coffee. But it was just what she needed to help regain some control. A knock on the door yanked her back to the present. With the back of her hand she dabbed at the rest of her tears and called, "Enter."

Marcus Beckman, a polished cover your ass, political maneuverer, cleared his throat. His star was trending at the agency and he knew it, "Hey, hi," he said. "Welcome to the GSA. So you're the new girl." He elongated out the last part of his sentence.

Codi couldn't see him over her boxes, so she quickly put on a so-happy-to-meet-you smile and stood to shake Marcus's hand. A quick furtive glance told her everything she needed to know about the six foot, olive skinned, overconfident man in front of her. Narcissist. *Great I've had my fill of those.*

"Lieutenant Colette Sanders, si–"

She caught herself mid-sentence. An awkward moment passed between them.

"We don't use that sort of formality here," Marcus said. "Colette, is it?"

"Everybody calls me Codi."

Marcus sized her up and liked what he saw. The new agent was about five-eight, brunette and stunning. She had an athletic figure and a perfectly proportioned rack that captured his undisciplined eyes. He quickly forced his eyes back up to her face and was met with intense brown eyes with flecks of gold. "I'm Agent Beckman, Marcus. Nice to meet you, Codi. I see they gave you Butler's old office."

"Butler?"

"Some loser who couldn't hack it." Marcus spoke as though he had personally fired Butler. "After you get your stuff settled, come by and I'll give you the 'tour.' Last office on the left."

"Sounds great," she said. If only she meant it. His words sounded fine, but the creep alarms going off in her head could not be ignored. And the way he said *tour* left no doubt as to his intentions.

Thankfully, after Codi flashed him her fake smile, he left.

Codi followed him to the door and turned the lock as he closed it behind him. She mechanically let her fit muscles lower her slowly to the floor, knees bent, back pressed firmly against the door. She absently rubbed her left ankle as an emotional wave engulfed her. Hopelessness and despair swelled, threatening to take on physical proportions. A dark place called to her and Codi fought to stay the hell away. It was a battle she had lost and won over the last six months.

Back then, things were a bit different for Codi.

"Down, down! Cover fire!" someone shouted.

Codi dropped flat and rolled right into a small depression in the mud just as a three-round burst stitched the ground where she had just been. The twenty-six-week SEAL qualification training program was almost over. She had excelled where others had failed. Being the only female in her group didn't help, since the entire program was clearly modeled after a boys' club.

Other females had paved the way and she was determined to carry on. The BUD/S (basic underwater demolition) School was relatively easy for her, as she was a natural in the water and always had been. But she had to overcome her fear of heights to complete the parachutist course. Once she was chosen for SEAL training, she felt like she could do anything, even if most of the other candidates wouldn't give her the time of day.

This was competition personified and nothing punctuated that more than the bell of shame, a brass bell that hung on a post where morning musters took place. When you couldn't take any more or go on, all you had to do was ring the bell. She had watched as several other soldiers had succumbed to the rigors of the training, each eventually just wanting to make it stop. With the pull of a string they were done.

Truth be told, night after night, in freezing cold conditions, without sleep, there wasn't one applicant that hadn't considered ringing the bell, but the walk of shame up to that bell left a permanent stain. For Codi, failure was never an option. No matter what, SEALS don't fail and nothing could sway her in that direction.

She had something to prove to herself and to her father who had been taken when she was just thirteen. She used him as a spirit guide in her life and more than once had pushed herself beyond her limits to please the figment in her mind. The relationship had worked and in spite of a high-priced psychologist, she had held on to her imagined father and used him to gain inner strength. Together they had succeeded where others had failed.

Codi popped her head up just long enough to get off two three-round bursts down range on target and then dropped back down as return fire nicked the ground around her head. She gripped her colt M4A1 assault rifle with its 5.56mm NATO rounds. This was it—go time. "Cover me!" she screamed as she jumped up to storm the bunker they were trying to breach.

A klaxon sounded as a voice came over the loudspeakers. "Stand down; end of drill. I say again, end of drill. All cadets meet in the war room for debriefing."

Codi sloughed off the excess mud that clung to her like a hungry parasite. Somehow she had survived another exercise where her team leader had given her the shit job. Two previous encounters had proven that most of these macho soldiers had no respect for her and did whatever they could get away with to pressure her into quitting. What they didn't know was that that sort of harassment only made her dig her heels in deeper and fight even harder. After all, she'd made it through hell week and often beat them at their own game.

Growing up north of San Diego, most people would think that Codi had had it easy. But after her dad passed, she became a latchkey kid with a mother who would dip into depression and disappear for days at a time. They moved every year or so, her mother in search of a new job. In time, Codi found that the only person she could really count on was herself. She had used that as a motivator to find her independence and stand on her own. In high school, she found that few people were as fast as she was in the water and she capitalized on that ability to pay for college. After graduation, in spite of several promising opportunities, Codi joined the Marines as an enlisted soldier. She had something to prove and nothing would get in her way. Now, three years later, as a SEAL trainee, she was determined that no one or nothing would break her.

Codi's eyes snapped open. She had been asleep for only a short while. It was somewhere between one and three in the morning. It was cold and it was raining. They were fifteen miles outside the base on a four-day maneuver. Something was moving off to her right. She could sense it. The rest of her squad was still asleep. With the crazy hours they kept, one quickly learned to sleep when you could.

She tapped Corporal Westmire next to her, the one guy in the squad she really trusted. He was instantly awake. Codi gestured with her hands—two fingers pointed at her eyes and then pushed together pointing to where the intruder was, followed by three fingers held up: three possible tangos were headed to their position from the south. Westmire stealthily alerted the others and they were quickly on their feet and spreading out into a defensive formation.

The group was going on three hours' sleep in the last seventy-two hours. They were cold and mostly exhausted from the non-stop physical exertion. Appearing from nowhere, their instructor stepped from the dark followed by two assistants. He looked the squad over and barked, "Everyone up that tree now!"

There was a large tree twenty feet away. The lowest branch was at least fifteen feet up. The group didn't hesitate. This would require serious teamwork and they were ready.

Codi and the corporal set up a human platform that the other trainees used to attempt to scale the tree. The squad leader pushed off and got his hands around the branch, but it was wet. Just as he started to pull himself up, he slipped fifteen feet down, bounced off Codi and hit the ground flat on his back. Everyone stopped, not sure what to do. He struggled to get to his knees and take a breath. The instructor walked around the tree once and said, "Now you've got four minutes."

The squad leader sucked it up and tried again. This time he got a full grasp around the branch and hauled himself up. Others followed until it was Codi's turn. She pushed off with everything she had and got a firm grip on the squad leader's hand that was reaching down. She dug her feet into the trunk and held tight to his hand while he pulled her up. She slipped a bit on the wet trunk but recovered and continued to climb. Just as she was within reach of the branch, she felt his grip loosen. She looked up into his eyes and could tell something was off. "No, no, don't you dare!" she screamed at him.

She tried to reach for the branch and caught just a finger on it. But it was too late. The rain and the *male only* military mindset conspired together and Codi fell. She tried desperately to tuck and roll when she hit, but the cracking sound and the shooting pain in her ankle told her it was futile. She looked down to see the distorted shape of her ankle. It was broken and so was everything that mattered to her at that moment in life.

The bell of shame rang loudly and Codi wasn't going to let them see her cry. Then it rang again and again. What the... Codi snapped out of it as her cellphone brought her back to reality—her new office. She grabbed the phone and hit the green button. "This is Codi."

"Girl, you're here! I'm so excited. When do you get off today, cause we gots to celebrate."

Codi's BFF, Katelyn Green, lived in DC and worked for the office of Senator Hightower from Wyoming. She was outgoing and had been the genesis of several regrets over the years for Codi. They had met in a Poli Sci class at University of California San Diego and had been best friends ever since. Katelyn's curvy figure and carefree attitude got the boys' attention, but Codi's athletic build and genuine charm kept them around.

They set a date to meet after work at the Black Cat on Fourteenth NW. Codi hung up and stared at nothing for a second. She would put the past behind her for the moment. Even the last six months where darkness and depression seemed to rule the day.

Codi pressed into a standing position and opened her office door. "Okay," she said to herself, "time to show 'em what you got."

CHAPTER SIX

C odi slid into the last available chair in the conference room. Twelve people surrounded the faux wood rectangular table. Codi had only met one of them before, Ruth Anne Gables, who everyone called Boss. She stood and made the introductions, including how happy they were to have Codi on the GSA team.

The General Services Administration, or GSA, was a government agency tasked with leveraging the buying power of the federal government to acquire best value for itself and the taxpayers. They developed and innovated effective management policies and exercises for responsible asset management.

GSA has an enforcement division that sniffs out government waste and/or corruption and acts upon it. Codi was its newest member—a paper pusher with a badge. The GSA requires all their special agents to attend the basic twelve-week Criminal Investigator Training Program (CITP) at the Federal Law Enforcement Training Center (FLETC). Additionally, they must complete the three-week IG (InvestiGator) Training Program.

Agents also attend advanced training at FLETC for collateral duties such as Firearms, Control Tactics, Technical Surveillance, Advanced Interviewing, Undercover Operations and Leadership. Compared to her SEAL training, all of this was a breeze for Codi and she graduated at the top of her class.

Out of the corner of her eye Codi caught Marcus staring at her from across the table and tried not to let it bother her.

"Agent Sanders," said Boss, "I want you to get to know Agent Joel Strickman. You two will be working together and he will be your go-to guy for anything digital."

Codi glanced over to where Boss had gestured. Strickman, a tall wiry blond with glasses and a moppy haircut. He looked like a cross between a surfer and a super nerd. He smiled and nodded in response. "You mean like hacking?" Codi said.

"We don't do that word here at the GSA, Agent Sanders, but Agent Strickman is one of our best."

Director Ruth Anne Gables was a no nonsense bureaucrat who had used her political savvy along with her brains to rise to the top at the GSA. Her female, African-American heritage played little or no role in her advancement. She genuinely cared for her subordinates and was a full-fledged mother hen when it came time to protect them. It made her team trustworthy and very loyal, a rarity in Washington. Codi gave a mock salute to Agent Joel Strickman who nervously smiled back. Her first impression—cute.

The meeting finally broke up and Codi and Joel decided to do lunch to get better acquainted. Over fish tacos and soggy coleslaw, Codi pumped Joel for everything he could tell her about the job and its people. She pushed him for who could be trusted and who to watch out for. By start of the workday tomorrow she would be ready.

The rest of the day was uneventful, except for the tour the ever-so-helpful Marcus gave her. She had lost track of how many times she caught him undressing her with his eyes. After turning him down for a third time to grab a drink after work, Codi finally had a chance to unpack and arrange her office. Her ankle had completely healed, but the scar left behind was a good reminder of whom she should and should not trust—no one.

The brisk walk from her apartment on Queen Anne's Lane to the GSA's main office at 1800 F Street in DC had taken only ten minutes. But after her get-together with Katelyn the night before it was taking a bit longer. The path took her around George Washington University and past the World Bank. DC was an exciting town with politics and crime vying for the top position. The future of the world was being decided here almost every day and Codi hoped she could be of some value in that area. With a Starbucks on every corner, Codi stopped at one across from the office and grabbed two coffees.

The GSA, like most government agencies, was an inefficient business. More often than not, one part of the company didn't know what the other was doing. As long as they met their budget each year no one seemed to care. The enforcement division of the GSA was responsible for tax evaders and people or companies trying to defraud the federal government. This was specifically what Codi had been hired to do.

She stepped into Joel's office and handed him a coffee. "Thanks." He smiled.

She handed him a USB drive. "Boss wants us to start slow, so she gave us this file as our first case."

Joel popped it into his computer and did a quick virus scan. He leaned back and took a sip from his steaming cup. "Tastes like Moroccan roast."

"If you say so."

"No, seriously, hint of cardamom and cinnamon."

"Is that good?"

"It's great. I'm kind of a coffee nut and the coffee here is..." "Horrible and I'm not a coffee nut." The information from the drive populated his screen. "It appears to be a list of names connected to various VA incentive programs," he said.

Codi leaned over and said, "As in, I'm a veteran so I get preferential treatment on contracts?"

Joel nodded. "Exactly. How do you want to proceed?"

"I'll take M-Z and you can have the rest. Email me the files." Codi stood and headed to the door.

"Uh, I don't know your email."

Codi paused at the door. "You wouldn't be much of a special agent, Joel, if you can't figure that out." She smiled and left.

Marcus was loitering in the hallway chatting up a secretary. His plastic smile turned Codi's way as she headed to her office. He broke off his conversation, marched over to Codi and stopped right in front of her. "Special Agent Sanders, you're looking lovely today–"

Codi held her hand up to stop him mid-sentence. She knew this male personality trait well and if she didn't do something quick it would only get worse. Marcus paused briefly. "Perhaps we can grab some lunch a little later?"

Codi paused and using a slightly elevated voice so all around could hear, she said, "Thanks, but no thanks for the offer, Marcus and unless you have something to say about the assignment I'm on right now...not interested." She raised her hands as a point of emphasis. "If you have plans for a drink tonight after work...not interested."

Marcus glanced around and squirmed uncomfortably.

"If you're hoping to make me one of your work conquests...not interested. In fact, I think you should look elsewhere to get laid, as I am *not interested*." She turned and walked away leaving Marcus to look around nervously.

There was a collection of heads that had turned in his direction. He waved weakly and then called out to Codi, "Okay, we'll talk later?" Then, head down, he shuffled off to his corner office.

Codi rubbed the bridge of her nose and glanced away from the screen. It was slow going; every name had to be crosschecked and rechecked. The paper trail seemed unending. Identify the name, cross-reference it with a social security number, follow the numbers and reconfirm it with their tax return. Once that was done, she had to confirm their veteran status and that in itself was a nightmare. Other than "after action" or AA paperwork, this was the most un-glorified part of being an investigator. She opened a bottle of water, took a swig and moved to the next name on the list.

"Knock, knock." Joel popped his head into her office. "I think I've got something."

"Good, because I'm about to throw my laptop through the wall and quit." Joel looked at her nervously not sure if she was serious. "Not really, Joel. Show me."

Joel's office was the same size as Codi's, but that's where the similarities ended. Star Wars paraphernalia decorated the room. He had a very sophisticated set-up with two large computer monitors and a host of peripheral gear. The room was dark grey with two-foot-square foam baffles interspersed on the walls. There was a large TV on the wall where he could cast information up for others to see what he was working on. Codi stood over Joel's shoulder looking at his computer. A small rubber Yoda was stuck to the top of the screen staring with blank eyes back at them.

"Sandy Holcomb, Iowa City, Iowa." He cast the image up on the TV. "Married to Warren Holcomb, has no children."

"Does it say what she does for a living?"

"Yes, she and the husband run a construction company called WHI. It looks like they have received over eight million dollars in government contracts."

"Go on."

"They have a Service-Disabled Veteran-Owned Small Business Program designation for their business."

Codi leaned forward for a closer look. "That's probably how they're getting the government contracts. Makes sense. So what are we missing?"

"I couldn't find any mention of a disability in the military files we have access to."

Codi started back to her office. "I'm gonna give the Veterans Admin a call to see what's up."

"Hang on. I can do that here."

Codi moved back to Joel's desk and sat in a chair next to him. He looked over and smiled at his new partner. In an embarrassed reflex he scratched his nose, shoved his glasses up and went back to his computer. Codi watched him bang on his keyboard for a second. He was cute but definitely not her type.

Joel used his skills to bypass the firewall at the VA. "Just a little of this and some of that and—wha-la, we're in."

"Whoa, you are good." Joel gave her a half smile. She said, "You may not use the term here, but that looked a lot like hacking to me."

Joel quickly changed the subject. "It seems the VA has no record of either a Warren or Sandy Holcomb receiving a disability."

"Check to see if either has a military background."

Joel banged away at the keys for a minute. "Hmm, looks like Warren was a private in the Army, but that's it."

Codi leaned in closer to the screen. "No mention of a disability or Purple Heart from the army or the VA?"

"Nothing."

"Well, Joel, looks like someone's trying to defraud the US government."

CHAPTER SEVEN

The Iowa City airport is a large, unremarkable beige rectangular building with a single dogleg section sticking out onto the macadam for jet parking. It is not the sort of airport you can get a direct flight to. Codi's bag was the last one to come off the baggage claim. She grabbed it, pulled up the handle and wheeled her way through to the car rental agency to catch up with her partner. She had never been to Iowa City and was looking forward to some classic Midwest charm.

Joel and Codi left the rental lot in what she liked to call an Impala POS (piece of shit). The silver Impala was the most unrecognizable four-door made.

Codi turned onto Highway 27 and headed north. Joel looked over at her and smiled.

"What?" she asked.

He cleared his throat. "So, first mission together."

"So?"

"So I thought it would be appropriate to celebrate."

Codi glanced out the window as they drove past the Herbert Hoover Presidential Library and Museum. "What do you have in mind? Our per diem is good for about one drink with dinner and I'm afraid to see what our hotel looks like."

"I took the liberty to do a little web work and got us a free upgrade—two suites and a complimentary breakfast." Joel looked proud.

Codi smiled. "They're not adjoining rooms, by chance, are they?"

Joel's face turned fire truck red and he looked away. "No, never!"

"Never?"

"No, I mean I–" He was too choked up to speak.

"Relax, I'm just bustin' you, Joel. But what's your deal?"

"My deal?"

"Yeah."

Joel thought for a second and then piped up. "Well I grew up in New Brunswick."

"New Jersey?"

"No, Canada, St. John, specifically. My dad was part of a US/Canadian fishing co-op that was going on at that time. When he finished that, the US Department of Fish and Wildlife sent us to Great Falls, Montana."

"So, a lot of cold winters."

"Yeah, a lot of time indoors on a computer. Drove my mom crazy, but my dad always said it would be my door to a better life." They drove in silence for a few minutes.

"Now tell me about the Holcombs," Codi said.

Joel fumbled for his computer bag behind his seat and pulled the laptop out. For the rest of the trip to the hotel, he filled Codi in on the latest info regarding their suspects.

Sandy and Warren Holcomb ran a construction business out of an old Quonset hut, a steel building based on a British design called the Nissen Hut developed in WW1. With its semi-circular roof that went all the way to the ground in a half-circle design, it was a unique reminder of a bygone era. The business was based in Coralville, a small suburb of Iowa City. No kids, no pets.

Out of the eight million dollars in contracts they had received from the federal government, Joel estimated they ran on about a forty percent profit margin.

"That's $3.2 million!" Codi said.

"Yep and they're up for a remodel of the local VA office right now."

"So what is it that makes 'em tick?"

"Tick?"

"Are they members of any radical groups, or just two embezzlers who scam the government between rounds of golf and PTA meetings?"

Joel plowed through his laptop. "No mention of any subversive group memberships. But Sandy Holcomb does have two unpaid parking tickets."

"A real terrorist, huh?"

Joel, still getting used to his partner's sarcasm, picked up on this one. "Yep, one hundred percent lethal."

The two shared a laugh as Codi turned into a local Kum & Go. "I need some coffee," she said.

"Here?" Joel looked a little fearful at the thought of convenience store coffee.

True to Joel's fears, the coffee was terrible.

The hotel had upgraded their rooms, but the term "suite" in Iowa City is different than it is in Washington D.C. Dinner at the Golden Corral mirrored that fact. But Joel managed to get a bottle of Goose Island Bourbon County Stout that wasn't half bad. He ordered a second bottle knowing his per diem would cover the additional cost.

Codi started the conversation by saying, "I have a confession to make." Joel looked across his iced beer bottle at her. "I hate coleslaw—too much mayonnaise." She had pushed her slaw into a small pile at the edge of her plate.

"You should try my mother's coleslaw; no mayo at all."

"Really?"

"Yeah, she uses a light vinaigrette dressing."

Codi frowned. "Sounds like cabbage salad to me."

He said a bit defensively, "Well, she calls it coleslaw."

Joel hid behind his beer bottle for a second, thinking of something to say. "I have a confession to make."

Codi smiled up at him. "What's that?"

"Hotel beds, hate 'em. I have yet to spend a night in a hotel bed and not have some sort of problem."

Codi waited for him to continue. When he didn't, she asked, "Like?"

"Not during dinner. It's nasty."

Codi picked up her beer and raised it. "Here's to working for the government: cheap per diem, crappy rent-a-cars and bad hotels."

Joel raised his beer. "And the pay's not so good either." They clinked bottles at the neck and downed a gulp.

The adventure-and-outdoors-themed hotel lived up to its name, as the next morning two GSA special agents with very little sleep made their way to the Impala POS. Coffee and a proper breakfast was the objective. They had each taken one look at the complimentary breakfast and decided to check out instead.

Something outside Codi's room was scratching off and on all night. She was guessing an opossum or a rat. Joel's eyes looked puffy and a rash ran from his ear down his neck, to where it disappeared under his shirt. He scratched at it absently. They drove to the Bluebird Diner on Market Street in silence where they got their fix, including good coffee. They ordered refills in to-go cups and hit the road.

The WHI construction sign was small against the bright red front of the building. A solid wood entry door was centered between two metal roll-up doors that were trimmed in white. There was a row of six small windows about twelve feet high that ran across the façade of the building. The single large window next to the entry door had the blinds closed tight. An Open sign leaning in the sill was the only thing visible. Codi and Joel finished their coffee, got out of their rental and headed for the door. She kept her head on a swivel, not that she was expecting trouble, it was just so ingrained in her that it had become her SOP (standard operating procedure). Joel grabbed the doorknob, but it was locked. His mouth was dry, a quick glance over to Codi was followed by a go ahead nod. He banged on the door and yelled, "Federal agents! We'd like to talk to you. Can you open up, please?"

There was some muffled voices and a clunk sound. Codi went on high alert. She pressed her ear to the wall and heard the unmistakable clank of a pump action shotgun cocking. She dove at Joel, who was standing in front of the door, knocking him to the ground just as an eight-inch hole was blown through the door. The sound was deafening, but Codi, in one fluid motion, spun off of Joel, drew and fired her weapon back through the hole in the door. The gen-4 Glock 23 bucked twice.

There was a sound like a sledgehammer hitting the side of a pig and then a metallic clang as the shotgun bounced on the concrete floor inside. Immediately, a high-pitched scream sounded somewhere in the building followed by, "I give up, I give up, don't shoot!"

Joel looked totally rattled but managed to get to his feet. He checked himself for bullets—none. Codi was already kicking in the front door. He fumbled for his weapon and chased after her. She did a quick peek around the doorjamb and found one man down with a female wailing over him. "Hands in the air, *now!*" Codi said to her. The female complied, but her crying continued.

Joel burst onto the scene a few moments later pumped up on adrenaline and pointing his gun in all directions. Codi kicked the shotgun away from the suspects and handcuffed the female. "Call it in," she said to Joel.

He grabbed his phone and shakily dialed the local authorities.

Codi approached the man who lay on the floor. Blood was oozing across his chest. She checked his vitals. "Shit."

CHAPTER EIGHT

M rs. Holcomb continued to wail. Joel looked over at Codi, still a bit rattled. "You're bleeding," he said.

Sure enough, blood was oozing down her right hand. Codi took off her coat and saw three blood spots on her white shirt. She tore off the sleeve and examined her wounds. Sure enough, three buckshot holes in her bicep trickled blood. She grabbed a penknife from her pocket and flashed it open.

"What are you doing? The ambulance is on its way," said Joel.

"They'll make me go to the hospital to have these removed."

He looked flabbergasted. "That's how this works. You get shot, they take you to the doctor and he fixes you."

"Yes, but I can do it now and save me the trip and the aggravation."

"Are you insane? You've been shot. There are bullets in your arm!"

"Technically it's buckshot and going to the hospital for a minor wound is insane. Do you know how many germs there are in one hospital room alone?"

She took the smallest blade on the knife and used it to pop out one of the BB-sized slugs. Joel creased his face in disgust, but he couldn't turn away. "Besides," she said, "the door slowed the projectiles down; they're not in that deep."

She then used her ripped shirtsleeve to make a bandage. "Give me a hand."

Joel reluctantly tied the ends into a knot.

"There," she said. "No hospital. Plus, I hate leaving lead in me any longer than necessary."

Joel looked at her with disbelieving eyes. "You've been shot before?"

"Sure, haven't you?"

"No, I haven't been shot before; I haven't even discharged my weapon before."

"Never?"

"No, never—not at a person."

Codi seemed unfazed. Sirens were approaching in the distance.

The handcuffed woman on the floor suddenly stopped crying. "Who are you people?"

"Federal agents, Mrs. Holcomb and you're under arrest."

Once the local authorities were appeased and Codi's wounds were properly cleaned and bandaged by the paramedics, it was time to head back to DC and file their AA reports. The turbulence on the plane seemed relentless as Codi and Joel left Chicago O'Hare Airport on the second leg of their journey back. Joel was playing some computer game, trying to calm his nerves. Codi's arm was now throbbing. She wished she'd grabbed some Advil back at the terminal. She leaned her head back and her thoughts drifted back to the last time she had taken a bullet.

Afghanistan was a dreary place, a country filled with competing tribes that each had a different agenda. No one government or country would ever rule it. But as a US Marine, Codi was given a chance to try to bring sanity where none would ever exist.

The mission was simple, a supply convoy to Camp Leatherneck in the Hemland River Valley Province. It was a sixteen-hundred-acre Marine base that had all the modern conveniences of a home away from home. Since 2013, women have held numerous combat positions and have proven themselves commensurate. Lance Corporal Colette

"Codi" Sanders was one of these women and took pride in being an overachiever.

She was behind the wheel of a cargo truck and turned abruptly to avoid a large pothole. She looked over at her sergeant in the passenger seat. His head moved side-to-side looking for anything out of the ordinary. In Afghanistan that was a challenge, as everything seemed suspicious. A five-year-old girl could press a button and—boom—your day was ruined.

Private Moody was standing in the gun turret keeping a lookout from his higher vantage point. He was a nineteen-year-old redhead from Milwaukie, Oregon, the youngest of five brothers and the first in his family to join the military. His mother Pearl, had supported his decision on the outside, but on the inside she feared and prayed for his safety every day.

Private Moody bent down to say, "Hey, Sarge, when are you going to stop taking us on these punk-ass supply runs and get us some real action?"

Codi spoke up. "You mean like you and Kaufman back at the bar last night?"

The sergeant looked over. "That was you and Kaufman I saw in the corner booth playing grab ass?" Private Stevie Kaufman was one of the cutest new recruits on the base. She and Moody had just clicked.

"Sure was," Codi said, "and I hear there might be a ring in their future."

The sergeant looked perplexed. "Unbelievable," he said. "There's like a thirty-to-one ratio of guys to girls over here and shit-for-brains here gets one. And not just any one, but a real looker."

"It's the red hair, Sarge; a girl just can't say no," said Private Kaufman. She leaned close to Codi. "Isn't that right, Codi?"

"No," she replied without hesitation.

Kaufman leaned back, disappointed. "She's not a girl, Moody. She's a woman and a hell of a soldier."

Codi looked over at the sergeant. They held the look for a second too long. He was ruggedly handsome, she thought. Maybe? But the truth was, she'd been out in the desert for too long. She shook the thought away.

The first RPG slammed into the cab of the seven-ton MTVR. The large cargo truck quickly lost its way and dropped off the road. Kaufman yelled, "Incoming!"

Immediately, Codi took evasive maneuvers, just as the second RPG sailed past the spot on the road they had just occupied. The Humvee behind her took the hit and stalled out, smoke coming from a destroyed engine.

"Somebody take that guy out!" The sergeant yelled.

Return fire followed from the turret above. Codi flipped her Humvee around to provide protection for the guys in the damaged vehicle behind her. Small arms fire filled the air from both sides. What few civilians there were on the outskirts of town scrambled for shelter.

Codi looked over just in time to duck down as another RPG hit her Humvee broadside. It took off the protective housing, known as the GSK—Gunner Shield Kit—and with it, the top half of Kaufman's body. Blood was everywhere and Codi's sergeant lay motionless in the passenger seat. Through the ringing in her ears she could barely hear the distress call going out over the radio for evac and air support. Some of the guys in the other Humvee were returning fire.

Another explosion followed and then chatter over the radio, which told her the RPG had been taken out. But small arms fire continued to pepper away at them. Codi climbed over and up to the now unprotected M240 machine gun on the roof. The insurgents had gotten brave and were closing in on the two disabled vehicles. Codi wasted no time. Over the radio she yelled, "Clean up on aisle seven!"

She cycled the bolt, pulled the trigger and let the fifty caliber rounds free.

The combination of the two allied groups firing soon ended the threat, but not without cost. Five solders dead and two wounded, including Codi who had taken a round in her left shoulder and never realized it until the shooting was over.

Luckily, the bullet had done what's called a through-and-through, where the projectile passes through the body missing anything vital. Three weeks on the sidelines and Codi was ready to get back in action.

The Boeing 737 shook and then bucked, sending Codi back to the present. Joel glanced over at her. She had her head leaning against the port window and her eyes were closed, but she must have felt something because without looking over she said, "What?"

"You know you saved me back there," he said.

"What are you talking about?"

"You saved my life. That shotgun would have hit me dead-center if you hadn't shoved me out of the way."

"I see. Well, you're welcome."

"Seriously, I don't think I'm cut out to be in the field."

Codi looked over at him. "Then why are you in the field?"

"Boss thought I was ready, but–"

Codi interrupted. "Boss was right, that's why there are two of us. With four eyes and ears we are twice as likely to sniff out danger and put a stop to it. You bring things to the table I don't and vice versa."

Joel looked unsure. Codi continued. "That suspect shot first without warning. There is only so much preparation you can do for that. Mostly it's about reacting."

"But you got shot saving my ass."

"Yes I did, so you owe me." Codi smiled.

"Of course. Anything. What do you want?"

"A quart of Ben and Jerry's Chocolate Fudge Brownie."

"Wait. What?"

CHAPTER NINE

"I don't believe this. We haven't had a shooting since I've been director," said Ruth Anne Gables as she paced around her office like a squirrel in a box. Codi and Joel sat in matching blue chairs listening to Boss's rant. "We deal with budget waste and white collar fraud. Violent crimes are for other agencies."

"I assure you, there was no choice in the matter," Codi said.

Joel nodded to reflect Codi's words.

"Oh, I've read the AA report," Director Gables said.

The AA stands for After Action.

"How's the arm, by the way?" she asked.

"Fine," said Codi.

"Good." Director Gables moved to the front of her desk and sat on the corner.

"You two did some fine work out there. I guess I'm still amazed at what a cornered suspect is capable of." Ruth Anne grabbed a USB drive and passed it to Codi. "Here. I have something of a mystery. See if you two can make anything out of it. But first schedule an appointment with Dr. Roswell. You'll both have to be cleared before I can let you back in the field."

Joel looked up hopefully and said, "Good. I feel like that would help me tre–"

Codi kicked him in the leg and he stopped mid-sentence. She stood up. "Anything else, Boss?"

"No. Now get out of here before I suspend both of you."

Joel looked up, surprised and found Ruth Anne smiling at them. Codi flipped the drive to Joel and the two left the office.

Ruth Anne had a good feeling. Good agents were hard to find and when they worked as partners all sorts of drama came up. The stories she could tell, if only she hadn't signed the OSA, Official Secrets Act, when she was promoted to her current position. But these two were all right. Dr. Roswell was a pushover; they'd be cleared and back at it in no time. She went to her desk and picked up the phone.

"What are we looking at?" Codi asked. Back in Joel's office, she stared at the screen. "It appears to be the longest paper trail to nowhere."

Codi and Joel had been trying to make sense of the information in the files. There seemed to be a mystery payment that went to a company or person called T. Light. But its source and details were nonexistent. It was getting late and they were getting nowhere. Codi leaned back in her chair and rubbed her temples. Her arm still hurt. It was time to find some more Advil and break for the day.

The Ultrabar in Penn Quarter is a nightclub that boasts five distinct floors, each with its own event options. It has state-of-the-art lighting, sound systems and projection screens throughout. It's DC nightclubbing done right. Katelyn handed Codi one of two Washingtonian's she had carried back from the bar, a drink made of vodka, limoncello and Chambord. "Welcome to DC," she said.

The two girls had found a great little booth tucked off to the side, but they still had to shout to be heard over the thumping music. "You only brought me here for my badge so we could skip the line. You know I could get in trouble for that," Codi said.

"Relax. Drink up. Have some fun for once."

Codi looked down at her drink. "You know I'm not much of a drinker. I'm more of a beer girl."

Katelyn took a large swig of her drink and smiled. "It's like fruit punch."

Codi looked at her friend and realized there would be no stopping her tonight. Her champagne metallic ruched V-neck dress showed off all the right curves. She was moving to the beat and downing her drink while checking out every cute guy that passed. Codi let out a breath and then whispered to herself, "What the hell," and took a sip. Katelyn was right; it did taste like fruit punch.

"So what's the job like?" Katelyn asked. "What do they have you doing?"

"I'm not really allowed to talk about it."

"Come on, Codi, hit me."

"Fine." Codi took another swig and set her glass down. "I follow paper trails and identify possible fraud. They usually have local authorities follow up, but sometimes I get to go into the field. Now what about you?"

"Me? I work with a lobbyist group called Williams & Gillespie. It's a large firm that covers everything from tech to mining interests. I'm responsible for their web marketing." Katelyn finished off her drink in one final gulp. "Ok, let's find me a cute guy."

Codi just smiled and shook her head. Katelyn hadn't changed a bit since college.

How the fight started, Codi didn't know; probably two guys and one girl. What she did know was that Katelyn was on the dance floor and someone had just pushed her down. Codi was up and next to her friend in a flash. Katelyn had a red shiner on one eye and was trying to hide it with her hand.

"You okay?" Codi asked her.

"Yeah. Just caught some jerk's elbow, I think."

"We should go."

"Is that a proposition?"

"Funny."

The fight was getting out of hand. They needed to move. As Codi helped Katelyn to her feet she was slammed by one of the club's bouncers as he came flying through the air. The 250-pound mass of beef flat-backed her to the floor, leaving her spread-eagle in her Nanette Lepore red flared skirt. Codi shook her head and tried to clear the cobwebs.

The bouncer, rubbing his jaw, rolled over and stood on slightly wobbly legs. He offered his hand. "I'm so sorry. Some guy cold-cocked me." He helped Codi back to her feet, but just as he did, he was blind-sided again with a haymaker to his temple. He dropped to the floor like an overfilled bag of rice.

That was it. Codi spun and drop-kicked the assailant with an expertly timed round house. She then dropped to a crouch and uppercut assailant number two in the crotch. As he dropped to his knees Codi clasped her hands together and slammed them like an axe blade to the back of his head. So much for assailant number two.

She dusted off her outfit and looked around. There was another man in a business suit trying to put down a third assailant. But this guy was solid muscle and was hopped up on something of a chemical nature. The two were locked in mortal combat. Codi let out a frustrated sigh. This was not how she saw the night going. She was sure she would be helping Katelyn home and holding her hair back listening to her regrets in between bouts of throwing up. She shook the thought from her mind and got her head back in the game.

With cat-like quickness Codi was next to the fracas. The goon was just about to end it with the guy in the suit when she side-kicked him in the knee. The attacker dropped to his other knee in severe pain and the guy in the now-ripped suit came in for a front kick. The goon saw it coming and parried the man's foot away. The thug then forced himself back to his feet just as Codi dropped-spun and did a leg sweep, taking his feet out from under him. The man in the suit didn't hesitate. He used all his weight to drop an elbow on the man's face. Lights out.

The fight was over. Codi and the guy huffed and puffed and stared at each other for a moment. He wiped some blood from his mouth and rubbed his elbow. "I'm Special Agent Carter, FBI, but you can call me Bruce. Thanks for the assist."

Codi was still trying to assess the stranger. "Yeah, sure. No problem. I'm Special Agent Sanders, but you can call me Codi." They continued their stare-down as patrons began to shuffle back onto the dance floor. Then each let out a big smile that turned into a laugh.

Codi looked into his eyes. They were strong, believable and possibly the greenest eyes she had ever seen. "So, I know a place that makes a terrific hot chocolate." It all came flashing back, the career change, her new job, even being shot. What the hell, life is short, might as well enjoy it. She took his hand in hers and said, "That sounds perfect."

CHAPTER TEN

Codi walked into the office feeling the effects of the night before, half-flushed with contentment and half hung-over. Marcus Beckman was the first to see her. He was instantly nervous, like a trapped roach and nearly ran into the wall trying to turn around and go the other way.

Codi laughed at his antics and then put a hand on her head. Ugh, no laughing just yet. She needed some Advil. At least she would no longer be bothered by the office sleaze. Her phone vibrated.

She glanced down and checked the message. It was a text from Katelyn: "You are a wild woman! Call me WYC." Codi smiled at the text and the memory of last night. Special Agent Bruce Carter was just what she needed right now—fun, competent and uncommitted.

Her phone vibrated again, this time it was a text from Joel: "I think I have something." She texted back: "BRT," and picked up the pace on her way down the door-lined hallway towards his office.

"Wha'cha got?" Codi asked as she rubbed her temples and peeked over Joel's shoulder in a now familiar routine. He had come in early and was finally making some headway on the case. "Top right hand drawer."

"What?"

"Aspirin. Looks like you could use some."

Codi grabbed the bottle and popped a few in her mouth and dry-swallowed them. She rolled a chair back over next to Joel and looked up at the screen.

"I've gone back as far as I can go to where we no longer have a digital footprint."

"What do you mean?"

"T. Light has quite the history. The government has been sending checks every month for over sixty years."

"Whoa, does it say what the money is being used for?"

"Nope and the weird thing is most government checks follow a set structure and procedure, but this payment was initiated by someone very high up."

"What makes you say that?"

"It skips all the protocols and there's no digital origin for it."

Codi glanced over at Joel "How is that even possible?"

"I have no idea." Joel leaned back in his chair. "Looks like we'll need to get our hands dirty if we want to get to the bottom of this."

The National Archives building is more monument than office building. It has a stone façade, eighteen columns and a large portico. The main room inside, the rotunda, is a museum-like space that holds the charters of freedom, such as the Declaration of Independence and the Constitution.

The research entrance is much less grandiose. It's on the Pennsylvania side of the building and has a very specific set of rules for ingress and usage of the records. Once Codi and Joel got through security, they made their way to the consultant's desk. Joel picked up a request form, or pull-slip and started to fill it out.

Codi introduced Joel and herself to the research consultant and explained who they were and what they were looking for. The badge on the consultant's blouse said Irene Coldridge. The fifty-plus woman had a dour face, as if the prunes she'd been eating were not working. "I'm sorry," she said, "but no matter who you are, all researchers have to follow the rules."

"Look, Mrs. Coldridge–"

"That's Miss Coldridge."

"Sorry, Miss Coldridge. It is extremely important that we–"

Miss Coldridge interrupted Codi; she'd heard it all before. "Do you have a researcher's card?"

Codi's frustration was building, but she knew that bureaucracy was like King Arthur's sword in the stone, immoveable. "No, but we need–"

Joel cut her off, "I have a card."

Codi looked over at Joel with a single raised eyebrow.

He handed Miss Coldridge his card and the filled out pull-slip he'd been working on while Codi did combat with the old battle-axe. "Thank you," she said. "I'll be right back. You can wait in central research area, room 203." Then she walked off.

Codi sat there for a second and then said, "You have a library card to NARA?"

"Sure. If you want, I'll show you how to get one."

"Um, pass. Come on."

Room 203, or the central research room is a large open space with dark wood-paneled trim that surrounds the room for the first twelve feet up. Above that, on one wall is a row of large frosted windows; on the other is inlayed stone. Tables are scattered throughout the room and a watchdog guard sits at a raised station to oversee all.

Codi and Joel sat at a long wooden table that had a row of built in lamps down the center. "We're going to be here a while," she said.

"Why do you say that?"

"Because she doesn't like me and people like her find ways to get back at what they misperceive as a usurper."

"Like giving a redneck a badge."

Codi nodded. "Plus, she probably went home to feed her cats before pulling our files."

Joel shifted in his chair. "You should have more faith in people, Codi. Nine times out of ten they will surprise you and do the right thing."

"Did you read that in a fortune cookie?"

An hour later, Codi and Joel were each given a box of records and were going through them. Codi had given Joel an I-told-you-so look, but he pretended not to see it. Suddenly, Joel sneezed so loud Codi practically jumped out of her chair. Everyone in the room looked over. "What on earth?" Codi whispered.

"Sorry. It smells like Pine-Sol disinfectant and lemon zest had a baby. I think I'm allergic." He sneezed again.

She moved her chair a few more inches away from Joel and started back at it. Every piece of paper had to be read and often times deciphered. It was a slow and painstaking process. After six solid hours without any food or water it was time to give it a rest.

The next day went just as poorly, though with fewer sneezes from Joel. They requested a few more documents and the paperwork was pilling up. This was a classic GSA investigation and Codi was loosing interest. She prided herself on always giving a hundred percent, but historical paper trails held little interest for her. Was this really what she wanted to do for the rest of her life? She plopped down the page she'd been looking over. "I'm so done."

"Hmm," Joel said without looking over.

"Done, as in get me out of here; I can't keep doing this; my head is about to explode." She stood up. Several patrons glanced her way.

"Hey, hey, hey," Joel said."

"Hey what?" Codi slowly sat back down and glanced over at him.

"It says here that in 1952 Harry S. Truman personally set up an account to pay this T. Light company or person. Something called Project Skystorm."

He continued. "It looks like it was designed to pay ten thousand a month in perpetuity. Never seen anything like it."

"So who is this T. Light? Did he save the president's life or something?"

"I have no idea, but the checks are sent to a PO box, number eighty-seven, in Snowflake, Arizona."

"That's all it says?"

"See for yourself."

Codi inspected the paper. "Must have been some enterprise that fell through the cracks and has been lost to time. And there's no connection to the army or any of the federal government science divisions?"

"Nope. It's almost like it was Truman's own little secret. He left office in '53. I wonder if he just forgot he'd set this up?"

"Are the checks still being cashed?"

"Yep, every month."

"That's a lot of money over the years. Sounds like T. Light has some explaining to do." Codi pushed her chair back, "You up for a trip to Arizona?"

CHAPTER ELEVEN

The three-hour drive from the Phoenix airport was uneventful. But the scenery was majestic. Highway 260 skirts the Mogollon Rim, a 200-mile Grand Canyon-like rim that gives way to a green-carpeted forest with pines and quaking aspens. Once again, the agency had reserved a silver Impala POS for a rental car. This one smelled of bad cigar smoke and cheap perfume. Codi could only imagine what had taken place in the vehicle before they got it. Joel kept the window cracked to keep from sneezing.

As the sun dipped on the horizon, orange hues kicked off the sandstone hills. The town of Snowflake is located in the northern tip of the White Mountains. It was named after two Mormon pioneers, whose last names were Flake and Snow. After a long day of travelling, Codi and Joel felt like they had entered into a time warp. Everything in town had a fifties vibe. Streetlights were just starting to turn on along a very empty main street. They turned into a parking lot guarded by a large vintage neon sign.

Codi glanced out the driver's side window at the Cedar Motel with its white and teal trim and rustic fifties charm. Joel tried to ease her concerns. "Yelp gives this place two-and-a-half stars."

"Is this the best we could do?"

"This town is probably still on dial-up. I had to call a land line to get us this place."

Dinner was at the El Cupidos Mexican restaurant, where the food was fairly authentic and way too spicy for Joel. They spent the time going over their plan for the next day. Joel texted an update to Boss and the two retired for the night.

Joel sat on his side of the booth in The Skillet Café the next morning, scratching himself. "I think I shared the bed with a few friends last night."

Codi just smiled past the steam coming off her coffee mug that she held in both hands. "Did you notice how clean and fresh the air is here?"

Joel was in a mood. "No, I'm too busy scratching my ass off here."

Codi took a sip of the aromatic dark liquid. "Even the coffee is good."

Joel suspiciously sniffed his cup. "The check should be coming today or tomorrow at the latest, depending on the postal service."

"I'm thinking," Codi said. "Let's hit the post office first and see what we can find out. If that doesn't work we can stake out the place and see who opens the box. And remember, this is NRA country so watch your back."

Joel stopped scratching and looked around nervously.

They drove though the three-block-long town to get the lay of things. The most impressive feature was a large Mormon temple set on a bluff overlooking the municipality. Codi looked over at the majestic structure, completely out of place in the small town and said, "We're not in Kansas any more."

Joel piped in. "My niece got married in a place like that."

"You're Mormon?"

"No, but my uncle is."

Something caught Codi's attention. "Post office, three o'clock." Joel glanced over as they drove past it. A half-block later they ran out of town.

Codi flipped the Impala POS around and parked on a side street.

They had a good view of the front door, but were still slightly covered by trees along the lane. The perfect vantage point, Codi thought to herself.

Joel rolled down his window and grabbed the binoculars.

"Morning. Can I help you?" An older man with a cowboy hat and a threadbare flannel shirt was looking intently at them.

Totally startled, Joel jumped out of his seat and dropped the binoculars. "Jeez, you scared the crap out of me!"

"Sorry."

Codi looked over at Joel with a smirk on her face and then said to the man, "No. We're good. Thanks."

The local looked the car over. "Well, if you need a place to stay, the Cedar Motel is just down the street, real nice."

Joel just about choked at the gall this guy had to actually recommend such a place.

Codi gave the man her best small-town smile. "Thanks, but we're fine."

"Okay. You folks have a nice day."

"Well there goes our cover. Come on." Codi got out of the car and headed for the post office.

Joel jumped out and followed her. "What are you talking about?"

"Small towns. Within half-an-hour everyone in town will know that two suspicious people in suits are here driving a silver sedan, so we might as well own it."

The tree-lined street opened to a small brick-red clapboard building that served as Snowflake's USPS. Inside, they were met by an empty counter and the smell of dust. Joel rang a small bell that had a Ring My Bell musical lyric sticker attached. The bell twanged more than rang due to the sticker. He looked around at the vintage room. There was a metal grating separating the front from the back room that sat on top of an old worn wooden bar that also held an antique white scale for weighing packages. Joel called out, "Hello?"

Eventually, a young female with impossibly large eyes and red hair so curly it could have been an Afro, appeared. She scratched her freck-led nose and said, "Help you?"

Joel pulled out his warrant and explained the situation. As she lis-tened, her eyes seemed to get even bigger, if that was possible. "Yeah," she said. "I heard you were in town, but I didn't know you were feds."

Codi gave Joel a look: Yep, small towns.

"So, look," the woman said, "I don't really know nothin' 'bout nothing'. My dad normally runs the place. I just help out when he's off fishin'."

There was an uncomfortable silence. Then Joel prompted, "And he's off fishing?"

"Yeah, I just said."

"So here's the deal…" Codi looked straight into the girl's eyes and held her stare.

"Oh. Samantha. Samantha Wainwright."

"Here's the deal, Miss Wainwright. This paper gives us the right to look inside box eighty-seven. Now you can open it or I have the right to shoot it open."

"Seriously? Shoot it open? Geez. Okay, I can open it." Samantha left and went into the back room. Joel was having a hard time not smiling.

The part-time employee returned a moment later with a brass ring full of keys. She was flicking through them one at a time until she found what she wanted. She then handed it over to Joel. He quickly found box eighty-seven and opened it. Samantha stared anxiously. It was empty.

"I could'a told you it was empty."

Codi was trying to keep her patience. "What can you tell me about this box?"

"I don't know nuthin' about the boxes. I just fill 'em up when the mail comes."

"Who uses this box?"

"Can I see that piece of paper you showed me earlier?"

"You mean the warrant?"

"Yeah."

Joel handed it over. Samantha scrutinized it. "I don't see my name on here and if my name's not here I'm not sayin' nuthin'."

Codi took a deep breath. "We have the right to ask these questions, Samantha and we also have the right to haul you in for obstructing justice."

"I don't know what that is, but my granddad is an attorney and you can't make me talk. I want a lawyer!"

Joel tried to intercede. "You are not under arrest so you can't ask for a lawyer."

"Who says?" Samantha suddenly burst out crying.

Codi shared a look with Joel and waited for a moment. Finally she spoke. "Samantha, if you just tell us the name of the person who uses box eighty-seven we will leave right now."

"Honestly?"

"Yes."

"Well I don't know his full name, but he only gets one envelope a month and it says T. Light."

"Thank you, Miss Wainwright and goodbye."

As they left the building, Codi let fly a few expletives normally meant for battle situations. "Small towns, I hate 'em!"

For the next two days, Codi and Joel spent their time at the county records office, but there was no T. Light. They called DC to get a warrant for the local bank so they could track the checks being cashed. But because there was no known crime committed the process was stalled. They tried talking to everyone they met in town and finally ended up right back where they started, parked on a side street staking out the post office.

"I never did ask," Codi said to Joel, "is there a future Mrs. Special Agent Joel Strickman in your life?"

Joel looked up from his smart phone. Codi had the binoculars resting on the steering wheel and was looking through them. She had a good view of the post office and could just make out the PO boxes through the front windowpane.

"Hopefully. Not right now, but soon I hope."

"Any prospects?"

Joel looked helpless.

Codi continued without looking over. "You know, Aria in accounting has the hots for you."

"Seriously?"

"I could put in a good word for you."

"No, God no. Please."

Codi finally looked over at a very red-faced Joel. "Don't worry, I got your back. You're a good catch. I'll find someone for you." She smiled a devious grin.

"I'd rather do things my own way, thank you." Joel tried to change the subject. "What about you?"

Codi paused for a minute. "Let's just say, I like things less complicated right now." She handed Joel the binoculars. "Van."

"What? Oh."

A rust-brown minivan pulled into the lot at the post office. Joel placed the binoculars to his eyes for a look and said, "A woman, mid-thirties, carrying a baby in one of those wrap-around papooses."

The woman entered the post office and looked around nervously and then went to her box. Joel leaned forward, eyes focused on her actions. The woman took her key and reached forward, supporting the baby with her opposite hand.

"Crap," Joel said.

"What?"

"Box eighty-six."

Codi slouched back in her seat. Stakeouts sucked. She started drumming on the steering wheel. Joel lowered the binoculars for what seemed like the hundredth time that morning.

"Morning, agents."

Joel jumped again. Codi smiled and leaned over. "Morning, Hobbs." They were now on a familiar basis with the old man from before.

"My wife baked you some cinnamon rolls. I can't eat 'em, you know. Gluten does some very bad things to me."

He handed them over and Joel thanked him. Codi and Joel were now like two fish in an aquarium and everybody stopped by to take a look, some to chat. The old man waddled off for his daily constitutional.

Codi's cellphone rang. It was Director Gables. She put it on speaker. "What's the update?" Gables asked. Codi could tell Boss was antsy.

"So far everything out here has been a dead end."

"I see. I want you to head back tomorrow. We've spent too much time for no results. Besides, I have something else that needs your attention."

Codi had to agree; this investigation had stalled out and getting back to DC sounded great to her.

But Joel was quick to insert, "Boss, I just want to say one thing. The total payments that have been issued to date to this unknown person or enterprise add up to over seven million dollars."

There was a pause on the line. "I hadn't processed that. Thank you, Joel. Okay. Keep on it through the rest of the week. I'm going to request that the payments be stopped on this end."

Codi was not happy at the prospect of staying four more days in this small town chasing a cold case.

Boss hung up and Joel took a bite out of the cinnamon roll. "This is really good. Want one?"

Codi shook her head. "I'm ready for lunch."

Joel checked his watch and said, "We can try the burgers at Shepherds Kitchen and Thrift."

"There's a restaurant here with a thrift store in it?"

"Yep."

"I wonder if the food is also hand-me-down?"

Joel seemed to temporarily lose his appetite.

Codi reached for the keys and then changed her mind. "Thirty more minutes. Then lunch. We're probably wasting our time though as I bet Mr. or Mrs. T. Light has already been warned and won't come anywhere near their box."

"Fine by me. I say we blow this town and head back to D.C."

Cody passed the binoculars to Joel. She was starting to think he had the right idea when an old mid-eighties Ford F-150 pickup truck drove into the post office parking lot. It was two-tone green-and-white with a toolbox mounted in the bed. A tall man in jeans and a tee shirt flip-flopped his way into the building. He walked over to the PO boxes and checked three pockets before he found the key he was looking for. Joel yawned as he put the binoculars to his eyes, still chewing his cinnamon roll. He jerked forward as he watched the man open his box.

Codi picked up on his body language. "What?"

"Box eighty-seven guy."

The case just got hot.

CHAPTER TWELVE

Codi had oft heard of the road that leads to nowhere, but now she was on it. They had been following the truck at a very discrete distance for the last hour-and-a-half. For her, Arizona's beautiful high desert topography had lost its glamour. It was a mind-numbing sameness that appeared to never end. Without warning, the truck pulled off the two-lane blacktop onto a dirt road. Codi drove past the turn-off and down the highway a piece before pulling over. Following a suspect on an empty country road that was as straight as far as the eye could see, it was nearly impossible not to be spotted. But on a single-lane dirt road—no way.

The turquoise-blue sky was punctuated with cotton ball clouds. Joel watched through the binoculars as a small dust cloud migrated to red sand stone hills maybe a mile away. "I see some kind of structure. He just pulled in."

Codi flipped the car around and headed back for the dirt road. They turned and moved cautiously along the dirt strip.

A withered old green barn slowly came into view. It sat against a large sandstone cliff. Other than the green and white Ford pickup truck they had followed, the place looked deserted. They noticed some serious power lines connecting the barn to a string of poles leading off into the distance. Joel said, "A lot of power for a barn."

Codi drove the last three hundred yards to the building. They had to wind through old farm equipment that was strewn about to get to the main door.

The car stopped in a cloud of dust and Codi exited the vehicle.

Joel held back a sneeze and moved to the large barn door. He knocked, this time standing to the side of it. "Hello?" Nothing. He tried again. Still no answer.

Codi tried the door. It slid open about two feet on silent greased rollers. "Did you hear something suspicious?" she asked Joel. "I did."

She cautiously stepped inside and Joel followed with a frown.

The space was just dark enough that it took a moment for their eyes to adjust to the light. Codi's mind was racing to take it all in. Joel took a small step backward. The barn looked like a farm museum with a variety of old combines and plows, all categorically organized and each perfectly restored to a like-new condition. Ambient light streamed through skylights mounted in the roof and there was not a spec of dust anywhere. Joel walked over to a bright red combine and touched the cool metal fender. "You think all that money went to old farm equipment?" he asked.

"Not likely."

Codi moved through the displayed antiques. What really got her attention was the huge cavern that the barn connected to—a sandstone cave that went back over a hundred yards. There were three fourteen-foot-tall stainless steel cylinders that looked like giant metal phallic symbols pointing to the ceiling. They were placed in an open area of the cave about twenty-yards apart. Further inside was a host of mechanical and electrical equipment. Joel's jaw hung half-open with wonder. "These aren't the droids you're looking for," he mumbled.

"What?"

"Nothing."

Supertramp's *Bloody Well Right,* played in the distance and someone was trying to sing along. Codi cringed as the person singing hit the last word with a crack in his voice. It made her and Joel relax a little as they started towards the vocalist. About halfway there, Codi called out, "Hello?"

The man who'd been driving the truck stopped what he was doing, reached over and turned the music off. He looked genuinely surprised, but said nothing. As Codi and Joel walked towards him, the large towers started to hum. Codi could feel the hairs on her arm prickle. She sensed something was not right. "Federal agents. We need to talk to you."

The man calmly put his hands up and interlaced his fingers behind his neck, as if pondering the moment. "Agents," he said, "I don't know what you're doing here, but the place where you're standing right now? Think of it as a minefield and if you so much as take one step in any direction it will be your last."

Codi and Joel froze and looked around with their eyes only. She noticed the hair on Joel's head was now sticking straight out in every direction and she could feel hers doing the same. She put on a brave face and said, "We are federal agents from the office of the GSA and we are duly authorized to be here."

"Unless you have a federal warrant, I doubt it."

"And you, mister, are threatening an officer and will be brought up on charges."

He thought about things for a second and then dropped his hands. "Tell you what, give me your badge numbers and if they check out, we'll talk."

Codi and Joel looked at each other. What choice did they have? They each gave their badge number to the suspect. He typed in a few keystrokes on his computer and said, "It's okay, Terence, they're the real deal. You can turn it off."

The hum that was emanating from the steel towers died with a moan. Joel noticed that the hairs on his arms and head were no longer standing on end. Codi kept her eyes on the man as he moved in her direction.

Much to Codi and Joel's surprise, an older man with pure white hair stepped out from behind them. "I'm Terence Bridgestone," he said, "and that's my partner, Matt Campbell."

Matt walked over and Codi started to relax a bit when she saw that his piercing green eyes were set against a kind face. He said, "Sorry, officers. Just being carful."

After introductions and handshakes, Matt said, "So what brings you two all the way out here?"

Codi and Joel shared a look.

Terence interrupted with, "Tea, anyone?"

CHAPTER THIRTEEN

Terence brought out a tray holding four white porcelain cups of tea and proper English biscuits and set it on the table. They were sitting in a section of the cave that had been furnished much like the living room of a house. There were also bedrooms, bathrooms and even a kitchen, all sectioned off with walls. The concrete floors were stained and throw rugs were used as accents.

Terence selected a cup and sat down in an overstuffed leather chair that was distressed by actual years of use.

Matt looked his guests over. The female agent was quite a looker and had the figure to back it up. He noticed her brown eyes seemed to constantly be on the lookout, for information or danger, he assumed. Her partner seemed bookish and naive.

"So what can we do for you, officers?" Terence asked.

"You can start by telling us what it is you do here," Codi said.

"I'm afraid I can't do that."

"Can't or won't?"

Terence sat, unmoved.

Matt flicked his moppy hair out of his eyes and interceded. "If you tell us what it is you're looking for, maybe we *can* tell you something."

Codi took the opening and hit them with the truth. "We're following up on a payment that has been coming for over sixty years to a PO box that you visited today."

Joel added, "This check is from the federal government and it's our job to account for that money."

Matt turned to Terence and said, "Paper-pushing cops. I told you this day would come."

Terence just nodded.

Codi could sense they were getting nowhere and laid her last card on the table. "We know about Project Skystorm," she blurted out in desperation.

Matt burst out laughing. "Project Skystorm. Wow. Haven't heard that in a long time." He thought back for a second. "Project Skystorm was something my grandfather was working on for the war effort."

"What war?" Joel asked.

"World War II," Terrence said in a flat tone. "What we do here, agents, is classified. You may have some concern over an old money trail, but if you check with General Stanfield of the ARO, you'll see that we are legit."

Codi's head was spinning. "ARO?"

"The Army Research Office," Joel said.

"The only possible mistake made here," Terence said, "was the continuation of a payment structure that was put in place many years ago so that we wouldn't have to undergo any further scrutiny."

Codi took a sip of tea and used the delay to reformulate a plan.

Joel blurted out before she could stop him, "Okay. We'll check out your story and if it doesn't add up we'll be back with a warrant and enough agents to tear this place to the ground."

Terence set his teacup down and stood. "I think not," he said and walked away.

Matt just sat there staring at them. Codi took the hint. She tossed Joel the car keys and said, "Here. You drive."

Matt watched the two federal agents leave. He was not quite as confident about their current situation as his partner was. He grabbed a phone and started to dial.

ılı|ı

General Stanfield's cellphone buzzed. He glanced down at the screen. The name on the screen read Mickey Mouse. He immediately excused himself and got up from his place at the table. The meeting was The Joint Chiefs of Staff weekly briefing where each department advises and updates the Secretary of Defense. Homeland Security had pulled another no-show, but otherwise things were uneventful. He stepped outside, pressed the green icon on the screen and said, "Go."

The voice on the other end came through loud and clear. "Just had two agents tour our facility. They were following the payment routine we've been using. I sent 'em away, but expect a phone call and possible heat. Also, they know about Skystorm."

The general thought for a moment. "Where do we stand on things?"

"We can have everything finished by the end of the month."

"Good. I'll clean up things on this end and we can move to phase two. What agency were they from?"

"General Services Administration."

"GSA? Seriously? Okay, this won't be a problem. Thanks for the heads up." The general hung up and headed to his office. If Homeland Security could miss the briefing, so could he.

DC at night cleans up nicely after a good rain. General Stanfield enjoyed the few moments each night when he took AJ for a walk. The squatty French bulldog was busy peeing on every bush he came across. This was the time of day when the general liked to check out, but the call he had received earlier got him thinking. He cancelled the old payment structure they had been using and was now in the process of finding a new way to fund the project. He was so close to completion after what seemed like an interminable amount of time.

The general looked up in time to see a stunning beauty as she turned the corner up ahead. On a leash attached to her left hand was a dog almost identical to his AJ. The general forgot all about his issues and a big grin overtook his face.

"Oh, my gosh," the woman said, seeing the general's matching French bulldog.

The general introduced himself and said, "What are the odds? This is AJ, short for Andrew Jackson."

"This is Chloe and I'm Juliette."

The general was a very put-together man. His subordinates at the office had given him the acronym LACH, for Large And in CHarge. But once his eyes met Juliette's, he found himself at a loss for words, a very unfamiliar situation for him.

"So, do you live around here?" he awkwardly squawked.

Juliette smiled and jerked a thumb over her shoulder. "I'm in a brownstone just around the corner. I just moved here." The two dogs were busy doing the butt sniff tango. "Looks like Chloe has a new friend," Juliette said. The double entendre was not lost on the general and he actually blushed, but looked down at the two canines to hide it.

At that moment, Juliette stepped towards the general. She started to whisper something that the general couldn't quite make out, so he leaned closer. With crazy snakelike reflexes she plunged a needle into his neck.

"What the–" was all he managed to get out before he crumpled into Juliette's arms.

She grabbed hold of the two-hundred-plus-pound male and eased him to the sidewalk. A nondescript van had been on the approach and in less than five seconds it pulled alongside and the general and AJ were quickly loaded and closed up inside. Juliette jumped into the front passenger seat and the van drove off into the night, leaving a very curious Chloe standing on the sidewalk sniffing the air, wondering what had just happened.

General Stanfield blinked his eyes and forced his mind back to consciousness. His surroundings slowly materialized. He was in some sort of old cement room. His mouth was dry, like month-old road kill. Ambient light drifted from above, illuminating thousands of dust specks floating in the air. The floor was covered with water and in the distance he could hear dripping. There was a muffled conversation going on in another room somewhere. It sounded French, but he wasn't sure. He tried to get up, but realized his arms and legs were strapped to a chair.

This ignited a genuine fear in a man known for his calm under pressure. He wriggled and wormed frantically to free himself, but to no avail. He was caught. He took a deep breath and willed himself to have courage as the first fingers of real panic started to take hold. He took in his surroundings and decided that he was in some old fort or bunker.

A cart was pushed into the room by a man with a face not even a mother could love. It looked like someone had taken a blowtorch to his skin and while everything was still hot, it had been pushed and pulled in all the wrong directions. There was no hair anywhere to be seen and one of his eyes was mostly obscured with what looked like grotesque skin-colored cottage cheese.

The hideous being breathed with a raspy wheeze and seemed to support itself on the cart it was pushing. The general gripped the arms on the chair for all he was worth. Be strong, he told himself. He glanced over to the cart and saw its contents. This initiated a brief urinary incontinence. The creature glanced over, its one good eye assessing its prey.

The general put on his best face. "What's going on here? Do you know who I am??"

"I'll ask the questions," rasped the creature's voice with an off-putting accent. He picked up a rusty pair of garden snips and looked them over. "My name is Dax Cole and I have come to kill you." His eye moved from the rusty shears back to the general. "You know, I didn't always look like this. I was handsome once."

He moved closer to the general, his hunched posture working overtime to keep him upright. "Then a little thing called napalm took that away." He casually walked over and without warning, callously snipped off the general's right pinky finger. It wasn't a quick thing as the rusty shears had to be forced several times to complete their task. The general did everything he could to hold his voice and not give this SOB the satisfaction of a scream.

"Did you know it was developed in a secret laboratory at Harvard University?" Dax asked.

The general looked up, sweat pouring off his face that was twisted with pain. His finger stub was pissing blood. "You haven't even asked me a question yet."

Dax continued as if the general had never spoken. "I find the simplest ways are always the best, don't you?"

The general shook his head vigorously as his torturer snipped off his next finger. He let out a scream that echoed off the walls.

Dax paused and smiled through the gnarled slit in his face. He looked around the room. "The Army built hundreds of these bunkers to protect us from an invasion during World War II and we never needed 'em."

He snipped off the middle finger.

The general was on the verge of passing out. His head felt like it weighed a thousand pounds. "Please, I'll tell you anything, just stop."

"Oh, I know you will, but the fun hasn't even begun yet." Dax walked out of the room and returned with AJ. The little dog was shaking and whining.

"Now the real fun begins."

The general let out a gut-busting howl. *"No!"*

CHAPTER FOURTEEN

Dax walked into the adjacent room where there was a temporary table and chairs set up. He was covered in blood. Juliette and two other men, both dressed in black, stopped their conversation and looked over. There was an assortment of high-tech gear and weaponry lying around. Juliette, a striking beauty, was the opposite of the famous Oreo cookie. She looked sweet and delicious on the outside and on the inside—darkness.

Dax reached up and began to tear at his face. Fingers tore away prosthetic chunks until, underneath, appeared a chiseled eastern European male with dark hair and brooding eyes. He stood up straight and spoke perfect English. "That was amusing."

Juliette smiled and tossed him a bottle of water. "Did you get what we needed?"

"Oh yeah and so much more." He opened the bottle and used it to wash some of the blood off his arms. "Did you know that the general peed his bed until he was twelve?"

A smattering of reds and blues from Arizona's version of the Outback, flew past as Codi sat in the passenger seat staring out the window. She was mad; this case was nothing but a wild goose chase. "ARO, my ass!"

Joel said, "Army Research Office; it's part of the US Army Research Laboratory. They fund, well, shit like what we just saw."

"Well, this general and the two nerds we just met have obviously been using this long forgotten payment system to keep it under wraps. And you know what, Joel? We're gonna shut this little party down."

Her phone beeped. "Finally, a cell signal." They had been travelling for the last twenty minutes without a signal. She glanced down to see the text: "Tonight, u, me & 2 hunks, art viewing at the National Gallery????"

It was Katelyn. Codi got out of her funk and texted her back: "In AZ rain check." She decided her phone's signal was strong enough to call Boss and dialed.

"Director Gables."

"Hey, Boss, it's Codi."

"Where are you calling me from? You sound like a 1920's crooner singing in a tin can."

"First off, I wouldn't know what that sounds like."

"Very funny, Agent Sanders. So what's the latest?"

Codi and Joel filled Boss in on their current situation.

She listened and took notes. "Okay, I'm going to make a few calls on this end and see if I can get you a warrant that will at least allow for some clarity. The GSA will not sit by and let some self-serving general defraud the government. But know that politics come first in this town, so it might take some time."

Codi and Joel unconsciously nodded in unison.

"Head back to your hotel and I'll see if I can get that over to you in time to serve it up AM tomorrow."

"Okay, will do." Codi hung up the phone.

The thought of spending one more night in the hotel consumed Joel and he almost drove off the road. "Do you think bedbugs are covered under workman's comp?" he asked.

At four AM, Codi's cellphone rang, ejecting her from a restless slumber. She was instantly alert as she hit the green icon. "Your general took a dirt nap the hard way."

Codi recognized her boss's voice on the phone. "What?" she said.

"Somebody cut off all his fingers and gutted him while he was still alive." Director Gables added, "They either wanted something that he wasn't willing to share, or it was a fetishly sick person." She cleared her throat before saying, "Or both. It looks like they did God-knows-what to his dog, too. I want you two to get back out there and make sure there's no connection. Find out everything you can about what the general did for them and this project Skystorm as it relates to our case."

Codi was up out of bed and pacing. Her mind was processing the information as fast as it was received.

Director Gables continued. "This is a torture and homicide of the Director of the Army Research Office. The FBI will be all over this fast and we'll have to back off."

"Any luck on the warrant?"

"Nothing. This town closed ranks like the last note on an accordion."

"Okay, we'll do what we can."

"Get me some answers and then get back here in one piece. Oh and no shooting this time." Director Gables hung up.

Codi gazed at her phone for a moment and dialed her partner.

A flashing blue neon light leaked through the bathroom window il- luminating Joel's phone as it buzzed on top of the toilet seat. He reached over from the bathtub where he was sleeping and groped to answer it. Ten minutes later they left the Cedar Motel for the last time.

The hour-and-forty-five-minute drive to nowhere seemed shorter the second time around. Codi and Joel were treated to a magnificent sunrise that painted the sky every possible shade of red and orange. At five-thirty AM they hit the cellphone-free zone. Codi watched as her signal faded. She had brought Joel up to speed on the most recent developments and they had a plan in place. Twenty minutes later they turned onto the dirt road.

The sun was up and shining right into the windshield. Even with sunglasses Codi could barely see. But as they came over a rise and an- gled downward towards the barn the sun angle changed just enough to clear her vision. She hit the brakes and let a few choice expletives fly.

Three hundred yards away were two black four-door Jeep Rubicon's, both tricked-out for serious off-road use with raised clearance and thirty-five-inch knobby tires. But what really caught her eye was the smoke that was coming out of the barn.

She stomped on the pedal of the Impala POS. It spun out in the dirt and then lurched forward. "Something is very wrong here," she said.

Joel's hands were shaking as he pulled and checked his weapon. Codi was focused on trying to see the road ahead. Telling flashes from a rifle of some sort came from behind one of the Jeeps. "Get down!" she said to Joel.

Bullets tore at the front of their car and the windshield spider-webbed in every direction. Between the sun and the cracked glass, Codi was blind. The Impala flew off the side of the road and augured into the adjoining roadside ditch. The good news was the shooting had stopped.

"Joel, wake up!" Codi shook his unmoving form. "You okay?"

He started to move. "I think so," he mumbled.

"We got about two minutes before these guys show up and smoke us."

"Wait!" Joel tried to focus.

"Shut up, follow me and do what I say. Don't make me leave you here."

Joel immediately picked up on the urgency of Codi's tone and did as instructed.

Codi forced her door open and fell to the ground. The car was at a forty-five degree angle in the eight-by-twelve-foot ditch. It was leaking every kind of fluid, including steam from the radiator. She pulled Joel out and left him leaning against the vehicle. She scrambled up to the edge of the ditch and did a quick peek-a-boo to get her bearings.

She could see three men in tactical gear running towards them. Codi reached into the car and plunged the cigarette lighter to its stops. She grabbed her partner by his collar and slightly shook him, saying, "Joel, look at me." Joel was hyperventilating. "Look at me!" He did. "I need you to focus." He nodded his head. "Stay low and run in this ditch about two hundred yards that way."

"Are you crazy? That's towards the barn."

"They won't expect it. Oh and if you have to shoot—headshots—they're all wearing body armor. Now go!" Joel dropped a rare expletive and took off.

Codi grabbed the cigarette lighter and checked it for a red glow. She then closed the door and tossed it into a small pool on the ground formed by leaking gasoline. Flames began to spread. She stayed low and sprinted up the ditch to catch up with Joel.

Dax and two men approached the ditch with caution. He scanned for signs of life but found none. Dax had no time to fool with these amateurs. He turned to the man on his left and said, "Edwards, check it out.

Edwards moved cautiously down towards the wreck, his MP4 raised and ready.

The flames Codi had started with the lighter had worked their way up the undercarriage of the vehicle towards the gas tank. It was heating up. Edwards peeked into the rear window, his MP4 leading the way. Nothing. He turned to relay his findings to Dax.

The explosion turned the Impala POS and Edwards into assorted chunks. It blew Dax and the other man standing at the top of the ditch ten feet through the air and flat on their backs, leaving a black cloud mushrooming into the sky.

Codi and Joel had followed the natural wash as it arced around towards the cliff wall. It channeled them to within twenty yards of the left side of the barn. The explosion had Joel prairie-dogging to see what was going on. Codi pushed him back down and carefully crept to the edge of the ditch for a look. She peeked her head up to get a fix. "One down, two still out there, plus however many are inside."

Joel looked at the growing black cloud that used to be their rental car. "You told me I didn't need to buy the insurance. You said that it was a total rip-off. I used my personal credit card."

"Oops. Guess you got ripped off." Codi turned and moved up and out of the wash. "Come on."

"Yeah, but I–" Joel stopped mid-sentence as Codi was already out of sight. He climbed the steep bank and ran to the side of the barn to join her.

The two agents inched their way along the side of the barn towards the front, guns drawn. Codi could see the downed killers getting back to their feet and looking for bodies. Joel snagged his left hand on a splinter from an old board and tried to get it out with his teeth. Codi smacked him on the back of the head and signaled with her fingers for them to move. It was now or never. They stayed low using the perp's vehicles and old farm equipment as cover. They dashed the fifty feet to the barn's sliding door and slipped inside.

Director Ruth Anne Gables slammed her phone down. This was no way to run a government, she thought to herself. Director Calvin Jameson, her counterpart at the FBI, was a real SOB. His demeaning attitude towards other agencies was legendary and his inflexible style made it hard for anyone to work with him. He had pulled the trump card on her and was taking over the investigation. It wasn't that this was unexpected, it was just the way he went about it that pissed her off. The GSA was a real agency with real authority and he had acted as if they were some redheaded stepchild.

The news of the general's gruesome death had hit the press and the FBI was doing the full court press. Director Gables had been kind enough to provide Jameson with details unknown to the FBI and in return he had ordered her to stand down. Her agents were not to enter the premises in question until he could get his people there. The problem was, Codi and Joel had left cellphone coverage twenty minutes earlier and she had no way of contacting them. This information left the FBI director fuming and ultimately he had hung up on her. "Give a man a gun," she mused. Then her thoughts turned back to her two agents in the field.

Inside the barn Codi and Joel found cover behind a grey Gleaner Baldwin Harvester. The two-story tractor was totally restored and looked ready to harvest a field of wheat. Codi leaned over to Joel and whispered, "Those guys are going to be coming through that door any minute and they will be pissed. No mercy. Stay here and take 'em down first chance you get. If you play it by the book or give them any chance at all, they will kill you. Understand?"

Joel nodded his head.

"I'm going to see what's going on inside. Follow me when you're done."

"Wait!"

But Codi had already left.

She used the perimeter of the cave for cover. As she came across the shiny phallic-looking metal towers set in a box pattern she noticed that one was sheared in half and was emitting a column of smoke. Sparks jumped from broken wires. She moved left to the section of the cave that had been converted into a home. In the distance she could just make out three men, one holding Terence Bridgestone at gunpoint. They were yelling something that she couldn't quite make out. She needed a distraction so she could get closer. She looked around. There was a fire extinguisher on the floor by the kitchen.

It would have to do. Codi placed it on the kitchen's gas cooktop and lit the burners. She quickly moved closer to the action, trying to flank the mêlée before her IED (improvised explosive device) went off.

A sudden scratching sound caught her attention. She dropped to the floor and noticed a man crouched low on the other side of a metal cabinet. It was Dr. Matt Campbell. He was dressed in his ubiquitous jeans, tee shirt and sandals and was holding a fourteen-inch wrench in one hand. She crept closer and said, *"Psst."*

Matt turned, saw Codi with a gun and lowered his weapon in defeat. "I should of known these goons were with you," he said.

"What are you talking about?"

"You know," he imitated Joel, "'we'll be back with a warrant and enough agents to tear this place to the ground.'"

"This isn't us."

"Bullshit." He said the last word a bit too loud and Codi looked around tensely to see if they'd been compromised. She gave him the look to keep it down or they would be discovered. "Seriously, we came here to check on you, because...your general is dead."

"Stanfield?"

Codi nodded.

"Murdered?"

She nodded again.

"Who did you tell about this place?"

"No one," she said.

Matt was beside himself. A string of swearwords followed. "We're in deep trouble here."

"You think?"

"Where's that nerdy partner of yours?"

"He's covering the front."

Shots could be heard towards the front of the building. One was a semi auto pistol and the other was a full-auto machine gun. Codi felt a pang of guilt for leaving Joel to cover the front while she was sitting and chatting with Mr. Wizard. There was a brief pause in the action and then it started up again.

"Come on, that's our cue to get you out of here," she said to Matt.

"I'm not leaving."

"Oh yes you are. It's my job to keep you safe."

"You don't understand. This technology could be the most important development of the century. And if used the wrong way..." Matt's words fell away. "It could be one of the deadliest." He looked back up at Codi. "I'll die before I let it get into the wrong hands."

"Great, then we're probably both gonna die. Come on."

Matt moved off in the wrong direction. "Hang on a sec."

"What are you doing?" Codi said.

"Just give me a second." Matt stealthily moved to a wooden workbench. He stayed low and raised a hand to feel for an old toolbox. He opened it up and withdrew a funny looking pistol.

"What is that?"

"A Welrod."

Codi looked puzzled.

"A silenced nine-millimeter, a donation from a previous insurgent back in my grandfather's time." He pulled the rear bolt and nodded his head for Codi to take over.

They moved in an arc around the men who were holding Terence, slowly closing the gap. The gun battle up front had stopped. Codi hoped the outcome was positive. She realized that one of the fanatics was not a man but a woman. And she was doing all the talking. "Come on, professor, we haven't got all day. Well, actually we do since there's not a cop around for a hundred miles." She looked in a different direction and yelled. "I'll give you to the count of five to come out or there'll be one less dweeb on the planet."

Just then, one of the men from outside walked in holding his left arm. Blood could clearly be seen oozing between his fingers. Codi had a sinking feeling that Joel hadn't made it. The man walked over to the female and whispered something to her. She nodded. He then shouted, "My name is Dax Cole and I am not here to kill you, Professor Campbell." He looked at Terence. "You, however, that's different." He raised his gun and without remorse, shot Terrence in the head. Codi could tell by the way the body dropped, like a puppet with its strings cut, that Terence was dead.

Matt gritted his teeth and got ready to charge. Codi grabbed him and pulled him back. "There's nothing we can do for him," she said.

The metal canister of an overheated fire extinguisher had reached its expansion limit and exploded. Codi yelled, "Run!" They started firing into the group. Each shot was reasonably well aimed, or lucky in Matt's case, she wasn't sure. Two black-clad gunmen were down within seconds. Dax, the man who had shot Terence, dove for cover and the girl who had the fastest reflexes Codi had ever seen dodged her third bullet. Was that even possible?

The woman dove behind a metal worktable and pulled out a cellphone. She showed the screen to Dax. There were flashing red dots set on a map of the cave. She called out something to Dax and he nodded in understanding.

Codi grabbed Matt by the arm, "They're trying to out-flank us. We need to move."

Dax fired a volley off to the side of where his targets had just been, encouraging them to move in a specific direction. Juliette tapped on one of the blinking red lights and the view magnified. It included additional information along with the flashing red light. She selected ARM, nodded to her brother and hit the green button.

The explosion rocked Codi and Matt's world. One second they were moving along behind a stack of steel canisters and the next they were propelled through the air. They say it's not the fall that kills you but the sudden stop at the end. Codi had one last thought as she flew though the air. She had failed everyone. Then everything went black as she came to that sudden stop at the end.

Dax waited for the dust to clear before coming from behind his cover. He and his sister Juliette walked over to see the results of their duplicity. Codi and Matt had landed in a heap on the floor, a very compromising-looking heap. Dax stepped up and looked down at the mock orgy that was going on, saying, "What a lovely couple."

Juliette took out her cellphone and took a picture. She inspected the photo carefully and said, "Good. This will definitely make my scrapbook."

CHAPTER FIFTEEN

Growing up under the social protection system in France hadn't been a problem for Dax. He had quickly figured out the players and what they could do for him and when a foster parent became too abusive a little deadly nightshade in their vino did wonders. It caused just enough sweating and paralysis to get them taken away.

By age thirteen, Dax had had enough of the system. He lit the house he had been living in on fire and disappeared into the night, never looking back. The past held no interest for him. He made his way to Paris and was overtaken by the bright lights and tall buildings. Living off the street was a natural for him, but there was something more, something missing. It drove him to deeper and darker crimes. Smuggling, B&E, even murder, until there were no lines left uncrossed and nowhere he could show his face.

The Police Nationale, formerly known as the Surete was closing in. Even the Milieu or French Mob was after him. There was only one possible outcome in his future, so he changed the playing field and left for America, the land of opportunity.

There, he had made friends with the Russian mob and found work as an assassin for hire. He had no interest in rising through the ranks of the mob. For Dax it was all about the money, which brought a freedom he had never experienced. He grew his business by learning from his past mistakes. Over time, he became a ghost, a rumor within a legend. His work made him rich, rewarding him with the freedom and independence he desired, but still a void remained.

Something was missing and no matter how many lives he took, or women he bedded, it still left him hollow. So he had immersed himself as a student of the black arts—poisons that were virtually untraceable, hand-to-hand combat, how to dismember a person while keeping them alive. It helped and the deeper he went, the happier he believed he was. Each job became a challenge to out-do his last hit in the most outrageous way. It became his identity, a calling card so to speak.

One man, he helped drown in his own tub by using only his pinky finger. He had given the man a temporary paralyzer that worked from the neck down. It had been most satisfying. Another was a woman whom he had seduced and then slit her throat during her climax. If he could have bottled the look on her face—priceless.

Juliette came into his life on June twenty-third, a day he would never forget. She brought with her something Dax could never have guessed was possible: love, sisterly love and better still, a twin. Juliette had been looking for him ever since she learned of his existence.

They were born to twenty-two-year-old prisoner 32857 and had been placed into a French orphanage system on the day of their birth. Juliette was adopted right away and Dax, never.

Juliette had grown up in a wealthy home on the outskirts of Paris. Her parents made sure she had everything she wanted, except an emotional attachment. Presents and gifts were their only way of conveying their love. In spite of it all, Juliette managed to succeed in a business family where others might have failed. She received top marks in school and was an aspiring Olympic slalom skier.

But from the moment Juliette learned she was adopted, something changed inside her. She had a brother out there somewhere. Her parents had adopted her, but not him. They had split up twins, an unforgivable betrayal in her mind. And a malicious seed took hold that day and started to grow within her. She began to lose interest in school and skiing, determined to find her brother and reunite.

The moment she found Dax, it was like two magnets coming together. It was that missing something Dax had been looking for all his life and he recognized it instantly. He was hesitant to let her into his life at first as she was from the right side of the tracks. But in time, he took her in and showed her his ways, marveling at how quickly she shed her societal norms and adapted to his world. They vowed to never separate; the bond between twins overpowered all. Individually they were ferocious, but together, unstoppable.

Chapter Sixteen

Juliette and Dax struggled to get their prize loaded into the back of the second Jeep. They closed the rear hatch and returned back inside. Matt and Codi lay motionless on the concrete floor. They were zip-tied and had been injected with a powerful narcotic. Dax looked down at their hostages. "One or two?" Juliette flipped a coin and caught it. Her reaction showed disappointment "Two," she said. She reached down and grabbed a handful of Codi's hair and started dragging her to the Jeeps.

They had lost three good men, but the prize they were packing would more than make up for it. Juliette slapped an explosive package on the old Ford pickup, started her Jeep and drove off with Dax following behind in the second Jeep. They stopped about a hundred yards out and positioned the vehicles for a courtside view.

Dax picked up his Iridium 9575 Extreme satellite phone. He pressed send and leaned back on the headrest. Juliette stepped out of her vehicle and slid into the passenger seat of the Jeep Dax was driving. The ringing stopped on the fourth ring and a voice in French announced, "Talk to me."

Dax filled the voice in on their progress.

"Impressive," the voice said. "That was smart to get out to the desert so quickly. Make sure you leave no evidence or witnesses behind and then bring our guests to the fort." The voice was gone as quickly as it had come.

Dax glanced over at his sister and said, "You heard the man, no evidence or witnesses left behind."

Juliette loved this part.

Like a grand conductor directing the London Philharmonic, she pushed the buttons on her cellphone to the rhythm of a beat only she could hear. One by one, blasts from inside the cavern destroyed what was left, obliterating all evidence and partially collapsing the cavern. She finished off with a final flourished swipe and the green and white Ford F-150 turned into a ball of fire. Smiles all around from Dax and Juliette. Then she hopped back into her Jeep and both vehicles drove off, the wind obscuring their tracks almost as fast as they made them.

CHAPTER SEVENTEEN

Joel woke with a coughing fit and a plume of dust. He was alive, but the impact of being shot had taken a severe toll. His right arm no longer worked and he was having trouble breathing. He forced his eyes open and took stock. He was lying under a piece of corrugated steel tube that had both pinned him and protected him from the explosions. Using his good arm and maximum effort, he wormed his way out from under the pipe and sat up.

Now he could breathe better. With his left arm he removed his tie and made a sling. He used his hand to put pressure on the bullet wound in his shoulder. He looked around for his gun; it was nowhere. Then he noticed there was a large rusty nail sticking out of his left thigh. He reached to pull it out, but it made him feel squeamish so he decided to leave it in. The back of his head was bleeding and he couldn't remember being hit there. His mouth was parched and his eyes were full of grit. But he was alive.

The barn had collapsed and from what he could tell, not much was left standing in the cavern. He tried to investigate, but there was no easy way to climb the rubble and get into the back of the cavern in his condition. He tried calling out for Codi or Dr. Campbell, but his voice croaked out only a whisper.

He sat down and dropped his head. He had failed. Boss was wrong; he wasn't ready for fieldwork. Tears rolled down his face as he thought about his situation. He was in the middle of nowhere and shot. His partner was gone and the bad guys were nowhere in sight. He laid his head back and let the darkness take hold.

Three minutes later he opened his eyes. *What am I doing?* he asked himself. Codi would never allow this. Get up and get going! He sat up and ripped the sleeve off his shirt and wrapped the bullet wound on his upper arm, using his teeth to help tie the knot. He stood up, wobbled a bit, but found his balance and shuffled a few steps.

While he paused to catch his breath he leaned against a restored 1950 Farmall M V-12 tractor covered with timbers from the barn's roof. The red tractor with white grill and cowling looked as though it was ready to be sold new at a showroom. An idea born of desperation struck him.

Joel cleared some of the wood away. He checked the fuel tank and the ignition. She turned over fine but would not start. His brain started processing and he remembered that old diesel engines needed their glow plugs heated before they would start. He looked over the knobs and pulled the one with the correct symbol. He silently counted to thirty and fired the ignition once more.

Pop! Pop! Pop! The old diesel fired up and within a minute it was purring. It took him a few tries to figure out the clutch and gears, but soon the old gal was humming away from the debris that was once a barn. He got to the end of the dirt road and turned left. Next town, fifty miles. At a top speed of twenty-two-miles-per-hour it was going to take a while. Joel's bleeding had mostly stopped, his newfound determination anything but.

CHAPTER EIGHTEEN

The Tibetan Singing Bowl rang loud and true, followed by an overwhelming need to vomit. Codi cracked open an eye. The ringing in her ears was constant and was the only proof that she was still alive. She was lying on an old cement floor. The air was damp and smelled of the sea with a fetor of urine. She tried to sit up but her head started spinning, so she laid back down and rolled over. She could just make out Matt who was throwing up in the corner.

"What did they give us?" she asked him.

"Probably ketamine and by the adverse reactions we're having," he threw up again, "a lot of it."

"Isn't that used as a horse tranquilizer?"

Matt held his thumb up in reply, as he was too busy puking to answer.

Codi finally sat up and tried to focus on her surroundings. She rubbed her temples. Her headache was as serious as a public hanging. Matt came over and sat down next to her. They were in a ten-by-ten cell. It was solid concrete other than a small square window with rusty metal bars and a reinforced metal door with slats. Codi walked over and tried the door—locked.

"I think it's an old prison." Matt pulled himself up to the small window and looked out. "Yeah and it's on the ocean."

"What?" Codi climbed up to the window to see for herself. The view through the small stone square opening showed nothing but ocean for as far as she could see. "We're a long way from home."

Nial Brennan was in his late sixties. He was clean-shaven and still had a full head of dark hair. He was, what some would call, fit for his age. His piercing dark eyes like a moonless night, looked out from the passenger seat of his metallic charcoal grey Eurocopter 130.

The sleek design and unique tail rotor gave it a range of 370 miles and a top speed of 180 mph with a little tail wind. He had paid two-point-seven million euros for it and considered it one of his favorite toys. He was a firm believer in the adage, with a twist, "He who *lives* with the most toys wins." And he wasn't afraid to get his hands dirty to achieve it.

Nial glanced down at his most recent acquisition in wonder. That is, one of his many shell corporations' three-layers-deep recent acquisitions. Fort Boyard was an old abandoned French military fort built on a mostly submerged pile of rocks on the Pertuis d'Antioche strait, five miles off the west coast of France. The structure was a 223-by-100-foot oval five stories tall, like a concrete layer cake with a hollowed-out center. It sat alone in the middle of the ocean, a testament to man's desire to tame Mother Nature.

Fort Boyard had a single access dock and a raised cylindrical glass observation tower that stabbed up above everything like an airport control tower. The fort was originally built to keep the English at bay. But by the time it was completed France was no longer at war with the English. Fort Boyard was abandoned at the turn of the nineteenth century. It was re-commissioned several years later and used as a prison until World War II.

It was built of stone and concrete with walls six feet thick. Inside was a large courtyard flanked by an arched walkway for each level. The old gun ports had all been converted into cells and most recently a helicopter pad was attached to the parapet-style roof, truly a giant cement and stone island.

Fort Boyard was finally put up for sale at a government auction and Nial, through an attorney, had maneuvered successfully to acquire it.

Nial had started his most recent career in Angola bartering guns for diamonds. He transitioned from that into becoming a full-fledged arms dealer. He had a flamboyant personality and used it to his advantage. With the demise of Russia as a powerhouse, he was bright enough to see the writing on the wall and he diversified.

As the bulk of black market weapon sales became penny ante when others were forced to cut margins and ultimately choose another profession, Nial thrived. He had specialized in the big stuff and was soon the go-to guy. He had made powerful contacts in Russia and played middleman to some of the biggest black-market military sales in the last ten years.

His Irish roots had given him a hatred for the status quo. Belfast had been a dangerous place to grow up in the sixties. As a child, Nial had watched as British soldiers mowed down innocent civilians in retaliation for a bomb at the Everglades Hotel where several high-ranking officials had been staying. The tensions had never been higher between the two countries.

Seven-year-old Nial was on his way to the local theater with his mother and nine-year-old sister to see H.G. Wells' *The Time Machine*. He had saved the two schillings he would need to get in and his mother would cover the rest. It was an unusually cold and rainy day as the three ran from awning to awning in a hopeless attempt to keep dry.

As Nial paused for a brief second to look at a shiny red bicycle in a storefront window, his mother and sister turned the corner just in time to become part of one of the largest massacres of innocents in recent Irish history. They were dead before Nial could run around the corner to see what happened. His world ended that day. Teeth chattering from the rain and cold as he despondently watched the crews move among the carnage to haul it all away, his dad finally arrived on the scene and together they cried their way home.

His father buried his grief in cheap Irish whiskey, leaving his son to fend for himself. Nial had struggled between his Catholic faith and his hatred for the British. In the end he could not forgive them. What he *could* do though was make them pay.

Nial turned to the IRA who gave him a new home. And for his first assignment he was given that red bicycle he had been admiring in the storefront window. They loaded it up with explosives and asked him to ride it into the local recruitment office.

Nial Brennan peddled for all he was worth. For the first time since his family had been taken from him, he smiled. The bomb-laden bicycle looked like any other bike laden with packages. Nial had selected his favorite outfit for the job, a superman costume. When he hit the stairs leading into the building he nearly crashed, but sheer determination righted the bike and willed it into the building.

The recruiting office was a brick and wooden two-story flat that had been converted into offices. Once inside, Nial released the bike and turned to run. He could hear a shout from behind him as he exited the stairs two at a time. The explosion rocked the entire neighborhood, leveling the first floor of the building and causing the second to collapse on top of it.

Nial was blown across the street and nearly killed. Two key members of the IRA scooped him up and left the area. The bombing had killed five British soldiers and demolished their recruiting station. Nial had paid the price—he was disfigured as a piece of shrapnel nearly took his head off. It ultimately left him with a deformed ear and a prominent scar that ran across his face and down his neck.

The IRA applauded his bravery and Nial was hooked. After several more successful attacks, young Nial became a very wanted man. With the help of his new family, the IRA, he relocated to Africa. There, he continued to hone his skills until he cut his first deal—ten Kalashnikov rifles for one four-caret diamond. He used his connections back at the IRA to pawn the diamond. The rest was history.

CHAPTER NINETEEN

The door to the cell slammed open with a metal clunk. Three men in black with French FAMAS AA-52 machine pistols entered. The unique weapon was a bull-pup design with a channel sight that could also be used as a handle. Codi could tell by the way they carried their weapons that these men were professionals. With a Slavic twinge to their broken English, they ordered Matt and Codi to kneel down and put their hands behind their heads and interlock their fingers. Codi glanced over at Matt, unsure of their intentions.

They had made the effort to haul them to wherever they were, hopefully not to just kill them. One of the men flex-cuffed Codi's hands behind her back and then Matt's, while the other two stood watch a safe distance away, guns poised. Codi and Matt were then escorted out of their cell and down a hall.

The hall was an enfilade of cell doors. Codi took it all in and judging by the rust, this place had been long forgotten. The two prisoners were pushed through a seemingly random door and into a larger room with a bulky chair-like device in the center. The frame was made of wood with metal slats that crisscrossed the seat and back. It had raised armrests complete with tie-down straps and a set of wires that ran to a nearby table.

Matt was first to be strapped in and no matter how much he wriggled, he was caught like a mouse in a swimming pool. Codi was handcuffed to a steel ring on the opposite wall that was just high enough that she could not sit. The three guards left, but not before the leader said,

"Stay here," which caused all three to laugh as they slammed the iron door closed and locked it.

Codi could hear them laughing as they moved down the hallway. Matt's eyes were firmly planted on the electrical device on the table. He had no illusions; this chair was a torture device. Codi broke the silence, "I don't know about you, but this place is a bit Neo-Gothic for my palate."

Matt turned his head to the right so he could see Codi. She was smiling. "Yeah," he said. "It needs a few throw pillows and a nice settee."

"A nice place to hang out," Codi said while shaking the chains above her head.

"I could sit here all day, the view is so amazing," Matt countered. It made them both laugh for a brief moment, but the gravity was not lost on the prisoners and soon the room was filled with silence.

Dax opened the door and stepped inside. To Codi, it felt like all the oxygen fled the room. He smiled and looked them over like a wolf before its meal. "My name is Dax Cole and I have come to kill you." Things suddenly got real. "But first I have a few questions." Dax walked over to Matt and stared him down. "And if you answer them to my liking, how you will die...let's just say there will be a lot less begging involved."

Matt tried not to look directly into his eyes.

Dax breathed in the moment like a wine connoisseur with a rare bottle of Bordeaux. He circled Matt like a predator and then turned and moved over to Codi. He leaned in close for a good look, his eyes lingering on certain parts. "You cost me some good men. So I'll take my time with you."

Matt took on a brave tone. "Leave her alone, it's me you want."

"Oh, so I was right, there is a little something going on here."

Codi looked incredulous. "What, us? No, you're mistaken. I'm a federal agent and you're both under arrest."

Dax backhanded Codi with a swipe so vicious it split her lip and left her dazed.

He turned and casually walked over to the table and turned the knob on a large potentiometer that was connected via wires to the chair. The high-voltage current flowed through Matt's body with such intensity that he almost bit his tongue in half. His body became so stiff that you could have driven a car across his midsection without damage.

Codi screamed.

Dax took a whiff of air and said, "Something's burning."

He lazily looked at the second hand on his watch for a moment and killed the power. Matt dropped back into his chair, head lolling. Dax walked over to him and lifted his chin. He was a mess. Dax smiled. He moved over to Codi.

She glowered at him with hate-filled eyes.

"Okay, who's next?" he said as he rubbed his hands together, relishing his next move. He took her badge from his pocket and looked it over. "Special Agent Colette Sanders of the GSA. General Services Administration, I always thought that was a paper-pushing agency. No real authority. But your badge seems real enough. I wonder if they'll miss you."

"Bring it on, you son-of-a-bitch," Codi said.

Dax flicked out a stiletto that had materialized as if by magic. "Oh, I plan to."

A voice in French pushed through the static on the radio that was clipped to his belt. "Dax, we have inbound." He sighed at the lost moment. "Do you copy?"

Dax turned and abruptly left. As he opened the door three guards appeared. "Caleb, kill them both," he said in English for the benefit of his guests. Then he was gone.

The three men in black moved into the room with military precision. Two kept their distance, while the other unhooked and replaced the flex cuffs on Codi. He unhooked Matt who simply fell to the floor, his body like a wet noodle. The two soldiers grabbed Matt and dragged him out of the room. Caleb pointed his weapon at Codi and gestured for her to follow Matt. The group moved down a narrow flight of stairs towards the bottom of the fort, Caleb keeping his distance and vigil. Matt had regained enough body function that he was now walking on unsteady feet with the help of only one guard.

The word garbage is the same in French as it is in English and that word was just visible through the rust on a large metal door. Guard One kicked the door open and flung Matt inside. Codi and the other two followed. The room was blackened with age and the only identifying asset was a gated garbage shoot that led out to the ocean.

Caleb pushed both victims to the floor and pulled his forty-five-caliber FNP pistol out of its holster and took aim. He paused, stepped back and motioned to his cohorts. "They're all yours, boys," he said. "You've earned it." He leaned back against the wall and crossed his arms to watch the festivities.

Codi said, "You shoot a federal agent and you'll have the whole United States up your ass!"

Caleb smiled. "Up your ass. I like that and I suggest that's where we start." He was met with a laugh. One of the men handed his gun to his partner and moved to Codi with a glint in his eyes. She tried to get to her feet, but he kicked her leg out from under her before she could stand.

The skid of the Eurocopter touched lightly down on the purpose-built pad. Nial hopped out, instinctively keeping his head low, even though the blades were well out of reach. He dropped down the stairs to find Dax and Juliette waiting for him. "Report."

Juliette didn't hesitate. "We've almost completed reassembling Project Skystorm, though we're not totally sure what it does."

Nial smiled and with a grand gesture of his hands, said, "It does the most amazing thing." Dax and Juliette shared a look. Their latest boss had a flair to his personality that they found repugnant. "Excellent," Nial said. "And the prisoners?"

"In their cell, though I don't know why we have to keep them alive," Dax said.

"This is very cutting-edge stuff. Once we get a successful test, you can do what you want to them, but until then we may need them alive, well at least the male. Though the girl may provide leverage with him." He tilted his chin in the air, thinking. "Keep 'em both alive for now."

Dax negligibly nodded to Juliette who picked up a small handheld radio and stepped away. Dax held out his hand. "Right this way."

Juliette stepped out of earshot from the others and pressed the button on her radio to transmit. "Caleb!" she was met with nothing but static. She pressed the button and called again more urgently. A very static-filled voice came back. "Go for Caleb."

"For God's sake, please tell me you haven't shot them yet."

What seemed like an eternity passed before she heard, "Ah, hang on."

CHAPTER TWENTY

Joel walked into the office to a multitude of stares and mixed comments. His arm was in a sling and he walked with a slight limp. In general, he looked like hell. He didn't get twenty feet before he was met with a voice. "Agent Strickman, in my office, stat." The boss was in one of those take-no-prisoners moods and everyone else had been avoiding her. Joel slowly eased himself into the chair across from Ruth Anne's desk.

"What are you doing here? The doctor said two weeks, no work. This is not a request, it's required procedure."

"Yeah, well screw procedure. We need to be doing everything we can to get Codi back."

Ruth Anne tried to hide a smile that was tugging at the corner of her mouth. This was not the nerdy computer genius she had hired. This was a determined field agent ready to take on any task. "How are you feeling?"

"I've been better."

"It sucks getting shot."

Joel wondered if everyone he knew had been shot before. "With all due respect, Boss, I can be invaluable to this investigation."

"What investigation? The FBI has completely taken over. We are out."

"That's bull crap. It's our agent who's missing. We need to be part of the solution."

"Joel, you know as well as I that we don't investigate murders and kidnappings." Ruth Anne looked across her desk at the serious expression on Joel's face. She decided to play her final card. "I have, however, after much effort, convinced the FBI to allow one of our agents to play an advisory role in their taskforce. As you are the only agent to have been on-site during the action, I'd like to send you."

Joel looked up at his boss. "If this has anything to do with getting Codi back, I'm in."

"Glad to hear it." She looked down at some documents, selected one, signed it and handed it to Joel. "I'm temporarily assigning you to the FBI. You'll be our liaison, both eyes and ears."

Joel stood. "Nobody takes one of our agents and gets away with it."

Ruth Anne appraised Joel for a brief second and said, "Damn straight."

The FBI offices in DC are housed in a large rectangular limestone building with a domed top. It houses some of the brightest investigative minds in the world. The interior offices are compartmentalized by category and case. Agents work in teams and or in pairs.

Joel looked up at the building and put on his most serious face. He took the stairs two at a time up to the main door. After passing through a vigorous security check and receiving a visitor's pass, he met the task-force working on Project Skystorm and the murder of one government employee and the kidnapping of two.

The agent in charge, Special Agent Brian Fescue, was a task-focused leader who had a long list of convictions to his record. His cappuccino-colored skin and slight Jamaican accent was the only hint of his island past. He was about an inch shorter than Joel, but he was built like a tank. He introduced Joel to everyone, including Special Agent Annie Waters. She was on loan from the cyber division and was Joel's counterpart at the FBI. After reading Joel in on the case, they all listened carefully as he gave the details of his exploits at the barn.

Joel was able to give a vague description of the man who shot him and whatever details he had on Project Skystorm.

Agent Fescue nodded in appreciation and said, "That's good information. We're working two angles on this: first, what is Project Skystorm and what can it be used for; and the second is, where on earth are our agents. That has to take top priority. But working both might get us closer to an answer. Joel, I'm going to have you work with Agent Waters; she's a wiz on the computer like you. I'm counting on the both of you to get us something actionable. Then bring it to me and we'll handle it from there."

Agent Waters introduced herself to Joel. She was a slightly chubby, raven-haired Hispanic with a focused charm. Her brown eyes seemed to bore right through Joel and he glanced behind himself briefly to make sure she was actually looking at *him*.

He sat at his new terminal right next to Agent Waters. His leg and arm were aching, but he'd be damned if he let it show. She began going over every detail they had so far in an attempt to get him up to speed. She kept glancing over at Joel who was trying to concentrate. Finally, she blurted out, "So what's it like to be shot?"

Joel beamed. Finally someone who had *not* been shot. He puffed up with pride, leaned back in his chair and looked up. "Getting shot is like having your heart ripped to pieces by Carolyn Flynn twenty minutes before prom starts." He then went on to share every detail of his gun battle and how he had shot one perp before the other one loosed a wall of full-auto lead at him. Agent Waters listened intently. He shared how an explosion dumped the entire roof on his head and if a large piece of metal tubing hadn't hit him in the head and landed on top of him, well...he was lucky to be alive. Her eyes sparked at Joel's every word and he was loving the moment.

Their workstation was set up with two desks set side-by-side at a slight bevel. It allowed agents to work separately but also quickly share information. Joel followed a hunch he had until something gave.

"Check this out," he said. "An unidentified bogey crossed into Mexico across the Arizona border."

Agent Waters took the info and drilled down.

She opened a digital map that had multiple flight patterns for the area in question. "It looks like someone was flying low across the border."

"But right here they got just a little too high."

"And they showed up on radar."

"Yep." Joel double-checked his notes. "The timeline fits."

This was the first break. "I'll let Fescue know," said Agent Waters.

She stood to leave and Joel turned back to his monitor, determination in his eyes. "I'll follow this trail into Mexico and see what I can find," he said. He started checking every private jet that came in or out of Mexico during the two-day window prior to finding the radar blip.

She found Agent Fescue standing next to a table with two other agents rehashing the evidence. "You got something?" he asked her.

"I don't think they're in the US anymore."

Agent Fescue paused before saying, "That's not good news. Where are they?"

Codi kicked out at her assailant. He kept just out of reach, circling for the right opening to pounce. It was a game he was enjoying because he knew the final outcome, a little rape followed by an extended execution that ended with a bullet to the brain. Caleb leaned back against the cell wall watching the action with amusement.

His radio sounded off with a static-filled garble. He lifted it up into the air in an attempt to get a better signal. The thick stone walls were hard on radio waves. And being in the very bottom level made communication almost impossible.

Codi managed to connect with her foot, sending the guard stumbling back.

104   BRENT LADD

All three of the men in black laughed. This one was feisty. This time, the French voice on the radio could just be understood. "Caleb!"

He moved the radio to his mouth and said, "Go for Caleb."

What he heard next made Caleb react. *"Nous avons besion en vie. Arreter!"* he shouted.

The guard stopped his assault on Codi, saying, *"Ah, Merde."*

Codi and Matt were unceremoniously tossed back into their cell. Matt was beginning to feel more like himself. Codi bent her ankles up to her butt and wriggled until she managed to get her zip-tied hands in front of her. She went over to the small barred window and used the stone edge to saw through her bindings. The whole process took twenty seconds.

Next, she helped Matt break his zip-ties and helped him over to a wall so he could sit and lean against it. She sat down next to him pondering their next move. "I think it's time we had a chat."

Matt looked over, all his previous barriers gone. "What do you want to know?"

"All of it."

"This is the main housing. It can be mounted onto a helicopter, or any fixed aircraft really." Dr. Didier Comstock was giving Nial the tour. He was the lead scientist on the project. He was an Ethiopian by birth, but an English passport and an Oxford education had freed him from his country's clutches. His long curly grey hair and matching beard gave merit to the term "mad scientist."

Nial looked at the strange refrigerator-sized box. It had four tubular bars that stuck out of the front. They were each tipped with what looked like a four-inch chrome ball. He stood back and took in everything. Savoring the moment, he absently licked his lips with anticipation.

They were standing in a large room supported by several

floor-to-ceiling cement-arched columns. Temporary lights had been set up that gave the room once used to feed prisoners a yellowish-green glow.

"The control panel is over here." The group moved to a large folding table. "We should be able to operate Skystorm remotely within the next few days."

A collection of wires came out of the base and led to the control unit the size of a loaf of bread with three levers and an extended keypad with a small digital screen in the middle.

"Have you been able to make it work?" Nial asked.

"We have a few questions we need to ask, but everything seems to be here."

Nial flicked Dax's shoulder. "See, that's why I wanted them alive, just in case."

Juliette and Dax shared a look.

Nial turned back to the doctor and said, "Make a list of your questions and Dax will get your answers." Dr. Comstock nodded to one of his assistants who ran off to get the list. Nial was extremely pleased, the twins had come through for him and he wouldn't forget.

He then looked at a large wire that went to a large metal box with perforated holes. "What's this?"

"It's the power source," Dax said.

"Doesn't look very portable," said Nial.

"It's not," Dr. Comstock said.

Nial glowered, but Dr. Comstock held up his hand before he could go off on him. He said, "We have anticipated your need for portability and are putting the final touches on a capacitor-based recharging pack. It will give you two sustained pulses and then you will need to wait two minutes for it to recharge."

Nial processed the information.

"It's the size of a piece of luggage," Dr. Comstock added.

Nial's pout quickly changed to a grin. "That's why I hired you! Amazing, simply amazing." He did a little it's-going-to-work dance jig.

Dax looked on, but kept his thoughts to himself.

CHAPTER TWENTY-ONE

"It started off as a death ray," Matt said.

Codi perked up. "Seriously?"

"Yes. Back in the forties, my grandfather had some remarkable results with creating and controlling ball lightning."

"Ball lightning?"

"It's a rare but naturally occurring phenomenon in nature."

"And your grandfather figured out a way to recreate it?"

Matt nodded as he readjusted himself on the hard floor. "So much so that the president set him up in a secret off-the-map lab to perfect it."

"The barn?"

"Right. He was able to use the recreated ball lightning as a weapon that could disintegrate all organic matter and leave everything else untouched."

"That's incredible, how come it was never used?"

Matt turned and faced Codi. "Initially, the range was too short. The best he could do was about a hundred yards." He paused and then continued. "In 1945, they had a break-in, an attempted sabotage by the Germans. My grandfather's assistant was killed. It made him very paranoid and he stopped giving updates to his superiors. Once the atomic bomb worked, his research was put on the back burner. Honestly, he kinda got lost in the shuffle."

Codi nodded. "Secret projects back then were often so compartmentalized it would be easy to get lost in the post-war shuffle."

"My granddad went to Truman and convinced him to keep Thunder

Light alive." Matt stared out at nothing, remembering the story. "That was the name of the project," he said.

A light went on in Codi's mind. "That's what the paper trail was about—T. Light."

"Yes. They set up an off-the-book payment system and he reported directly to the president. They became good friends and when President Truman left office, he made it permanent."

"So this whole thing is about a death ray?"

Matt squirmed slightly. He had been sworn to secrecy and even now the words were hard to share. "Not exactly. My grandfather believed that within the ray itself he could create cohesion at a molecular level."

"Cohesion?"

"Like electronic glue. That's the work I have taken on and improved upon. Terence was my grandfather's replacement assistant." Matt stared off again for a moment, reliving his past and his friend's death.

"Go on," Codi said.

"After my grandfather died, Terence was my connection. I finished at MIT and he got me started on the path to completing the work." Matt took on a sad expression that Codi could see in his eyes.

"I'm sorry about Terrence."

He nodded solemnly. Matt had shared a lot of time with Terrance. He would be sorely missed and hard to replace. Matt tested the gash in his tongue with his teeth. The bleeding had stopped but it still hurt like hell.

"Tell me what Project Skystorm evolved into and remember, no science mumbo jumbo, please; keep it simple."

"First we were able to change the beam's configuration and use the infrared spectrum to make the ray invisible. Then we used a particle combiner, that was Terrence's name for it and we were able to achieve molecular cohesion."

Codi gave him a sideways glance. Matt put his hands up in surrender and continued. "Molecular cohesion is a process that allows us to beam microscopic particles over distance directly into a living organism."

"Wait, what?"

"For example, we could fly over a town and vaccinate every person in it."

"Like a microwave beam that shoots out a million microscopic injections?"

"Basically," Matt said. "It's much like the principal of helium gas in a balloon. The molecules are so small that, over time, they escape through the balloon. With Skystorm, we can instantly beam microscopic particles so small they go right through the skin and into the body."

"Without you knowing?"

"Yes."

Codi thought about the ramifications of the information. "Vaccinate or infect every person, right?"

Matt hung his head in shame. "That's what I'm afraid is happening here. And the problem is, because it enters the organism on a cellular level, everything works twice as fast."

"What do you mean?"

"Say you inoculate a group using stage four measles pathogens."

"Stage four?"

"The final stage, when the body is in recovery and has made weakened or killed forms of the microbe. Because it enters on a cellular level, they are immediately vaccinated against the disease. If they already have it, they're healed within twenty-four hours."

Codi quickly grasped the alternative—using stage one pathogens. "And vice versa."

CHAPTER TWENTY-TWO

Joel was onto something. Agent Waters and he had tracked the private jet in and out of Mexico through a surveillance camera at the Saltillo Airport in Coahuila, Mexico. The private jet had then flown across the Atlantic to Bordeaux, France. That's where the trail had gone cold. Agent Fescue ordered two agents to Bordaeux to check out the airport. He and the rest of the team packed up and headed to the FBI offices in Paris.

The FBI has agents stationed in over seventy-five cities around the globe. Their purpose is to build relationships and share intelligence with those countries' law enforcement agencies as it relates to protecting American's and their interests. They are not allowed to dispense justice without the local authorities' involvement. That line, however, sometimes gets crossed.

The long-range Gulf Stream 650 touched down on the runway at Charles De Gaulle airport. It was met with no fanfare as it taxied up to a non-descript metal hangar. The early morning crew sauntered out of the darkness with a yawn to chock the wheels and open the jet's hatch. Joel checked his watch, three AM. Two black SUV's pulled up alongside the jet and the FBI taskforce did the unload, reload shuffle.

The FBI office in Paris is located at thirty-two Rue Planchat, just off the Seine river. Joel and the team had worked during the flight over and everyone was beat. It was time for a brief stop at the hotel and then Agent Fescue wanted everyone back at it in four hours.

Joel noted the four stars the Hotel De Seine had received on Yelp and relaxed. The FBI travelled first class. He could get used to this. His room overlooked the famous river where he could see joggers and strollers by the water's edge. It was a perfect sunrise. The city was awake and on the move. He wondered where and what his partner was going though. It must be hell. He closed his curtains and went to bed.

Agents found the suspect jet in the back corner of a private hangar. The forensic unit was making a thorough pass, but it looked thin at best. The shell company that had rented it led nowhere. Their best clue was the dead pilot shot in the head and left to rot in the cockpit. Luckily, his license was still in his pocket.

Four hours later everyone was back at their new office and hard at work. Agent Fescue took in the information and relayed it to his team. "I need everything you can get on a pilot named Adrik Kudashov."

The cell door opened with a clank. Dax walked in with his stiletto held loosely in his hands. Two guards followed and stayed back with guns drawn. Codi and Matt could see the intensity on his face and knew they were in trouble. Dax looked at the couple sitting next to each other. "Ah, the two love birds," he said with a disingenuous smile. "Time to start squawking." He held up a piece of paper with writing on it. "Here is a list of questions I need answers to." Dax dropped the piece of paper on the floor near Matt.

"Doctor Campbell," he said, "you will write down the answers to these questions or I will shoot your treasured cellmate and start carving you up into little pieces until you do." Dax tossed Matt a pencil and left the room. Matt picked up the paper as if it were laced with cyanide. After reading the first question his worst fears were confirmed.

The assistant struggled to get the bleating goat into position. It had fought him on the dock, on the boat and now in the lab. He found himself in a tug of war that could go either way. Finally, he inched the beast forward and tied it to a stanchion. Victorious, the assistant insulted the goat and headed for the bathroom to wash his hands and shoes. Dr. Comstock glanced up from his work at the new arrival. It was finally time for a test. He requested the Skystorm device to be focused in the goat's direction.

Dr. Comstock typed a few keystrokes on his laptop and smiled. "Test subject number one. Load the Caseous Lymphadenitis." Caseous Lymphadenitis, or CL, was a nasty goat virus that was harmless to humans but eventually a death sentence to a goat. Gestation was several days and death would take anywhere from one to three months.

An assistant opened a small aluminum case and pulled a vial from it. He took a syringe and filled it with the clear liquid from the vial. Then he carefully opened a panel on the Skystorm and drained the contents into it. "Loaded," he said.

Dr. Comstock had been watching from across the room. "Half-charge," he instructed.

Another assistant connected the charging unit. "Charging."

Dr. Comstock slid his safety glasses on and ducked slightly behind his table. He held his breath and called, "Fire!"

The device made a snapping sound like a mean rubber band on a plastic table and then went silent. There was no flash, no boom, not even a visible light of any kind. The goat, however, exploded in a mass of flesh and hide that covered the room in Jackson Pollack-style gore. The assistant who had just walked into the room from the washroom bore the brunt of it.

Nial had been watching from the observation area. "Get my chopper ready," he said. "I'm leaving. Forty-eight hours, Dax. Get the doctor's answers and get it to work the way we wanted." He left before Dax could answer.

Joel blinked his eyes and rubbed his temples. He was getting a head-ache. The pilot in question was a Russian-born Soviet Air Force pi-lot that had gone AWOL two years ago. The most recent information showed him in the employ of a high standing member of a Mexican drug cartel. He'd been caught skimming three months ago and had managed to disappear, his life on the run apparently coming to an end and the cartel's contract for his demise fulfilled. It was another dead end, literally.

Agent Waters banged her hands down on her keyboard.

"Whoa, easy there, that's government property," Joel said, smiling at her.

"It's just that this is so stupid!"

"What?"

"I've been going over this all day and I'm starting to see patterns that aren't there." She blew a loose hair from her face. "The shell corpo-ration that rented the plane has no holdings, no officers, no nothing." Agent Waters was at a loss.

"Yes, we know."

"There has to be something."

Joel considered her thought. "Like who set up the shell corporation."

"The attorney!"

"Of course, that's public record."

Agent Waters typed like her life depended on it for about three minutes. "Get Fescue. We'll need a warrant."

Matt paced back and forth in the small cell, weighing his options. Codi's eyes tracked him like a slow-motion tennis match. She knew their options were limited, but her never-give-up attitude pushed her for a solution. Matt strolled over and plopped down next to her. "I'm sorry," he said.

"For what?"

"For accusing you of all that stuff back there."

"You know, I could be a plant placed here to see what I can learn and manipulate you into doing what they want."

Matt shot her a look and Codi smiled. "I've seen a lot of plants and none of them looked like you," he said.

"That's because you're living in the desert. All your plants have thorns." They both laughed nervously.

"I think you should kill me," he said.

Codi looked at him like he was crazy.

"Seriously. It's the only way. I won't be able to hold out and we can't let them get ahold of a working Skystorm." Matt looked down at the paper. The thought of seeing Codi die and being chopped up into little pieces was haunting him.

"What's the chance they'll get it to work without you?"

Matt looked up at the ceiling calculating an answer. "Thirty, maybe forty percent."

"We need to get out of here." Codi glanced at the pencil in Matt's hands. She had used less to defend herself in SEAL training. An idea born of desperation was growing in her mind. "Give 'em the answers. I need you to buy us some time."

Matt nodded almost imperceptibly as he picked up the paper and began to write.

Nial Brennan scratched at the scar on his neck. He was so lost in thought he missed the spectacular sunset across the ocean as he headed back to the mainland. It was eighty-five miles back to his chateau just outside the city of Bordeaux. The home was leased under one of his many shell companies and he rarely got to spend time there.

The magnificent port city built on the Garonne River has many charismata and was just far enough away from Paris to have its own personality. Also known as Sleeping Beauty, Bordeaux, with its neo-classical architecture and high-tech public transport system is Unesco-listed and a must-see for any traveler. But Nial had something else in mind for the city.

Two years ago, Nial had come to a crossroads in his business. The acquisition of certain weapons, the kind worth millions, had become more and more difficult. The demand was good but supply was modicum. And with international crackdowns on big-ticket items, his future in this category was undetermined. He had done some business with a hacker who dealt mostly in information, the one commodity that seemed recession-proof. The hacker went by the avatar Chameleon.

Nial and Chameleon had done several deals together and had both profited nicely. About six months ago, Chameleon approached Nial with an offer he truly couldn't refuse. The hacker had gotten in financial trouble and needed some quick cash. He had been developing a program that took existing software and mimicked it. The programs literally looked identical. The duplicate would look and work the same as the original. The difference was that Chameleon's program could capture and send key words invisibly through a back door. It was, essentially, very similar to the key word recognition the NSA uses for cellphones. The program was much less robust and information typically had to be collected from multiple sources to get the full picture, but over time it was astonishing what you could learn. And because it only sent out fragments of information at a time, it was virtually untraceable.

The result, over time, was an insider's view of a corporation, or a few extra secrets from a government. The program was called Trevi, named after the developer's favorite fountain in Rome. It took Nial only a second to realize why. It was a fountain of ever-flowing information. In the last six months it had become the most powerful weapon Nial had never sold. Rather than sell it, he used it for his own benefit across multiple platforms. He knew when to buy or sell a stock just like an insider and predicting government trends became child's play.

Trevi had led to the discovery of several top-secret weapons programs and with the help of a few associates, Skystorm was the first of his acquisitions. Now he could literally change the world and his position in it.

Chapter Twenty-Three

"What are you doing in here?" Hans Muller barked. The fifty-year-old barrister had taken affront to the intrusion. He couldn't decide whether to stand or sit.

"Mr. Muller, we're with the FBI and we would like to ask you a few questions," Agent Fescue said as he walked over and sat in one of the leather high-backed chairs that faced the desk. He crossed his legs, leaned back and looked around.

"Sorry, Mr. Muller," the barrister's secretary said. "They just barged in."

"I can see that."

Agent Fescue's men escorted her out of the office, closed the door and stood nearby.

The room was heavily paneled with dark rich wood. "Questions about what?" Muller said, sizing up the intruders, his coal black eyes boring into the FBI agent.

"We need to know everything you have on a jet that was rented through a corporation you set up called Hastings Aeronautical."

Hans' reaction gave nothing away. He sat casually back in his chair and deliberately removed his glasses and cleaned them. "I know nothing about any Hasting's Aeronautical. Besides, I don't have to tell you anything. Now please leave my office."

Agent Fescue pulled out a folded paper that was in his coat pocket. "True, but you see, I have here this little piece of paper that allows me to place you in general lockup with a bunch of real criminals, tear this office apart and dig into every one of your clients. We will then contact each one of those clients individually."

The micro reaction was slight but enough that Agent Fescue caught it. He continued. "Interpol has been watching you for quite some time. Apparently, you have been doing work for some very bad people and now it appears you are complicit in murder and the kidnapping of a federal agent."

Muller crossed his arms. Slight beads of perspiration began to pop up on his shaved head. "Murder? Kidnapping? You're insane. I'm not saying anything."

"Have it your way." Agent Fescue flicked a finger and the two agents who came in with him left their post by the door. They went around the desk and grabbed Muller.

"You can't do this. Mallory!" he called to his secretary. "Call the police!"

The scrawny, slightly plump barrister struggled for all he was worth. But once he was subdued and handcuffed, the gravity of the situation hit. The blood drained from his face and he broke. "Okay, okay, I'll tell you whatever you want. Please don't do this!" He started to sob. Agent Fescue placed the blank folded piece of paper back in his pocket. The ruse had worked.

"Let's go over everything we know," Agent Fescue said as he stood in front of an oval table back at the Paris office with his entire team. He was using a smart board to list all the facts of the case. He had drawn a line down the middle of the board and placed a word at the top left—FACTS.

"We know unidentified individuals stole government technology called Skystorm, kidnapped one scientist and one agent of the GSA," one agent said.

Agent Fescue noted that on the board. "What else?" he asked.

An agent on Joel's right, Agent Colleroff, spoke next. "We know that they used a private jet to fly them, or at least the technology, to a hangar in Bordeaux." Everyone looked up at the implication that there was a very real possibility that Matt and Codi were dead, probably shot and dumped somewhere along the trail.

Agent Fescue pressed on. "What else do we *know?* Facts only, people."

"The pilot of the jet was shot with a single GSW to the head after they arrived."

"And someone named Nial Brennan owns the company that hired by a barrister by the name of Hans Muller to arrange for the plane," Agent Waters added.

"Okay, we'll need to find out everything we can about this Nial Brennan. I want to be in his presence, giving him the squeeze within the next twelve hours. Anything else? Facts only."

Silence.

Agent Fescue turned back to the smart board and added a new category, this time in the right margin—GUESSES. "Okay, what do we *think* we know?"

A female agent across the table started. "We think that General Stanfield of the Army Research Office was tortured and killed for the information that led to the incident in Arizona."

Joel said, "We believe Codi and Doctor Campbell are still alive."

Agent Fescue looked at Joel and cocked his head. "How do we think we know that, Agent Strickman?"

Joel continued. "Logic. They were taken, not left behind with the other bodies. So I think they still need them."

Agent Fescue nodded his head while he processed the possibility out loud. "Agent Sanders for leverage and Doctor Campbell to put Skystorm back together and make whatever it is work."

"I think I have an idea what it is." Everyone turned to Agent Waters.

"I was finally able to get the general's assistant to go through his files. He was old school, kept everything on paper locked in his safe.

Skystorm is, well, it's very technical stuff, but essentially it's an energy beam capable of shooting microscopic biologicals contained within its beam." The group looked a little confused, so Agent Waters continued.

"For instance, I could shoot you with this beam from a mile away and infect you and everyone around you with the plague or the vaccination for the plague, without you even knowing it had happened. And I could also completely disintegrate you if I dialed up the frequency and focused the beam." The room went quiet.

Agent Fescue broke the silence. "This is now the agency's top priority—find me this Nial Brennan, people." He circled the name on the board. "We need to stop whatever he or they have planned. No sleep. No breaks. Not until we have some answers. Got it?"

Yes sirs were mumbled about. Agents scampered off to get to work. Agent Fescue picked up a phone and dialed. "Director Calvin Jameson, please."

Joel plopped in the mesh chair at his desk. His mind was bouncing off every possibility. He closed his eyes trying to focus. Then he adjusted his glasses and with a look of determination, he typed Nial Brennan into the search engine.

CHAPTER TWENTY-FOUR

The air was thick with moisture though there wasn't a cloud in the sky. Juliette drove a faded white cargo van with two mercs for company. It was the rainy season in Durban, South Africa and everything was especially green. Palm trees lined the street and children played rugby in a small park. Durban was a city whose Indian population had grown so much, it had taken on a decidedly Delhi feel.

They turned off the N3 expressway and crossed a set of light rail tracks to Vusi Mzimela Road and headed south. The bustling town gave way to a different world. This was an area to avoid. Ruffians grouped on street corners and cracked asphalt merged with trash-filled gutters. Juliette barely missed a giant pothole. She turned down a sketchy one-lane road that died at an old cement warehouse with no windows.

After pulling around to the loading dock, she exited the van. Her associates followed. A well-hidden camera amongst the garish graffiti plastered on the walls alerted the occupants to their presence and soon the giant metal roll-up door lifted on worn rails, protesting all the way to the top.

Juliette raised her hands in the air as three men brandishing Milkor BXP submachine guns appeared. They were the newer more compact and versatile version of the MAC 10. They herded the threesome into the building keeping their distance and sight picture intact. Juliette immediately picked up on their professionalism and wondered if her brother had given her the right information. It was too late now, so she did what she did best and led the group inside, ready to strike at a moment's notice.

"What's the meaning of this?" Juliette asked, but the men were all business and gave her no quarter. Fluorescent lights replaced sunlight as the roll-up door squeaked closed. One of the armed guards stepped forward and relieved Juliette and her men of their weaponry and cell-phones, while the other two kept vigil.

She said, "I thought we had an agreement," and was met with a silence so complete it absorbed her words.

From out of the shadows came the clicking of practical shoes on cement. It was followed by a tall red-haired woman wearing a lab coat and a frown. She put on a pair of black-framed glasses and circled like a hungry lion after a kill. Finally, she stopped and removed her glasses. "I have no issue with the agreement," she said, "just with the way business associates of Mr. Brennan's have a way of dying in lieu of a final payment."

She flicked a button on a remote in her left hand. A spotlight popped on, illuminating two crates loaded with metal canisters. "Feel free to inspect them if you like; we've all been inoculated."

Juliette hesitated and then lowered her hands and orbited the crates. On each side of the crates were six stainless cylinders the size of a scuba tank, making a total of thirty-six tanks per crate. They had a threaded top that was capped, the valve sealed with metal tape. Juliette glanced down at the biohazard sticker prominently displayed on each tank.

"I had originally planned to sell this lot to the Saudi's," the red-haired woman said, "but I will be mixing up a special concoction for them instead. It's funny..."

Juliette looked over. "What is?"

"Seems the more the population grows, the more everyone wants to kill each other." She shrugged her shoulders. "More business for me, I suppose."

Everything looked as discussed and there was no way Juliette was opening one of the canisters here to check it. "Appears good to me," she said, "but if this turns out to be anything but what we agreed on, I'll be back in a very different capacity."

"I would expect nothing less." The woman's smile looked more like a challenge. She pulled out an I-pad mini and swiped at it. "Preliminary results were better than expected, topping out at just above forty percent."

"Human subjects?"

"Of course. See for yourself." The woman flung the I-pad over to Juliette who caught it one-handed. "Keep it," the woman said.

Juliette inspected the screen. There were dozens of pictures showing a steady progression of patients—first, red with fever, then with their epidermis covered in pox and finally death.

"You'll find additional specs and formulations as well," the woman said.

Juliette flicked through several screens and confirmed this was the case.

"So?" Juliette reached slowly into her pocket. The armed guards tensed. She pulled out a pouch and flung it to the woman who caught it and hefted it in one hand, testing the weight.

She poured the contents onto a table and flicked on the nearby desk lamp, randomly selected several diamonds from the pile and carefully inspected them through a loupe. After what seemed like the longest five minutes of Juliette's life, the woman scooped up the diamonds. "You know," she said, "it's ironic, diamonds making it all the way back here."

Juliette was losing her patience. "We good?" she asked.

"Just one more thing." The woman nodded to one of her guards who walked over and handed Juliette a small briefcase. "The vaccine. You might want to give yourselves a shot before you handle the crates, just in case."

She turned and left, saying, "Nice doing business with you."

The guards followed her out, leaving Juliette and her two mercenaries alone in the room. Juliette looked at the crates and the briefcase. She opened the briefcase.

Codi slid the pencil up her sleeve. Her mouth felt like the Gobi Desert; she couldn't remember the last time she'd had anything to drink. Matt's usual sparkle in his eyes was extinguished and his electrocution hairdo would be the envy of any garage band. He was staring blankly out the window. "You okay?" she asked him.

Matt gazed over at her with only his eyes. "Sure, never better. My life's work is in the hands of a lunatic, I've been blown up, shot at, imprisoned, electrocuted and now I'm about to hand over the final piece of the puzzle so this douchebag can wipe out or kill God knows what. So, yeah, I'm feeling pretty fuckin' good right now."

Matt glanced around. He was standing and mad before he realized that Codi had just manipulated him out of his funk. He sat back down and smiled over at her. "Thanks."

"Sure. So how does a guy like you end up in a place like this?"

"Hard to find a good man in DC, huh?" Matt smiled and the gleam in his eyes was back. Their connection was interrupted by the sound of footsteps.

Codi tried to discern how many were coming and tensed for action. The door slammed open and Dax marched into the room. He looked at Matt. Pathetic, he thought to himself. The paper he had left with him was lying on the floor. He glanced at the woman who glared back with intensity. Too bad he was so busy; it would have been fun breaking her.

Dax picked up the paper and looked it over. No words were needed. Matt looked up at the man named Dax and saw hatred in his eyes. He knew that if his answers were wrong, at the very least, Codi would die. Dax turned and left the room, the clang of the bolt on the door echoing in their cell. Matt squeezed his hands into hardened fists. He needed to do something but was currently helpless to do so.

"Odds are, the next time they come in here will be the last," Codi croaked.

Matt nodded in grave understanding, still staring at the space where Dax had been a few seconds before. Codi stood and started to pace. "I, for one, am not going to lie here waiting for a bullet." She double-checked the bars on the window and the door—nothing. "This is what I'm thinking."

CHAPTER TWENTY-FIVE

Getting contraband out of South Africa is much easier than getting it in. Six hours in the twenty-six-foot Steiger Ocean Craft at thirty knots had just about killed Juliette. Her kidneys were throbbing and her knees were tired of playing the role of shock absorbers. The trip from Durban to Maputo, Mozambique, had started with Juliette in a bikini on the bow waving at the SA Coast Guard as they left Durban Harbor. From there they skirted the African coastline northward. The choppy Indian Ocean made for a very bumpy ride.

Originally a Portuguese Colony, Mozambique gained its independence in 1975. Maputo, the largest city, sat on the coast of the Indian Ocean across from Madagascar. Palm and jacaranda trees bordered white sandy beaches that gave way to high-rises and Mediterranean-style architecture. Once in the port, Juliette could use money to get their contraband unloaded, put on a jet and flown back to France.

Dr. Didier Comstock pulled his eyes from his laptop and looked across to one of his assistants. He had received the missing technical information and they were in the process of re-tuning the amplitude and frequency of the pulse generator. This was supposedly the missing piece they needed.

His grasp of the project was short a few lines of code and he was trying his best to get up to speed. Dr. Comstock was anxious to complete this endeavor, get his money and get out before the boss got trigger-happy, one of the many risks of working for a narcissistic psychopath.

Dr. Comstock had put into place a time-release computer virus that would cause a terminal error. It required him to enter a seven-digit code every twelve hours. It was his safety net. No one can screw me now, he thought. He would email the boss a permanent override once he and his money were safe. This was Dr. Comstock's way of keeping honor among thieves.

He watched as goat number two was attached to the stanchion. This one had been much easier for his assistant to get into the lab. Dr. Comstock readied the machine and had one of his assistants reload the vial. A quick countdown and a press of the firing button followed. It made the familiar snapping sound that signaled a discharge of the weapon. There was nothing else. No light, no exploding goat, not even smoke. He rose up from behind the relative safety of his table and lowered his safety glasses.

The goat bleated and looked around, seemingly unfazed. Dr. Comstock motioned to one of his helpers and told him to do a physical inspection. The man walked over and checked the goat for change. He went through his procedures and then looked up. "Nothing," he said.

Dr. Comstock called out, "Draw blood and process it."

The assistant selected a syringe and drew blood from the seemingly unaffected goat.

After the centrifuge came the microscope. Dr. Comstock wiped the sweat from his eyes as he rotated the lens to a higher power and pressed his eyes to the ocular lenses. He knew the people he was working for had a low tolerance for failure and he was on borrowed time. He was trying to think of a good way to blame the American as he rotated the fine focus knob.

Dr. Comstock suddenly paused. Thousands of tiny organisms swam in the goat's blood. Almost to himself, he uttered, "Number two shows a high concentration of Caseous Lymphadenitis. Test successful."

Dax called out from the back of the room, "What'd you say?"

Dr. Didier Comstock pulled back from the microscope, now fully aware of what he had done and stood straight up. He repeated himself. "Test subject number two shows a high concentration of Caseous Lymphadenitis. Test successful." He was over the hump. Now for phase two of his plan—get out and get paid.

A loud bleat broke him from his deliberations and he looked over to see that the goat had collapsed to the floor and was struggling. Foam was coming from its mouth and the legs were shuddering. Dr. Comstock looked over at Dax who had walked over to stand beside him.

"It worked," Dax said, his voice slightly incredulous. He smiled and picked up his cellphone.

The goat had stopped moving. The assistant reached in to check the animal for signs of life—nothing. He looked back at the group and gave the universal headshake for dead. Dr. Comstock checked his watch. Ten minutes had elapsed. A genuine smile could not be contained. He had done it.

The naturally distressed wood plank floor set against a green patterned wall was Nial's own choosing for his office. Light streamed in from windows on three walls, each giving a view of the greenery outside. *Come on Eileen* was playing in the background as Nial finished off his lunch at his desk, a working meal, as he liked to call it. He was a big fan of eighties music and found it to be the one thing that helped him relax and distract him from his funk.

After seeing the goat explode rather than become infected, Nial had to consider that the plan had failed. He was at a loss as to his next move. He knew he needed to exercise patience, but that word was not in his nature. The collective data he had acquired through Chameleon promised a much different outcome and he'd been battling with which direction to go with it.

The thousand liters of Variola Major he had sent the team to collect in South Africa had cost him dearly and was scheduled to arrive the next day. It was a variant of smallpox and promised a forty percent mortality rate. It was just what he was looking for to establish proof of the weapon's effectiveness and to allow him to bask in the glory of revenge. His mind drifted with images of screaming and dying British fools. It was enough to brighten even the darkest day.

The waiting part he absolutely hated and Nial knew better, but he couldn't help himself. He was a man who wore his emotions on his sleeve. His severe ADD caused him to experience extreme highs and lows at the flip of a switch that, at times, his natural intelligence couldn't thwart. He banged the table in frustration.

He stared and finally picked up his chrome-plated Walther PPK S380. He stared intently at the pistol, rotating it in his hand, finally looking straight down the barrel. An unseen force pushed his hand up and placed the tip of the gun into his mouth and then under his chin, finally landing on his temple.

He willed himself to stop, but he was powerless. He envisaged what it would be like to join his family. He tried desperately to hear the song that was playing and sing along, but…nothing. His finger pushed against the trigger. A ringing sound cut through his madness and the ephemeral thought vanished.

Nial forced the gun away and repeatedly pulled the trigger until the gun was empty. Harmless. A nearby vase and window were destroyed by the outburst. Nial screamed at the top of his lungs, stopping only when he was out of air. He took a second to compose himself. Finally, he glanced down at his ringing cell. The call was unlisted.

He grabbed the phone and stabbed the button. "Yes?"

There was a banging on his office door. A muffled, concerned voice was calling to him. "Hold on," Nial said to the caller and hit the mute button. He called out, "I'm fine. Go away!" The banging stopped and he unmuted his phone. "What?"

"We just had a successful test," Dax said.

In that single instant everything changed for Nial. "Tell me every-thing," he said.

Dax filled him in on the details, Nial hanging on Dax's every word. "So the goat died within ten minutes?" he asked Dax.

"That's right, apparently receiving the virus on a cellular level hyper-activates the efficacy."

Nial started pacing. "This is fantastic news," he said to Dax. "Make sure you know how to work the weapon and test it a few more times to be sure. Once you're sure, no witnesses unless they are absolutely crucial. I'm on my way." Nial hung up and danced a jig, singing along to *Friday I'm In Love* by The Cure, which was now playing, his erstwhile plight long forgotten.

Dax hung up and looked over as his twin, Juliette, burst into the room. "You're back early," he said.

"And you're going to want a shot of this vaccine," Juliette said while placing the briefcase on a worktable. She opened it and pulled out a syringe. She had just gotten back with the canisters of Variola Major and the good doctor was having his lab assistants haul them up from the dock and into the room.

"Any problems?" Dax asked as he rolled up his sleeve and held out his arm.

Juliette pointed the needle skywards and flicked the air bubbles out. "Unfortunately, we lost our contact over at the customs office in Merignac. He took one look at our canisters and wanted more money."

"It was a loose end that needed tying," Dax said casually.

Juliette responded by jabbing Dax with the needle and injected him with the serum. "Ouch! You are a bad girl."

She smiled wickedly at him. "I know. We need a cleanroom to handle the virus. It's pretty nasty stuff." Dax absently rubbed his arm. "Get a list from the doctor on what you'll need and make it happen." He brought her up to speed on the successful test of the Skystorm.

On the third successful firing of the weapon Dax felt confident he no longer needed his hostages. He considered his options, finally deciding to let the two guards he had previously stopped from having their fun do with the prisoners as they wished. It would be good for morale. "Just make sure you dump the bodies in the ocean when you're done," he told them.

The two soldiers moved without hesitation. Having been stopped before, they were anxious to get back at it. They discussed their plans as they took the stairs two at a time. Each had a little something special in mind for the woman. They couldn't decide whether they would kill the man first or make him watch. Finally, a flip of a coin resolved their biggest concern of who got to go first with the female.

Codi could hear footsteps approaching. Matt looked over at her a little wide-eyed. It sounded to her like...she raised two fingers. Two soldiers were coming. She whispered, "Get ready." Matt stood up and moved to the center of the cell, his hands slightly shaking.

He had been in relatively few life and death situations. And now there was a very real possibility he would not live through the next two minutes. He tried to concentrate to make the rational/scientific part of his brain take over. Codi took out her pencil and hid behind the door. Matt quickly unzipped his pants.

As the bolt on the other side slid open with a clank, Matt let out a large breath and willed himself to stay calm. This was not the time for stage fright. Codi's plan was simple, all he had to do was be the distraction. He reached in and grabbed his penis and thought of running water as he tried to pee. The two guards moved into the cell, flush with thoughts of how they would rape and kill the American woman. Each had his own personal perversion running through his mind.

The sight of the man urinating right out in front of them completely took them by surprise. Matt gave them a sheepish smile and the two killers lowered their weapons just a fraction as if to say what the hell? That was all Codi needed; she bolted from behind the door and jabbed the pencil with all her might, burying it right up through the soft tissue in the first man's bottom jaw.

His look of surprise was the last thing to register before he slumped to the floor, lifeless. Before the other guard could react, Codi had both hands wrapped around his neck. She dropped backwards with all her weight pulling the man down with her.

The stunned guard swung his weapon towards Codi and started firing. Matt danced for his life as bullets ricocheted around the room making their way to Codi. He tried frantically to get his penis back in his pants and the now-jammed zipper to work while doing the bullet dodge and diving for cover.

Codi's momentum dropped the guard on top of her. She continued to somersault backwards and used her legs to launch him in the air. The guard never got a chance to aim his gun in her direction and before he knew it, he was upside down and airborne. The cracking sound when his head impacted the concrete wall echoed through the cell. It was the last thing he ever heard.

Codi grabbed the first man's weapons and checked outside in the hall for others. The hallway was empty in both directions. She slipped back into the cell and closed the door most of the way. She checked the two bodies to confirm the outcome.

"Are they…?" Matt asked.

She glanced up at him and said, "Yeah. You okay?"

"Well, I kinda feel like a fool."

"What?"

"I zipped up more than just my pants in all the commotion." Matt rubbed his crotch, while Codi smiled at his embarrassment.

"I'll kiss it better if we get out of here."

Matt's eyes bugged in surprise and his face flushed. He tried to think of something clever to say but nothing came out.

Codi could tell there was something special about Matt. She really liked him and if they ever got out of this place she hoped to have the chance to see what the possibilities were.

She started taking the dead guard's pants off and Matt wondered what she had in mind, but she had gotten them this far, so he kept his questions to himself. He collected the other guard's gun and picked up his radio. Codi tossed the pants to Matt. "Bring 'em," she said.

They quietly left the cell and headed back down the hallway following the same path they had been hauled down before. The blackened garbage room was small and the barred chute inside it was empty. They could hear the sound of the ocean close by. "What are we doing?" Matt asked.

"You're getting out of here," Codi said as she took the pants from Matt and began tying the legs in a knot. "Once you hit the water, blow air into the waist. They'll inflate and support you till you get to land."

"Are you nuts? I'm not jumping into the ocean."

"Look, I'm responsible for your life and staying here is not an option."

"It's as good an option as jumping into the ocean. I could just as easily get swept out to sea, or eaten by a shark."

Codi considered his point. Matt went over and looked at the chute. The bars were hinged to rotate up and allow for trash to be tossed out. But what caught his eye was the shiny brass padlock holding them together. "Besides," he said, "the bars are locked."

Codi glanced over at the lock. She could easily shoot it off, but maybe Matt was right. She leaned against the wall, the adrenaline in her body wearing off, making her hands tremble. "I could really use a drink of water."

CHAPTER TWENTY-SIX

Joel leaned back in his chair and closed his eyes in frustration. The man, Nial Brennan, was dirty. After a brief stint in Africa running guns he had branched out. And according to Joel's contacts, he had transitioned into large-ticket items. The problem wasn't in finding what he had been up to, it was finding his current location. Every lead had proven to be a dead-end.

Agent Waters was tracking his various businesses and had come to the same conclusion. She had discovered several virtual companies five layers deep with no humans behind any of them, compliments of information they had gotten from Nial's barrister. But that information was followed by a series of generic voicemails that were never answered and addresses that were false.

Joel looked at the time, three AM. He needed some rest. He took off his glasses, laid them on his desk and moved over to a space on the hardwood floor by the window to lie down. He closed his eyes for a second and rubbed his temples. Something clung to his mind like a starving leech. He couldn't shake it or understand it. He was missing a crucial piece of the puzzle. But what?

Agent Waters came over to lie down next to him. The cool floor and the horizontal position felt good. Joel could feel her body heat radiating in his direction. It was not often a woman had been this close to him and he tried not to squirm. He cracked open one eye and looked in her direction.

She had a beautiful profile. His eye shifted down and a really nice rack. He closed his eye tightly and tried to forget he had just visually copped-a-feel.

"I'm at an impasse," Agent Waters said.

"Me, too," Joel said, forcing himself to look up at the ceiling.

Agent Waters smiled and closed her eyes for a moment. Joel finally relaxed.

"So how did you end up in the FBI?" Joel asked. Agent Waters crossed her arms and cocked her head. "The usual. Got caught hacking into the DOD as a teenager and was given an ultimatum."

"Let me guess, come work for us or life behind bars?"

"No, the CIA tried to kidnap me and fake my death. The NSA got wind of it and used the CIA's illegal actions to leverage me over to their side. I told 'em both they could drop dead."

Joel looked over at Agent Waters, completely taken aback. "Then what happened?"

"They dumped me in a black site, no trial, no lawyer and six months later I completely broke down and gave in. By then, the NSA and the CIA had moved on. So I ended up here."

Joel sat up on one elbow and looked over at Agent Waters, unsure of what to say or do. His lower jaw dangled open. Agent Waters looked Joel straight in the eyes and held the gaze. Then, ever so slightly, she cracked a smile.

"Wait. What? You're kidding, right?"

Agent Waters burst out laughing and Joel soon followed.

Codi tried to make small talk with Matt. "Where did you grow up?" she asked.

"I'm a Texas boy raised by my mom in Plano, just outside Dallas."

"With cows and horses?"

"No, just a bike and a skateboard." They were still in the garbage chute room. The sound of the constant wave action gave the dreary room an audial plus. They knew it wouldn't be long before the dead guards were missed, but they needed to catch their breath and figure out a plan.

Codi inspected a scrape she had on her left elbow. "Tell me something no one else knows about you."

"Like?"

"Like I ran naked through my mom's dinner party or I peed in my roommate's grape juice. You know."

Matt thought about the question for a second. "I killed my neighbor's cat."

Codi looked surprised.

"It was an accident. We were playing Stuntman."

"Stuntman?"

"It's a game my cousin and I used to play when we were little. It's where you had to out-stunt each other."

Codi looked slightly confused, so she asked, "Like the game Horse on a basketball court?"

Matt nodded. She got up and peeked out the door to make sure the hall was still empty.

"My cousin rode his wagon off his roof onto a ramp we had built and jumped this tree that was in his back yard." Matt demoed with his hands. Codi came over to Matt and sat back down. "So I decided to tie a rope to the top of his chimney and swing off his roof and onto the neighbor's roof. I called it the Batman express." Codi was all smiles listening to his story. "About halfway through the arc, the chimney gave way and I landed in a pile of rose bushes."

"Ouch."

"Yeah. Broke my arm and cut the crap out of my skin."

"What about the cat?"

"Mr. Boots? The chimney fell on him, smashed him flat. My cousin and I buried poor Mr. Boots among the rose bushes and swore each other to secrecy."

Codi couldn't help but laugh at the mental image. Matt's smile was uncontainable. "I would never have taken you for a cat killer," she said.

"There's a lot more to me than just killin' cats."

Codi inspected the man with the amazing green eyes and perfect smile. "I bet there is."

"What about you?"

"Me?" Codi looked at the ceiling for a second. "I gave myself bangs to hide a zit.".

"A little vain, are we?"

"It was high school and I had my first date, Curtis Rowe. I had a friggin' third eye on my forehead and nothing was working. So I chopped my hair and *voila*, bangs." Something electrical passed between them as the two stared into each other's eyes.

Codi was the first to break the connection. "You know we can't stay here."

"I know. We were gonna die anyhow. But I was really enjoying this moment and I'm not in any hurry for it to end."

"Same here," Codi said as she got up and opened the door.

Matt stood up and followed. But as soon as he got to the door, Codi rushed back and whispered, "We've got movement and it's heading this way." She looked around, already knowing there was no way out but the sea. Shooting off the lock now would just send the guards running in their direction. They were trapped.

Caleb and another guard were pushing the dead goat in a small two-wheel garden cart. They were talking back and forth, each complaining that they had been left out of having a go with the American woman. But with the money they were being paid on this job they would soon be able to buy a few of their own and do with them as they pleased.

Matt tensed as the door to the room opened. From his position lying on the ground behind the door, he saw the cart enter first. He hesitated only a second before slipping the barrel of his rifle onto the spokes of the cart's wheel. The wheel rotated and then jammed to a stop as the metal rifle barrel wedged against the base of the cart and the wheel's spokes.

The guard pushing the cart doubled over on the rear push-bar as it unexpectedly came to a halt. Caleb, who was walking behind him was exposed. Codi reacted instantly, rolled into view from beside Matt and popped off several 7.62-millimeter slugs in his direction. Caleb reacted faster than expected and ducked behind the guard who was now folded over the cart handle. Codi tracked with Caleb and stitched a line across the first guard's torso, causing it to jerk wildly

The first guard collapsed with all his weight onto the push-bar of the garden cart. Caleb stuck his FAMAS G2 assault rifle over the back of his fallen comrade and returned fire, shooting blind in Codi's direction. The weight from the now dead guard on the rear push-bar caused the garden cart to cantilever, sending the front end into the air and all of Caleb's shots into the now exposed dead goat. With the front of the cart buoyed up, Codi's view of Caleb was completely blocked and vice versa. She stayed crouched down using the cart and the assailant's dead buddy for cover. Caleb was leery of popping up at the wrong time and being met with a bullet in the brain.

Codi inched her way closer to the cart; her weapon at the ready. Each shooter was daring the other to make a move or a mistake. Matt, thinking the battle was finished, leaned around the corner of the door. "Is it over?"

A surprised Caleb spun towards Matt and pulled the trigger. Bullets flew wildly from Caleb's FAMAS towards Matt, who flung himself backwards as fast as he could, trying to emulate Neo in the Matrix movie. The assault rifle bucked in Caleb's hand and then died out. Codi reacted instantly and as soon as Matt's unplanned distraction happened, loosed her weapon in Caleb's direction. He took several hits to the chest. She finished him off with a double tap to the head. Caleb slumped to the floor, motionless, beside the other dead guard.

Matt climbed from the hard greasy floor and checked himself for holes. "Holy shit, where did he come from? And why is it I'm always the one getting shot at with your stupid plans."

"You were supposed to stay behind the door."

Matt inspected the bullet holes in the door that had saved his life. "The shooting stopped, I thought it was over."

"Over? You nearly got yourself killed."

"Yeah, well, I see that now. Oh and thanks for saving me—again," Matt said with an extra helping of sarcasm.

The two stood staring at each other for a second waiting for the adrenaline to subside. Smoke and the sting of cordite filled the room. Codi walked over to check the bodies. "Remember this, if you want to stay alive, it's never over until I say it's over. Are we clear?"

"Sure." Matt smiled and Codi's anger abated. She rummaged through Caleb's pockets and came up with a set of keys.

"So you think they heard that?" Matt asked.

"Everyone heard that and right now they're sending more guns this way to investigate. Time to move out of here."

Matt looked at the carnage on the floor before him and made a sour expression. "Bad day to be a goat."

CHAPTER TWENTY-SEVEN

Joel jerked awake from a fitful rest. He looked around to find he was alone on the floor. Agent Waters was back at her screen. "I didn't want to wake you," she said without taking her eyes off her screen.

Joel rubbed his throbbing shoulder and rose stiffly. Nothing like sleeping on a hardwood floor to aggravate a bullet wound.

Agent Waters looked over her shoulder and asked, "How you feeling?"

"Other than the aches and pains that come from getting shot coupled with a shrieking headache, I'm ready to get back at it."

"Good, 'cause I found something."

Joel sat down at his desk and leaned over to see what she had; Agent Waters slid a cup of coffee over to him. Joel sniffed it warily and took a sip. She was fixated on her screen. "I found a group of buildings that this shell corporation here," she pointed to a name on her screen, "Accor-Lafayette Limited, has recently purchased. Lookit."

Agent Waters drilled down. A list of twenty names and addresses popped up on the screen. Joel said, "I'm not totally awake yet, so you take these fifteen and I'll take the other five."

"Slacker," Agent Waters said as she smirked. With a few keystrokes she sent the list to Joel and began her search.

Joel smiled, grabbed his glasses, refocused his mind and began his search. His five buildings were very dissimilar. One was a tilt-up warehouse on the outskirts of Rome. Another was a ship's dry-dock in Hull, England. There was an office building in Paris, an old military fort

139

stuck out in the ocean off the coast of Bordeaux and a cement plant in Ballymena, Northern Ireland. He drilled down for more information on each and made a request for satellite imagery covering the past month.

"How big *is* this place?" Codi asked after she and Matt had been walking for five minutes, still yet to see any targets.

"Great. Right back where we started," she said. She had purposely left the door to the garbage room open as a marker so they could track their progress. The hallway looked the same in both directions.

"At least we now know we're trapped in a giant oval," Matt said.

"That's helpful." Codi leaned back against the wall and lifted one foot up against it. "I may have been premature. I don't think they heard those gunshots."

"It's like a crypt down here."

"And we're the only ones in it."

Matt scratched at chin whiskers that hadn't been shaven in a week. The hallways were barely lit with bare bulbs mounted every fifty feet. There were more pools of darkness than light.

"Okay," Codi said, "one more time around and this time we check every door."

"I got the right side," Matt said as he reached for the first door on the right.

"As you can see here," Joel said as he pointed to a helicopter pad being built on the roof of the old fort. "There's definite recent activity."

The taskforce had gathered back in the conference room to review and update findings. Joel flipped to the next picture. In another overhead view men were moving large crates from a boat onto the fort's dock. "And in this image here, if we drill down…"

The picture zoomed in closer on two blurry men, one facing towards the camera and the other away. The pixilation gave way as the image resolved into Nial Brennan's face. Agent Fescue perked up. "That's him!" He leaned in closer. "So what is he up to out in an old abandoned fort in the middle of the ocean? And who's the other guy?"

"No idea," an agent from across the table replied. "He could be building a B&B for all we know."

"Come on." Joel's frustration showed.

"Without something concrete we can't go in guns blazing," said Agent Fescue. "I'll need something solid to be able to act."

"We don't have that kind of time," Joel said. "Codi, I mean Agent Sanders, could be in very real danger right now."

Fescue paced the table of the temporary conference room.

The agent next to Joel added, " I know we're only supposed to assist the authorities over here, but that fort is six miles off the coast. We could do a fly-by under the ruse of information gathering and see if there's anything that would give us probable cause to land and investigate."

"That might also alert them and get our two vics killed," another agent said.

"Come on," said Agent Fescue. "Thoughts, people."

Agent Waters spoke up. "Joel, try zooming into the glass on the helicopter."

As Joel did so, a very rough reflection of Dax Cole appeared on the big screen. Joel let out a cry. "That's him! That's the guy who shot me!"

Agent Fescue tented his fingers in thought. "Let me make some calls," he said and then turned and left the room.

"Got stairs," Matt said.

Codi stepped over to inspect. The stairs were carved out of stone and headed upward into darkness. "Stay here," she said. "I'm gonna take a look. I'll be back."

Matt nodded and watched as she moved like a wraith up the steps. He couldn't help but let his eyes linger on a very defined and shapely backside before it disappeared into the gloom.

As he stood staring at nothing his mind shifted to Skystorm, his life's work and the very real possibility that it was being perverted. Matt had worked his whole life to help make a positive for mankind. He had always worried that he might someday lose control, but the positives were so great he had led himself to believe it was worth the risk.

"Go see what's taking Caleb so long," Dax said. "I need everyone here and ready." The mercenary left to investigate. Dax was on edge as things were coming to a conclusion. He wanted to make sure everything was perfect. He couldn't do it all himself, but this wasn't his first cookout and between his sister and his trusted men, he felt confident in their success.

A squawk of his radio told Dax that Nial was inbound. Juliette stopped what she was doing and left to go meet him on the helipad. Since reuniting with her twin brother, she had found her life's passion, even after everything her parents had done to raise her the way they believed was the right way. Juliette could focus her talents like no one else. And as it is with most twins, the efficiency of their unspoken language doubled their productivity.

Nial jumped from his helicopter with a skip in his step. Juliette met him and welcomed him back. They moved off the landing pad flat roof and went down the creaking metal staircase that led to the third floor of the old fort. The stone and concrete fort was built like a tank that had doubled-down on its armor.

"Everything's on track," Juliette reported. "I have a team ready to start mounting the Skystorm on your helicopter. The remote is working and our witness situation is being dealt with right now."

"Great news, Jules. You know, this is my favorite part." She glanced over at Nial. "The part when all the pieces come together and the music plays."

Nial moved his hands like a conductor lost in the third couplet of a melody.

Juliette said, "The Variola Major has been loaded. You should get a yield of about ten minutes at, say, sixty miles an hour with a swath of two to three hundred feet, depending on your altitude."

Nial stopped and gaped at Juliette for a moment, processing the information. "Good to know. This has been a long time coming and I'm going to savor every moment."

She nodded as she pushed open the door to the main control room and followed him in. Dax was holding a slip of paper that he handed over to Nial. "Here are the coordinates for the pilot."

Nial looked it over. "Perfect. You know, I've been thinking, Variola Major is such a medical sounding term. We need to come up with something more interesting to call it."

"You mean like a code word?" Juliette said.

"Yes, I was trying to come up with something on the way here, but nothing really worked."

"Black Death has already been taken," she said, "so how about D3 for the diarrhea, delirium and death that are all part of the symptoms."

Nial thought for a moment and then clapped excitedly. "Okay D3 it is. Load six canisters of D3 into the helicopter just in case I feel the need to do a second test."

Juliette nodded and left.

Dax brought Nial up to date on the latest tests and other pertinent information. He then leaned in confidentially to show him a list he had made of essential and non-essential personnel. Five from security and three from the lab were highlighted. Nial studied it, made a few alterations and gave Dax the green light.

Codi wound her way up through the maze of corridors and stairs. The old prison was a formidable gal in her time, she thought. The concrete floor curved around to the left and didn't allow for a long sight picture, so she had to be very careful. She was vulnerable in the open hallway. She stayed close to the wall and moved like a cat.

About halfway to where she assumed the next set of stairs were, she heard a noise. Someone was coming. Codi dropped to a prone position next to the wall within a shadowed area and held perfectly still. A large man casually carrying an AK-74 around his shoulder walked briskly her way. When he got to within thirty feet she could see his bald head and purposeful gait. She popped up to a kneeling position and made herself known. "Federal agent. Drop your weapon."

The man didn't hesitate and dove left, pulled up and aimed his weapon in a flash. Codi anticipated the move and ended the man's actions with a three-round burst to his chest.

She ran forward, her gun raised, to confirm the kill. She was getting tired of people always trying to shoot her when she announced herself. Maybe the GSA should request a policy change—shoot first and identify yourself second.

The smell of ozone mixed with damp sea air hit Codi as she moved up the next set of stairs. She crouched low and peered over the first step trying to perceive as much information without being detected. The stairs opened to a large room. It had probably been a cafeteria at one point. But now it was filled with equipment and people. Several temporary lights raised on stands lit the room. There were three or four men wearing lab coats focused on the equipment and at least five men with French FAMAS watching.

She could see steel canisters stacked against the wall close to where she was hiding. They each had a biohazard sticker affixed to the side. As she scanned the room she got a glimpse of the man who had taken her and Matt. He was large and very much in charge. One look and you could tell this man killed for a living. She lined him up in her rifle's sights. The girl from the barn in Arizona walked in with another man. The way she and the large man treated him made it clear he was important.

The woman picked up a briefcase that was lying on a table and selected a syringe and vial out of it. She then filled it to the halfway mark. With a practiced flick of the needle she held it up to the man she had entered with. He reluctantly allowed her to inject him. The SEALS had a name for the situation Codi was now in, SNAFU: Situation Normal: All Fucked Up.

Movement to the left caught her attention. A man in full biohazard gear was coming out of a room that had plastic sheeting encasing the double doors. Codi figured it was some kind of temporary clean room and that this was a story too important to keep to herself. She had to get help. She lowered her weapon and pulled back down the stairs, returning to the bowels of the old fort.

Matt waited at the entrance as one minute turned into ten until finally he couldn't wait any longer. He banged his fist against the wall and made a decision. He took off up the stairs.

He managed only a few steps before he heard footsteps coming back down. He tensed and pointed his weapon at the direction of the sound. A shadow came into view and Matt pulled the trigger. Nothing happened. "You have to cock it first," Codi said as she stepped into the light. Matt let out a sigh of relief.

"You scared the crap out of me," he said. "What took you so long? I thought you were dead." The words fired out of his mouth in rapid succession.

Codi just looked at him with her perpetual smirk.

"What?" Matt said.

"Nothing. It's just you're cute when you're angry." Matt was taken off guard, but before he could comment, Codi said, "So here's the situation. There is a small army up there and the only way out is through them; so no dice. We are definitely in some kind of old prison that was built on the ocean. So we are not in the good ole US of A anymore."

"I think it might be an old military fort," Matt said.

"The bad news is they are using your Skystorm as a biological weapon of some sort."

Matt slumped. "We've got to stop them."

"Yes, but we'll need help to do it. The only way I see us getting some is taking the garbage chute to the ocean." She reached over and cocked Matt's gun for him. "Try not to shoot me," she said as she started back down the hallway.

Matt ran to catch up. "Am I really cute when I'm mad?"

Codi just shook her head—men.

Dax's men were in the loading process. The roof of the old fort looked like a running track, flat and oval. The center dropped off into a court-yard three stories down. The helipad was a raised platform opposite the glass observation tower on the west side.

They placed the requested six D3 canisters into the back of the helo and using part of the skid infrastructure, affixed the Skystorm unit to the space between the two runners on the bottom of the chopper. It looked like a small black refrigerator with four probes extending down from its door. A set of cables snaked their way to the power unit inside the helicopter where the rear seat had to be removed to make room.

Watching everything take place from an elevated position was a guard in the observation tower. Visibility today was close to five miles and with the newly installed ship-to-ship radar mounted on the roof, he could see almost four times that distance. His vantage point made him responsible for the fort's security.

The ocean breeze kicked up as Nial climbed into the copilot seat and started to buckle in. The telltale whine of the Arriel 2B1 turbine engine starting forced Dax to yell. He handed Nial the Skystorm remote and leaned in. "We'll take care of everything here and meet you with all the essentials in forty-eight hours."

Nial nodded.

"Bon Voyage," Dax said before closing the door. He gave a subtle wave as the helicopter blades started to push the craft into the air. Dax knew there was no turning back now and it was time to make sure things were covered on his end. That meant no loose ends.

CHAPTER TWENTY-EIGHT

Matt keyed the padlock open and strained as he swung the rusty grate up. He and Codi shoved the bodies of two killers, one annihilated goat and a shot-up garden cart down the now blood-covered chute. "If they come looking, there'll be no evidence we're still alive. Here," she tossed the pair of pants with the legs tied in a knot to Matt and then did one for herself. "Okay, feet first, I'm right behind you."

Matt looked down the chute and tried to will himself to go. It looked like a long way down. "Come on, newbie," Codi said. "You can do it."

He tried to crawl down a ways so the fall wouldn't be so dramatic, but he slipped on the blood trail and disappeared with a muffled cry.

He hit the water hard, jarring his whole body. The ocean was surprisingly warm. He kicked to the surface and headed away from his landing spot. Codi hit next and was bobbing on the surface by the time Matt got his bearings. They had a fish-eye view of the old fort. It looked massive and impenetrable, with no land or dock in sight. Codi took the pants she had brought along and showed Matt how, once wet, you could fill them with air to use as a floatation device. Once they were both floating in the ocean, she picked a direction. "Let's try right. Stay close to the wall; we'll be harder to see that way."

They both began to scissor-kick around the stronghold slowly making progress. The water was choppy, but the current was mild. After ten minutes, a dock servicing the fort came into view on the opposite side. Tied to it was a pair of thirty-one-foot Ocean Master sport cabin powerboats. The hardy aluminum ocean vessel was extremely seaworthy and the twin outboards made it fast and economical to operate. Codi and Matt ditched their flotation devices to give them a lower profile in the water as they approached the dock.

Nial made a B-line for Bordeaux. The sky was clear, not a cloud to be seen. He had a particular target in mind and he couldn't wait to see the results. Since his ill-conceived bout of melancholy, he was now feeling on top of the world and he allowed his mind to wander. This was the moment he had envisioned. He had transitioned Skystorm from a theoretical weapon into a practical one. If today was successful, not only would he strike back at the government that killed his parents, but he could increase his asking price for Skystorm by 300%.

The United Kingdom's consulate was a beehive of activity in an otherwise sleepy city. The large four-story French chateau sat back from the street. It was a combination of gothic revival meets neoclassical, with natural pink granite set against rows of tall white windows, all crowned with a dark pitched roof. Nial flew over the building once to get a proper view of the target. He was practically laughing, he was so giddy.

The second pass was done five minutes later to avoid rousing suspicion. The pilot dropped to five hundred feet. And just as they crossed the property line, Nial hit the green button on the remote Dax had given him. He heard and saw nothing but counted to fifteen before releasing the button, slightly unsure of his success.

The helicopter turned and headed for home. I guess only time would tell, he said to himself as he pressed his face to the widow and looked back at the receding edifice.

The reflection of Solimon Granger rippled in the polished teak tabletop. He sat down and answered his phone. His ever-present ascot complimented his teal eyes. The sixty-year-old had become a bit lost ever since his beloved wife Asima had died six months earlier. She had been his rock and his partner. Together, they had helped men to become presidents and governments to be overthrown. They were a true power couple and much of their rage and focus died with her cancer.

This was going to be his last move on the world's chessboard and then he would retreat to someplace quiet, maybe even warm and wait to join her.

He thought his latest acquisition was crucial to his plans, but the man he had to deal with was much too surly for his tastes. Asima would have told him to drop it and move on. But a weapon of such novelty was exactly what he needed: maximum effect while leaving no trace.

He stepped outside and was rewarded with a strong algid ocean wind. The North Sea defined cold this time of year and Solimon liked nothing more than the occasional shock it provided to refocus his mind. He watched a plethora of ocean whitecaps dance to the silentious symphony.

His seventy-eight meter ultra-luxury yacht cut through the slate-colored water with ease. It had every modern convenience, from the helicopter on deck to a thirty-foot tender that trailed in its wake. It had been custom-made for him in a dry dock west of Helsinki. Solimon made sure they spared no quality in the process, having to fire and hire several times to guarantee it.

His hand-selected crew of five knew his idiosyncrasies and were generally one step ahead of his needs. The steward stepped out and handed him a café latte served in a simple white porcelain cup. Solimon nodded to the steward and held the cup with both hands as he sipped in silence. Soon, Asima, soon.

Two UH-60 Black Hawk helicopters kissed the surface of the sea as they left the main coast of France heading west. Inside sat a joint task-force consisting of French-based Marine recon operatives and five FBI agents. The Marine group was used to doing things hard and fast and each one used the travel time to target in their own way. Two were dozing, another was cleaning his weapon for the third time and the fourth was playing a game on his smart phone.

Their leader sat in the copilot's seat of the second chopper and mentally checked and double-checked the plan. They were all geared up and ready for a fight and nothing would keep them from their end game.

Agent Fescue was in the copilot seat of the lead Sikorsky. He had been in some scuffles during his career, but a full assault on an island military fort with a joint Marine squad was a first. He could scarcely keep from smiling at the thought of it all.

The Pentagon had acted surprisingly fast to the information Agent Fescue relayed up the chain of command. Losing American weapons technology was one thing, but having it stolen and used by an aggressor was unacceptable. The fact that this mission would take place six miles off the coast of France also helped with the decision to keep it an all-US taskforce for now. The powers-that-be preferred to get their technology back now. Agent Fescue presumed that the US would rather ask forgiveness of the French for the intrusion as opposed to asking permission first and therefore having to share it with them.

Agent Fescue rightly surmised that he was only in charge due to his team's knowledge of the case they were working and the immediacy of its execution. But he knew that if they could pull this off, he'd be a legend at the agency.

The versatile helicopters were a natural when it came to flying NOE, or nap-of-the-earth missions and these pilots were equal to the task. "We want to come in low and swoop up to the roofline for a fast evac," Fescue said over the headset.

"Roger that, low with a pop-up," the pilot repeated. He lowered the

Black Hawk to within a couple feet of the water and the second pilot imitated his action.

Joel leaned with the helicopter's motion on his screen as he and Agent Waters watched the proceedings through their monitors back at the Paris office. Each team member had a small camera on his or her person and it was streaming live images via satellite back to headquarters. The effect was ten small videos pasted together on the screen, like a picture collage in a scrapbook. They could also choose any one of the images and have it pop up large on a single screen. "This sucks," Joel muttered.

"You want to be out there?" Agent Waters asked.

"Yeah, I feel responsible. They were taken during my watch."

"You were shot and unconscious."

"I know, but I just feel–"

"It's okay. You've made a big difference already. We'll get 'em back." Agent Waters placed her hand on Joel's shoulder. She doubted they were still alive, but hope springs eternal.

He nodded expectantly and turned back to the screen, fully engaged.

CHAPTER TWENTY-NINE

The observation tower on the fort was made up of hundreds of glass panels arranged in the shape of a large Dixie Cup. It had a domed metal roof and was supported by a twenty-foot-tall tubular cement column with an internal spiral staircase that allowed access to the tower. From a distance, the tower looked like a glass-covered sucker on a stick. The guard on duty inside was obsessive about his job with only one exception: when his home team, Lille, played PSG (Paris Saint Germain) in football, or soccer, as the Americans called it.

He never missed a match. In fact, he held a couple superstitions he believed helped his team to win. For one, he always watched the game standing, often pacing; and for the second, he wore his red-and-white team scarf no matter how hot it was.

The game was tied one to one and PSG was pushing hard for the go-ahead goal. A shot was parried left with the outstretched paw of the Lille keeper. That was close, the guard thought. He stepped closer to his tiny fuzzy screen to watch the ensuing corner kick, his back to the radar screen, using his body to help block the sun's glare on the screen. That's when the warning alarm sounded. He reached over and turned it off without looking up. The darn thing had been acting up all day and he was needed to help his team defend this corner kick.

With fingers crossed and mental focus maximized, he watched as the ball was placed in the small triangle in the corner of the field. Then the second warning alarm went off. What? That alarm never went off. He turned quickly to check the radar screen. Two intermittent blips were heading on a direct path in their direction. He grabbed the radio and called it in, "Two targets closing fast," and returned to the screen in time to hear the cheers for a goal scored by his team's nemesis.

Dax did not have time for this right now, but they had planned for every contingency. He quickly ordered his defenses to take their positions and as a precaution, called for one of his most trusted men. "Find out what's taking Caleb so long and tell him to get his ass up here and load my boat with six canisters of D3." He left Juliette in charge of security in the lab and ran to the roof to facilitate the surprise defense attack.

Codi and Matt pulled themselves up onto one of the Ocean Master boats. The stern had a large open area for fishing and hauling gear. The bow had a small cabin backed by a cockpit for operating the craft. In the distance Codi heard two helicopters approaching. But the best part was the hint of coastline that could just be made out in the distance. She took a moment and drained the saltwater out of their weapons and field stripped them both. Matt took the two clips he had collected from the dead guards and inverted them, watching as a trickle of water exited. He looked over as Codi stripped off her shirt and started to wring it out. Matt rarely saw attractive women in his line of work, but Codi was something else. With her wet hair and athletic build and a set of perfect breasts that were trying hard to push out of her bra... he tried not to gawk but found the view spellbinding.

Codi put her shirt back on and laughed just a little on the inside. Men—so predictable.

She quickly glanced up at Matt, who tried to bring his eyes up to her face. "Can I help you?" she asked.

"No, it's just that I don't see that every day in Nowheresville, Arizona." She gave him a playful concerned look. Matt's face turned red and he tried to cover quickly. "A girl with a six-pack—and all her teeth."

Codi loved his embarrassment and his wet tee shirt did him no injustice, either.

They shared a smile each one knowing perfectly well what the other was thinking about. "I want you to stay here. I'll be right back," she said.

"No way," he said. "I'm in this as much as you are and I'll be damned if I'm going to wait here and do nothing while you're off risking your life for me."

"This is bigger than the both of us," she said, but pondered for a second. "You're probably right, I can keep a better eye on you if you come with me."

Matt followed as she turned and headed up the dock back into the fort. He tried frantically to get his mind back on the job at hand, but failed.

The clasps on the case were open in an instant and hands grabbed at the weapons within. Dax called out to the men to take their positions. He picked up one of the venerable rifles that launched rocket-propelled grenades, more commonly known as RPGs and jammed home the ordinance as he headed to the tower for a clean shot at the intruders. He had not heard from Caleb and his other men on the radio. He thought it was because of the thick stone walls and assumed they would soon join the fight. For now, five men would have to do.

"Sixty seconds to target," the pilot broadcast across the headsets. The giant cement buttress loomed large in the Black Hawk's windscreen. A flash from the lookout tower caught Fescue's attention. Three others followed.

"Incoming!" he screamed as three unknown weapons rocketed their way towards him. Instantly, an alarm sounded in the cockpit and the pilot yanked left on his stick and rudder. "Four bogies inbound breaking right, possible RPG ordnance," the first pilot said to the second pilot behind him in a voice calm as stone.

The RPGs harmlessly scraped past the fuselage and continued to the second helicopter. Fescue nearly gave himself whiplash tracking them past his window.

The instant he heard the warning, the second pilot broke to the right as years of training had taught him to do. But the late reaction would be costly. The first two missed, but the third RPG hit the rear cargo area and detonated.

A ball of fire and aluminum expanded as the mortally wounded Black Hawk seemed to freeze in the air for a millisecond. It tilted forward, catching the front skids on the ocean, causing it to cartwheel in a violent jumble of flesh and steel.

One Black Hawk down. This was not the outcome Agent Fescue had predicted. Someone was going to pay.

Special Agent Joel Strickman and Special Agent Waters reacted as several of the streaming feeds lost their signal. *"No, no, no!"* Agent Waters cried out. She immediately did a diagnostic to make sure it was the real deal. It was.

"Pelican Two is down," the pilot reported using the code word for the taskforce's second Black Hawk.

"Weapons hot, come in firing!" Fescue yelled as the chopper swept up over the lip of the Fort and flared to allow for maximum return firepower. The roof looked like a NASCAR racetrack with the center an open courtyard to the floors below. Bullets flew in multiple directions as the skid swept up over the lip and hovered on the heliport. Fescue and his men returned fire and were out the doors and gone in a matter of seconds.

Dax rushed to reload his launcher while his men laid down a withering barrage of lead in the direction of the invaders. At least one target dropped to the ground mortally wounded.

Dax fired at the stationary helicopter. It was a sitting duck. As the last man launched from the Black Hawk, the pilot immediately lifted off by banking and dipping off the top of the fort using the large structure as a shield from further RPGs. One just missed his tail rotor as it slipped below the roofline of the fort. He rapidly retreated, heading for a safe holding distance. Fescue and his three remaining men took cover behind the helipad and returned fire.

From the lookout tower, Dax swore as he reloaded his RPG-7 and took careful aim at the retreating helicopter once again. He was the only person high enough to still have a view. He exhaled slowly and gently squeezed the trigger, releasing the firing pin on the primer. The booster motor ignited and pushed the VP-7M warhead out of the tube.

At that point, stabilizer fins engaged and stabilized the rocket. The sustainer motor, or main rocket motor ignited and propelled the grenade to a velocity of 300 meters-per-second. The blue-grey smoke trail pointed to a place in front of the retreating Black Hawk. Dax had anticipated the positioning of the bird and aimed accordingly.

"Control, be advised we are under heavy fire and have–" The pilot's words were cut short as the two-stage armor-piercing warhead penetrated the cockpit's interior and detonated. There was a bright flash followed by a rapid expansion the Black Hawk could not contain. In the blink of an eye, the esteemed flying machine went from a high-tech weapon of war to a scrap of useless parts that only a recycling center could appreciate.

Pelican One was now also down, leaving Fescue and his dwindling team with only one means of egress.

Dax took one last look at his work, watching the scrapheap drop into the sea. He then turned to the matter at hand. "Keep them pinned down!" He ordered over the radio to his men as he ran down the stairs from the tower. Out on the edge of the fort's rim, he joined his force. He took careful aim and let his FAMAS Assault Rifle do its thing.

Special Agent Fescue called for cover fire and one at a time, his men made it to the stairs and out of harm's way, at least for the moment. They had lost one man and an entire Marine squad but there was nothing to be done about it now. The unexpected explosion in the distance behind him meant there was only one way out—forward.

The trespassers had made their way into the fort. Dax withdrew his men and led them on a course to intercept. "Approximately five armed men heading your way," he warned his sister. "En route to intercept. Hold and wait for us there," Dax tried one more time, without success, to contact Caleb and his missing men. Juliette had armed Doctor Comstock' assistants and placed them in positions to set up a crossfire. Dax and his men regrouped down one level using the opened metal doors in the hallway as cover.

The dock led into the Fort at a slight uphill angle. Codi and Matt tensed when they heard the first explosion on the far side of the citadel. They quickly made their way inside to reconnoiter. There was small arms fire in the distance and they knew this would be their best chance. Once inside, they stopped to let their eyes adjust. The distant gunfire was now muted. They were both dripping with saltwater and looked like they'd seen better days. Codi took a second to tie back her hair.

They moved in tandem, hugging the wall. Matt whispered, "When this is over, the first round is on me."

"Make mine a double," Codi whispered back over her shoulder. A moment later she raised her hand and made a fist, the operative's international sign for stop. Matt bumped into the back of her. "What are you doing?" she said. "You're supposed to stop when I do this."

"Nobody told me that. Remember, I'm a scientist, not part of your special ops club."

"Fair enough, but next time, stop when I do this."

Matt nodded.

They heard a clanking sound and ducked behind a metal structure that held a massive wench used for hauling cargo in from the dock.

Two men in lab coats were pushing a cart with several steel canisters. Matt leaned out to get a better look, but Codi pulled him back so he wouldn't give them away. They froze and waited for the two to pass.

"There are biohazard stickers on those tanks," Matt whispered. Codi nodded, she had seen them before.

The men were in a hurry and scampered off towards the boats to complete the loading. Matt and Codi turned and continued into the old fort, keeping their heads on swivel alert for any danger. A constant drone grew louder as they approached a room that housed a running generator. Matt pointed to the cables that ran out of the room's door and down a hallway.

Codi understood and followed the wires. They led to an entrance on the opposite side of the main control room that she had seen earlier. Codi got low and pushed the door open just a taste. She could see the woman from before organizing the other workers into a defensive position, each one holding a weapon.

Codi silently closed the door and motioned for Matt to follow. They moved back down the hallway out of earshot to make a plan. "These guys are under attack and I'm thinking its law enforcement. Once they get down here, we can help counterattack from this side."

Matt nodded.

"We just have to be really careful not to get shot, because it's very likely both sides will shoot at us."

Matt realized the situation—one side wanted them dead and the other didn't know who they were. "What about the two guys behind us?"

Voices in the distance alerted them that the two lab workers were returning. Codi cocked her head and pursed her lips at Matt—impressive. "Wait here," Codi said and then moved down the hallway, stopped in the middle and waited. Matt crouched where he was and looked on.

The two workers were so caught up in their conversation that they didn't see Codi until they practically ran into her. The sight of her gun pointed right at them created an immediate response and both threw their hands in the air. "Federal agent," Codi said. "Down on your knees." They complied. "Finally," she said. This was the first time she had said those words and not been shot at.

Matt and Codi escorted them into the generator room and used a couple of leftover extension cords to tie them up. They then moved back to their position at the control room door and waited. Codi outlined her plan to Matt.

Agent Fescue and his fellow agents methodically cleared rooms as they worked their way through the top floor of the old fort. They moved within the narrow part of the oval and were greeted with a curtain of lead. The agents dropped back and returned fire. Fescue knew they couldn't stay where they were and shoot it out, as their ammunition was limited. He sent two agents sprinting in the opposite direction hoping to catch the perps in a crossfire. Then he and his two other agents used sporadic volleys of gunfire to keep the thugs engaged.

Dax used his superior manpower and weaponry to press his advantage. "They only have a few men; keep firing," he told them. Bullets countered bullets in a fruitless interchange.

Joel and Agent Waters watched helplessly as the camera images slowly faded into snow. The battle had worked its way inside the fort and the video signal became too weak to escape the thick stone walls. There was nothing more they could do but wait and hope. Joel picked up his phone and dialed Boss, this was an update he wasn't looking forward to giving.

Finally, Dax was getting somewhere. A ricocheted bullet found its mark and one of the infiltrators dropped and screeched. He pushed his men forward for the final kill. Agent Fescue worked his bone-mic trying to find the status of his other two agents. But the radio was useless in such a place. He thought of his days at Quantico and how they had forced him to think outside the box and suddenly found himself praying that a man who typically lived by the book could think of a way to save his men.

He leaned around the metal door he was using for cover and fired off a quick burst. A short static squelch caught his attention. The radios had returned to within line of sight and a static-filled voice said, "In position." Agent Brian Fescue knew this was it, perhaps an answer to his prayer, but whatever it was, it was do-or-die time. He coordinated his counterattack with the other agents, leaned around the wall and opened fire.

The air filled with lead and the smell of cordite. Fescue grimaced as he took a bullet to the thigh. He sucked it up and kept up the return fire needed to keep from being completely overrun.

Dax moved left for a better field of vision to the target. A bullet whizzed past the spot he had just left. He instinctively dropped and rolled as more bullets, this time from the opposite direction chewed into the floor around him. A fragment of flying cement took out a chunk of his cheek, but he barely registered the wound.

Bullets cut through his men, as they were also caught off-guard by the FBI's pincer move. They were surrounded and in trouble. Dax flipped around and dropped into a prone position and squeezed off a three-round burst that eliminated one of the rear shooters. "Concentrate on the rear!" he barked to his men.

Agent Fescue had heard the distinctive sound of his men's AR-15. He urged his men forward concentrating his fire on the shooters ahead. Bullets met with flesh in an intense exchange that lasted only a few seconds.

Fescue looked around. He was the only member of his team left standing. But he checked his men anyway—no luck. The other bodies were in a similar state. But most troubling, there was no sign of Dax. A moan got his attention and he ran to find that Agent Colleroff had been grazed on his skull, but was still with him. The large amounts of blood belonged to someone else. "You okay?" he asked Colleroff.

"Honestly, Fisc, I've been better," he said as he checked his weapon. "But I can still shoot, hopefully straight." He blinked his eyes to help clear his head.

Agent Fescue ripped a sleeve from a nearby felon and used the cloth to wrap Colleroff's head. He then did the same for his leg. "Good. Let's finish this thing," he said.

Agent Colleroff nodded, but quickly stopped as the pain shot through his skull. His head felt like someone had taken a sledgehammer to it. Fescue helped him up and slowly and awkwardly they moved out.

Dax burst through the side entrance of the control room. He was alone and not happy about it. Four lab assistants almost shot him, they were so jittery. "Hold your fire!" Juliette yelled as she ran over to her brother from her fortified position.

"Status?" he asked.

"Shit, you're bleeding," said Juliette.

Dax wiped the blood off his cheek with the back of his hand. "It's nothing."

"We're ready to repel all boarders, providing they're carrying pitchforks and hoes," she said.

"Where's Caleb?"

Juliette held her hands up with an I-don't-know gesture.

"Dr. Comstock," Dax said to him, "you're with my sister; do not leave her side."

The doctor nodded and stepped next to her.

"There is one, maybe two left and the only way out is through here, so be ready."

The next two minutes felt like a lifetime as the lab assistants, shaking in their boots, held awkwardly onto their weapons, waiting to fire. Every creak in the room was followed by five rifles pointing in unison in that direction.

Fescue and Colleroff silently moved to the lab. They stopped in the shadows of the stairwell and took aim. Special Agent Fescue started things off with a shot to the head of a lab worker who had poked his head up like a prairie dog to look around. His gun fell beside his limp body having never been fired. That set off a hail of bullets in Fescue's direction, mostly fired by scared lab workers who barely knew which side of the gun to point.

Fescue and Colleroff dove for cover and countered in measured bursts that were deadly, dropping the less prepared with ease. Dax responded with accuracy that forced the agents to get their heads down and find better cover.

Codi and Matt slipped in behind during the battle and added to the devastation. Bullets were the main attraction for about another twenty seconds until those still alive had to pause to reload. Dax had conserved his ammo and used the brief interlude to end Colleroff as he reloaded. A well-aimed bullet sent him to the floor doing the twitchy dance of the dead.

Fescue returned a barrage of fire in the direction the shot had come from, but Dax had already changed positions. The wave of bullets had now become cat and mouse tactics until, with the addition of two new shooters coming in from behind, Dax had to change his strategy. It was time to leave.

Codi and Matt moved slowly to their left. Matt's gun was empty, but Codi had half-a-clip left. A well-concealed lab assistant took aim and loosed a torrent of lead in Matt's direction. Bullets sprayed all around Matt and he went down in a cloud of cement dust, dropping his gun.

The shooter was lying prone under a folding table stacked with equipment. Without thinking, Codi let out a scream of expletives and charged the combatant. She launched herself off a nearby crate and grabbed one of the tall temporary light stands and used it to pole vault through the air. She landed hard on the top of the table and it collapsed on the shooter breaking her fall and the neck of the man under it. The metal light stand crashed to the ground in a shower of sparks and light bulb explosions, dropping that section of the lab into total darkness.

Dax used the distraction to his advantage. He signaled Juliette with a head nod to get out. Then he laid down cover fire as she grabbed the doctor and slipped out the door. He quickly reloaded his assault rifle, grabbed the briefcase with the vaccine and followed behind. He released the pin on a grenade he was saving and tossed it back into the room as he closed the door and left with Juliette and the doctor for the dock.

"Grenade!" Codi screamed as she dove for cover. The room flashed white with a booming noise. Then all went black.

CHAPTER THIRTY

The ringing in her ears made it impossible to hear anything. Codi cracked her eyes open and forced herself to get up. The process was agonizing. Everything hurt and she was so dehydrated her body was starting to shut down. She leaned over and tried to smack some of the dust out of her hair.

Matt sat up stretching his jaw trying to equalize the pressure in his eardrums. He was bleeding from several small abrasions, but after careful inspection, he found himself still alive.

"You are one lucky SOB," Codi said.

Matt glanced at the source of the comment. Codi flicked her finger past him and he looked behind him. On the wall where he had been standing was a bullet pattern that almost perfectly outlined his torso. Each one so close, without one bullet hitting him. She came over and extended her hand. Matt grabbed it and shakily got to his feet. He glanced one more time at his body and noticed a bullet hole in the crotch on his pants. He quickly did an inventory.

"That was too close," Codi said.

Matt gave her a sheepish smile and his teeth glowed white against his dirt-covered face.

"Hold it right there!" A rifle came into view pointed in their direction.

Matt and Codi were in no position to react and knew this was it. Matt reached over and grasped Codi's hand, at least they would go out on their own terms. They slowly turned in the direction the voice had come.

The stranger looked at them in recognition. "Agent Sanders, Doctor Campbell?" Agent Fescue tried to say something more, but his adrenaline was gone, as was a large amount of blood. He fell to one knee and then to the ground, unconscious. Codi didn't miss a beat. "He's all yours," she said to Matt. "I'm gonna get us some water."

Fescue opened his eyes to see a man with a smile. "You're back," Matt said. He had bandaged Fescue's wound and propped up his head. He handed the agent a water bottle. "You've lost a lot of blood and will need to drink about three of these."

"How is it you're still alive?" Fescue asked.

"That's all on Codi over there. She got us out and planned the counterstrike to help you."

"Codi?"

"Special Agent Colette Sanders, sir," Codi said as she passed out a few snacks she'd scrounged and sat down next to Matt. Fescue watched the two eat like starving animals. They hadn't had any food or water for days.

Fescue sat up. "I'm Special Agent in Charge Brian Fescue of the FBI."

"In charge of what?" Matt asked, his mouth full. "We're the only ones left."

After regaining some of their strength, the three reconnoitered the area and confirmed they were in fact, the only ones left standing. Agent Fescue placed a jacket over the face of agent Colleroff and said a few words. He cleared off one of the tables and called Codi and Matt over. The three shared information and built a basic picture of everything they knew. Fescue then gave assignments to each. He used pieces of debris on the table as icons for his plan. He was used to being in charge.

Matt dug through all the equipment to see if he could discover what exactly Dax and his group were doing. Fescue collected as much paperwork and computer hard drives as he could. Codi was tasked with getting them out.

"It's not here," Matt said. Agent Fescue looked at Matt. *"Skystorm, it's not here. This is not good at all, they're probably getting ready to use it somewhere."*

"Use it how?" Fescue asked.

"That's the real question, isn't it?" Matt replied. Codi and Fescue shared an apprehensive look.

"Keep looking," Agent Fescue said. "Let's see if we can figure out what it is they're up to." He turned back to rummaging through a stack of paperwork.

Codi yelled from across the room. "Guys, I think you're gonna want to see this." Matt and Fescue stopped what they were doing and went over. Next to Codi were twelve steel cylinders, each with a biohazard sticker on it. Most troubling were two canisters that had taken bullets during the fighting and had leaked their contents onto the floor. "Shit," she said.

Matt backed away instinctively, but he knew it was already airborne. The three shared a knowing look and at that moment, whether they liked it or not, each was now committed to the death to see this thing out.

Matt took a couple of samples and used some of the remaining lab equipment to figure out what they were dealing with. Codi set her sights on repairing the remaining boat. It had been sabotaged and needed a lot of work to get it running. She checked on the two prisoners they had left tied up in the generator room, but they were gone. A close inspection showed their cords had been cut. Fescue tried to get a message out but there was no cell signal, even at the top of the fort. He soon discovered why when he found a cellphone repeater station that had been shot full of holes. These guys were covering their tracks well.

"It looks like smallpox," Matt said to no one in particular with his eye pressed firmly against the microscope. "But something is not quite right. We'll need a virologist to know for sure."

Fescue sat down and rubbed his leg; it was throbbing. When Codi walked into the room, Matt filled her in on the bad news.

"How's the boat coming?" Fescue asked.

"I need something to repair a cut fuel line. Otherwise, we're good to go."

She started rummaging through things looking for something she could MacGyver.

Matt stopped looking through the microscope and said, "I'm guessing about twenty-four hours before we see symptoms. The good news, if there is any, is that we would already be violently ill if we'd been given this virus via Skystorm."

"It works that fast?" Agent Fescue stopped what he was doing and walked over to Matt.

Matt nodded. "Skystorm forces material to enter the body on a cellular level at full-strength. The body hasn't had a chance to ramp up its defenses yet, so I'm guessing if they use this virus in Skystorm, you can expect a mortality rate of fifty to sixty percent."

"Oh my God," Codi said and stopped what she was doing. The gravity of the moment was not lost.

Matt changed the subject. "How long before they come looking for us?" he asked Fescue.

"Maybe a couple more hours, providing they can get the manpower," he replied as he grabbed a piece of pipe to use as a cane.

Codi found a tube to fix the fuel line and held it up. "Who's up for a boat ride?"

They loaded one canister, all the hard drives they could find and some of the paperwork onto the Ocean Master. Codi fired up the boat, Matt pulled in the dock lines and they left the fortress behind in their wake.

Once in cell range Agent Fescue checked in and brought everyone up to speed. A French biohazard team would be dispatched to recover and clean up the fort. A European APB went out for Dax, his sister and Nial. All of France went on full terror alert.

Agent Fescue's boss was furious. An international incident was brewing with the FBI at its heart. It was a CYA moment of epoch proportions. A new replacement FBI team would be sent out and within forty-eight hours they'd be up and running again, but this time with the French authorities in charge. Matt and Codi were to be debriefed and Agent Fescue was to report to the hospital.

"We're being replaced," Fescue said after he hung up the phone. "That's bullshit."

"They'd still be in the dark if it wasn't for us," Codi said.

"True, but the FBI has strict protocols, especially on foreign soil."

"How long before the new team takes over?"

"Forty-eight hours."

"This thing will be over in forty-eight hours," she said.

"I have my orders and so do you."

"I don't work for the FBI," Codi said.

"Neither do I," Matt added. "If you're unwilling to help us, then drop us off at the nearest town and we'll take it from here."

Codi looked over at Matt. Had he just said that? Damn, she was really starting to like this guy. Fescue stood in silence as the wind whipped through his hair. He turned very deliberately and said, "Okay."

Joel reached for the phone on the first ring. He and Agent Waters had been contacted earlier by Agent Fescue and brought up to speed. They were looking through satellite footage in order to track Dax's boat and his location. He paused what he was doing and put the phone on speaker. They were stunned at the news—he and Agent Waters were being recalled to the states. The whole thing had become an international incident and the FBI was getting the blame. It was circle the wagons time and the bureaucrats were in typical form.

He and Agent Waters powered down their computers in silence.

His phone rang again and it took him several seconds to even realize it was ringing. "Yes?"

"What in the hell is going on over there?" Crap, it was Boss. Joel recounted everything that had happened. Director Ruth Anne Gables listened with only a few interruptions asking for clarification.

When Joel finished there was a brief moment of silence followed by Director Gables saying, "The FBI really screwed the pooch here." Agent Waters leaned in by Joel's ear so she could hear. "Terrorist with a super-weapon. Seems like it's way too important to stand down, especially right at this moment. But orders are orders. Why don't you and Agent Sanders take a few days off and then get back here with a full report on Thursday."

Joel looked confused, said, "Ah... okay," and hung up.

"She wants me to take a few days off," Joel said.

"Seriously? You didn't get that?"

"Get what?"

"She basically gave you carte blanche to see this thing through."

Joel looked confused for a moment and then the light went on. "Yeah."

"And I'm going with you," Agent Waters said.

"But the FBI, you're under strict orders."

"Screw that, this is serious shit."

Joel looked at Agent Waters for a moment. With a serious nod, knowing what might lie ahead for them, he said, "Yeah, it is."

The news was spectacular. Workers at the British Consulate in Bordeaux had come down with an unknown strain of smallpox that hit so fast and hard it had health officials scrambling to contain and control it. They were working on a vaccine but had been unsuccessful thus far. The consulate was under quarantine and all business was being conducted though the Paris embassy. Local hospitals were busy making the populace aware of possible symptoms. France, as a whole, was on high alert.

Nial did a celebratory swoop with his arm through the air. "Yes!" The news was better than he had hoped. He glanced down at an alert message that popped up on his laptop. He opened it and carefully read the message. His smile dipped slightly. I guess life is full of good news/bad news days, he thought to himself.

He was a little surprised by the resourcefulness of the FBI. His mole program, Trevi, didn't allow for real-time updates. Its ability to remain stealthy meant the information was delayed in sending and Nial was just now seeing a pattern that indicated an attack on Fort Boyard was imminent. Luckily, he had placed several contingencies into his plan and now was the time to implement one of them.

He wasn't afraid of change. Plans almost never survived contact with the enemy, but Nial had loved that fort for all that it was and for what it offered. He was sad to see it rendered useless to him, but he still had the services of Dax, Juliette and Dr. Comstock, along with a small core of his best and brightest. He picked up his phone and texted: "Move everything to Rome."

Nial called his pilot and told him to prep the helicopter. He packed a bag and said goodbye to his chateau. He was going to take a little detour on his way to join them and, hopefully, slow down the FBI at the same time.

The sun sent a kaleidoscope of orange refractions across the city as it made its first appearance of the day. Paris, known as the city of lights, is a must-see for every tourist. With its fabulous museums and world-class eateries, the city is a cultural experience for the mind and body, truly one of the jewels of Europe.

The Eurocopter swept in from the south across the Seine river and on to the FBI headquarters. Nial could see the Eiffel Tower in the distance casting a giant shadow across the Palais De Chaillot. Now that he had gotten the hang of how to fire the weapon, he needed only one pass. The pilot dropped to five hundred feet and then leveled off. Nial powered up his remote and allowed his index finger to hover over the green button. As soon as they passed over the Seine, he pressed the knob, holding it down for a full ten seconds as they passed over the building. The pilot banked right and they continued on their way out of the country.

Inside the building, agents and staff were unaware that anything had happened. The replacement team had arrived and was in the process of unloading their gear in the bullpen. Those lucky enough to be deeper within the building would experience nothing, as the microscopic particles would never reach them, but the ones on the perimeter were a different story. Tiny traces of the modified smallpox virus entered their bodies on a cellular level. The virus took hold and replicated within minutes. Inside an hour, symptoms were not only presenting themselves, they were raging and the odds of the uninfected getting out of the building without coming in contact with the sick and thus catching the disease the old fashioned way, were remote.

The boat slowed and reversed engines as Codi pulled alongside the concrete dock in the Port de Bordeaux. The French Coast Guard had intercepted them about two miles offshore. The bright orange ship with a dark blue hull had made it clear that they were in charge and that no deviation of any kind would be tolerated. At the dock, Agent Fescue, Codi and Matt were met by a host of very serious looking

French constabularies, each trying to be in charge over the other and each blaming the trio for what was now considered a terrorist act on French soil.

Agent Fescue tried to explain, even warned them that they had been infected, but there was no interest. And once they found the biohazard canister on board the boat all hell broke loose. The three were summarily disarmed, de-badged and handcuffed. But worst of all, the canister, hard drives and paperwork were taken by some guys in tight-fitting suits.

Codi and her gang, as they were being referred to, sat handcuffed on a small wall surrounded by shortsighted bickering government officials. Everyone wanted a piece of them and pressed their status to the end. Matt was done watching the circus. He said to Codi and Matt, "What we need is Inspector Clouseau."

"No we don't, Matt," Codi said.

"What's going on?" Fescue asked, clueless.

Matt stood up and called out, "Hey, estupidos! We need to talk to Inspector Clouseau!"

Everyone stopped yelling and looked at Matt.

"Inspector Clouseau," he said. "We need to talk to him."

This started a whole new conversation amongst the French officials trying to place the name. After about five minutes a man in a blue uniform walked over to Matt and punched him in the stomach. "Funny man," he said.

"Are you insane!" Fescue screamed at Matt. He had lost his men, was being recalled and now his charge was making trouble. The day couldn't have gone worse.

Finally, the Police Nationale won the argument. A group of very serious looking men bustled Codi, Matt and Fescue into a blue police van and off to headquarters. They were each placed in separate cells and left wondering what was to come next.

Codi slammed her fist against the wall of her cell. The place smelled like vomit and bleach. She didn't have time for this and neither did the

French authorities. She had literally gone from one cell to another. After pacing for close to thirty minutes she finally gave up and sat on the inflexible wooden bunk, propped her hands on her face and let her mind focus.

Special Agent Kyle Hastings of the FBI sat at his new desk on the third floor. He was reading a personal email. His girlfriend was coming to visit him in Paris. He couldn't wait. His new promotion had moved him to an office with a view overlooking the Seine. It came with a lot of responsibility and he was looking forward to the challenge and impressing his girlfriend.

He considered three possible restaurants where he would propose to her. Finally, he settled on one, Le Mesturet. It was located on a quaint corner near the Royal Palace. Kyle had met Leesa at a restaurant bar on one of those few nights when trainees were allowed to leave Quantico. She was a buyer for a high-end clothing store and they had clicked right away. Over the last two years, a long-distance relationship had actually worked and with his new promotion, it was time. He would go ring shopping after work and make the reservation for the restaurant.

Suddenly and without warning, he began to sweat. He ignored it and picked up the phone to make a call. Muscle cramps took hold. He hung up the phone and doubled over in pain. The urge to vomit came on slow and steady. He left his office and headed for the bathroom down the hall. He was trying to remember what he'd eaten in the last twenty-four hours. Probably a mild case of food poisoning; he would be fine.

Within three days Special Agent Kyle Hastings would be dead.

The news broke hard and fast. The UK consulate in Bordeaux was intentionally attacked by some unknown super-strain of smallpox that had taken six lives already. The FBI headquarters in Paris experienced the same outbreak. A general sense of panic spread throughout the normally tranquil city. Steps were being taken to control the outbreak, but soon anyone with a fever jammed the already filled hospitals. Flights and all transportation out of the city was stopped while the world held its collective breath, hoping for containment. The police were quickly overwhelmed.

Codi awoke to the sound of her cell door opening. Two armed guards escorted her to an interrogation room where she was handcuffed to a metal eyelet on a steel table. She sat back slowly into the grey metal chair and looked up at the two cameras and the one-way glass facing her. The room was very utilitarian—muted green walls and a concrete floor complete with a drain in the middle that she hoped was a leftover item from years past.

The door opened and a short man with a dour expression and crewcut entered. He sat in the chair across from Codi and perused a file he had brought with him. Codi knew the tactic well and almost laughed out loud. The exchange started off well but quickly deteriorated. Codi protested her innocence and the policeman blamed her and her cohorts for the mess. Codi stood her ground and even used a few choice words to describe the bureaucrat. In the end, he closed the folder and left the room. Ten minutes later, Codi was released.

Matt walked out of the police national headquarters in Bordeaux at about the same time. His whole body ached and his mouth tasted like dead opossum. He couldn't remember the last time he'd brushed his teeth. Codi and Fescue shuffled over to meet him. "Wow and I thought our government was screwed up," he said.

"No kidding," said Codi.

There was a screech off to the left and all three reacted as slow as molasses at Christmastime.

Joel exited a vehicle and ran over to Codi. It took her a minute to realize who he was. A huge smile spread across her face. She said, "You look fantastic for a dead guy."

"Yeah? And how's that whole Stockholm Syndrome working for you?"

They hugged. Joel held in a grimace from the pain that shot through his shoulder. Codi pushed him away and said, "Oh crap. We've been exposed to some kind of biological. You should keep your distance."

"We aren't contagious until someone shows symptoms," Matt said, adding, "I'm guessing later today. I suppose we're all in it now."

Everyone paused to absorb his statement. Codi made the introductions and it was quickly apparent that, with the exception of Agent Waters, they were the walking wounded and soon to be the walking dead.

"I take it you're the one responsible for getting us out," Fescue said to Joel.

"It was a team effort," he replied.

The group moved to a park bench across the street and took turns getting everyone up to speed. The news of the attack on the FBI building in Paris hit Agent Fescue especially hard. Joel and Agent Waters probably owed their lives to being officially dropped from the case since they had left the building before the attack. The country of France was now in the process of closing its borders.

Special Agent Fescue, always the man in charge, was especially morose. After all, he'd gotten his entire taskforce killed and was being recalled back home to answer for it. And knowing what was about to happen to the populace, things couldn't be worse.

Codi tried to sum up their situation. "Okay, so we have a crazy Irishman with a hyper-efficient bio-weapon, whereabouts unknown and the team who knows the most about what is going on has been ordered to stand down."

Matt had a very concerned look on his face. "Don't forget hundreds of infected souls with no vaccine."

"Right."

She continued. "We did everything we could. If the French authorities won't listen, we'll have to find another way."

Fescue put up his hand. "We're not finding anything; we've been ordered to stand down."

Joel piped in. "Technically, *you* have, but we're on vacation and would like to see the sights."

Matt looked back and forth between Joel and Fescue.

When Joel cocked his head, Fescue started to catch on. Agent Waters pulled her laptop out of her satchel and powered it up. She double-clicked on the icon for the case and spent the next few minutes going over their "vacation."

Codi finally interrupted when her stomach growled for the third time. "I've got to get something to eat."

They all agreed and headed for a small street-side café down the block. After all, an army runs on its stomach. "And I need a toothbrush and some toothpaste," Matt announced.

After a delicious meal of chicken with thyme, small potatoes and onions, Codi felt human again. She said, "First thing we have to do is find a way out of this town."

"I agree," Joel said, "but with all that's happened, getting across the border is going to be tricky."

"We have a car and I did some digging," Agent Waters said. She opened her laptop. "Here."

Joel cleared some plates to make room on the table. She brought up a map and pointed out a few details. "There is a small road that drops off the D113 here. We could take it and intersect with the A62 here."

Fescue leaned in and said, "That would bypass the roadblocks."

"And we can take that to Toulouse," Agent Fescue added. He was finding new strength in breaking the rules. "Does Toulouse still have a working airport?"

Agent Waters nodded her head.

Codi was getting her head around the plan. "And we fly to where?"

"Joel, you remember that warehouse you were checking up on," Agent Waters prompted.

"Rome? What about it?"

"I did some satellite pulls before we were shut down and found this." Agent Waters clicked to a new screen. It showed an overhead view of a warehouse complex. One of the buildings stood away from the others and had two trucks backed up to the loading bay.

Fescue had a blank look and said, "Okay, so it's being used."

Waters added, "This was from yesterday."

"So?"

"It was Sunday."

Codi had completely lost track of the days with all she'd been through, but a working warehouse on a Sunday in a nearly all-Catholic country was a very weak lead.

Fescue wasn't buying it. "What else do you have?" he asked.

Agent Waters opened her empty palms to the sky and shook her head.

Joel said, "Look, I've been working with Agent Waters for several days now and I gotta tell you her instincts are good." A second or two passed before he said. "We got nothing else to go on. Besides, we need to get out of France before they completely shut everything down."

"So who's up for a ride?" Agent Fescue asked. "Remember, we are all disobeying orders and if this goes south we are probably looking at jail time." Agent Fescue watched as every hand went up.

Agent Waters left to bring the car around. Codi looked up to see a silver Chevy Impala POS pull to the curb and said, "You have got to be kidding me!"

"Shotgun!" Joel called out.

⑊

The office was utilitarian—drywall, bad art and a metal desk. Nial sat tapping his fingers against it while pondering his next move. The fly-over of the FBI headquarters in Paris was a brilliant move. The TV showed roadblocks and a complete quarantine on the FBI building. He flicked through several channels, all with the same story.

Paris was cancelling all transportation in and out of the city. Citizens were encouraged to stay indoors and wear a surgical mask if they absolutely had to go out. The government had set up stations to pass out masks.

This was world news and he, Nial Brennan, was the man behind the headlines. It was the sweetest music to his ears. That should slow 'em down, he told himself.

He had a fleeting thought. I should have invested in the company that makes those masks. He imagined what would be coming next and then picked up his phone and called his broker. After all, money never sleeps.

Nial had managed to get Dax and his remaining team out of the country and they had regrouped at his warehouse near Rome. The weapon had worked like a dream. It was now time for phase two, the part he was most excited about—a payday that would buy him a small island and peace of mind knowing he had done his part to help bring down the pompous British Empire—with an American weapon, no less!

There was a knock on the door, followed by Dax's head popping in. "Thought you would like to know we are just about back up and running. I've got a message out to a few guys I can trust to help reinforce our position. We should be all set within the next sixteen hours or so."

"Good work, Dax. We're almost to the point where you and Juliette walk away with everything I promised you."

CHAPTER THIRTY-ONE

The hour-long drive on a bumpy dirt road finally ended as the Impala POS turned onto highway A62 and headed for Toulouse. Agent Waters, as the only one who was not a total mess, drove. The vehicle was made to hold three in the back seat, but only if you were small of stature. Codi was smashed in the middle and even with the windows down the smell of three days in captivity without a shower was taking its toll.

"Please tell me that smell is coming from outside," Joel said. A new stink was permeating the vehicle. He rolled down his window to save his nasal glands.

The odor intensified instantly. "Joel, what the hell!" Matt said as he put his shirt over his nose, preferring his own BO to the smell coming from a large pig farm they were passing.

Codi shook her head. "You guys need to get out of the office more. This is nothing compared to 112 degrees at the dump that also serves as a raw sewage drain in Kandahar."

Joel looked back over his shoulder at Codi and said, "Gross."

Agent Fescue, who had been unusually quiet during the ride added, "Or finding a pregnant female who'd been burned to death by her husband and left in a closed van for a week."

The thought of that smell made Joel almost puke on the spot. He had to look away and hold his mouth closed with his hand. The next ten minutes passed in silence.

Codi's boss, Ruth Anne Gables, had used some back-channel

contacts and had a plane waiting for them in the private charter terminal. Director Gables was feeling the pressure of the international
incident, but had to trust her boots on the ground, her agents. She
reminded them that they were walking on very thin ice and that she
could only protect them so far. The French government was blaming
them specifically for the outbreak. But pressure from the American side
had prevailed for now.

The older Learjet 24 had room for six with two sets of very worn
bucket seats positioned back-to-back and a small bench seat in the rear.
The ragtag group boarded and most were asleep before the plane left
the ground. The pilot cleared with the tower and turned east, heading
for Rome. Joel spent part of the flight to arrange a few rooms at a hotel,
one hopefully sans bedbugs.

Within a half-hour of the trip, the first symptoms started to show.
Headache and fever hit Fescue and Codi. They each downed three
Advil and went back to sleep.

Once the plane cleared customs, the pilot called Codi to the cockpit. He lifted a section of the floor between his seat and the copilot's
to reveal a hidden compartment. He extracted a black duffle bag and
handed it to her. "All part of the service on Terminal Airlines," he said.

Codi thanked him and lugged the duffle bag off to meet up with the
others at the car rental center.

Agent Waters pulled around in a large black SUV. Codi smiled, now
we're talkin'. They loaded up and fought the chaotic traffic that most
Italian towns are famous for. Rome is a prime example of an ancient/
modern-juxtaposed city with structures from almost every century and
style of architecture, the most famous being the coliseum, which they
passed on the way to the hotel.

News of the FBI office being infected in the same mysterious way
as the British consulate was all over. France was in the process of completely shutting itself off to all transportation in and out. That made it
pretty clear that the team sent to take over was undoubtedly out of commission. The French were blaming the Americans and had refused their

assistance. A new FBI taskforce was now in London setting up. They were also about ten steps behind. Interpol was trying to coordinate a multi-national investigation and failing.

At the hotel, the group gathered in Codi's room. She called to update Boss. "By the way, thanks for the surprise package," she said before hanging up the phone. To the group she said, "Boss agrees with us that our lead is really shaky, but the rest of the authorities seem to be chasing their tails. That means she's backing our play—for now."

"It looks like your boss is trying to distance himself from this mess," said Codi.

"He pushed you two over to work with us." She pointed to Agent Fescue and Waters.

Fescue added with a hint of disgust, "He just needs a fall guy and that's me."

Agent Waters piped in. "That's *all* of us if we don't stop what's going on here."

"She also said and I emphasize this as to her mood," Codi said, "there is to be no direct action taken no matter what—no shooting, no blowing things up. If we get any actionable intel, it goes up the chain and to the local authorities."

Matt was bewildered. "Even if they shoot at us first?"

Codi held her hands out and said, "That's bullshit and you know it."

"Hey, I was just sayin'."

She looked around the room. "Everyone clear on our orders? No shooting."

They all knew none of this was their fault, but Agent Waters had to add, "Don't look at me." This started a chain reaction of much needed laughter.

Joel walked in with a several bags of food from a local restaurant and was caught off-guard by everyone laughing. "What did I miss?"

There was an awkward silence that followed, as no one knew quite how to explain it. Agent Fescue seized the moment and said, "Let's eat."

After the early dinner, Agent Fescue took everyone back through the plans one more time. Codi took a few minutes to go through the duffle bag: three AR15's, five handguns of various makes, enough ammunition to start a war and one night vision spotting scope. In the side compartment were tactical comms that used in-ear bone conduction mics. It was a lot of firepower for a no shooting policy. Codi racked one of the pistol's slides back, chambered a round and said, "I'd rather be judged by twelve than carried by six." She looked around. "Look, Boss has to protect herself. The onus is on us. Now's not the time to hold back. There are lives at stake, ours included. Let's find Mr. Brennan and shut him down."

The message was received loud and clear. They packed up their gear and left for the warehouse.

Matt started to show symptoms and Fescue's back started to ache followed by growing fatigue. Codi was now on a regimen of four Advil every three hours. Fescue looked over at her and asked, "You gonna be okay?"

"We just need to make sure we find something at this warehouse that leads to a cure."

Fescue nodded, knowing that the odds were not good.

Matt had explained that the normal progression of the disease was body aches, headaches, high fever, fatigue, sometimes vomiting and then red spots, lesions and blisters and finally death. Codi had a mild hammering in her head and was wearing an extra coat to keep from shivering. A clock somewhere was ticking down, but every one of them would take action over a hospital bed any day. They all knew what was at stake.

Dax and Juliette stepped into the office. "You wanted to see us?"

"Yes," said Nial. "Everything's in place. Please get Skystorm ready and loaded with a maximum payload. I will need you to grab everything else and drive it up to our final location. Our buyer will meet us there in two days and we can finally settle up and go our separate ways."

Dax started to turn, but sensed his boss was not finished.

Nial paused for a second to collect his thoughts. "I just wanted to say how grateful I am for all your hard work on this project." Dax kept his head on a swivel. He was sure Nial was up to something and he was ready for anything. But the flamboyant man came around his desk and vigorously shook both their hands. "Congratulations are in order to both of you. Wonderful job." Dax and Juliette shook his hand. Maybe he wasn't such a douche after all, Dax considered. "I expect no trail left behind, including the good doctor. Is that clear?"

Before Dax or Juliette could answer, Nial said, "And of course your fee will be wired into your account before final delivery. You can expect a cash bonus once I get paid."

Dax forced a smile at the mention of their money. He said, "The doctor, no problem. We no longer need him anyhow."

"Give us thirty minutes and the helicopter will be ready," Juliette added.

Nial picked up a bottle of 1989 Bollinger La Grande Année Rosé that was chilling on ice and popped the cork. He poured glasses for all. "Here's to the proof that crime does pay." Nial raised his glass.

Dax and Juliette each grabbed a glass and reflected. The old bugger was ending his career on a high note and just maybe that included them as well. Dax downed the smooth champagne and turned and left.

The sickly group drove past several Roman era arches attached to a cathedral that contrasted to its neighbor, a chrome and glass high-rise. The beauty and diversity of this city never ceased to amaze Codi. The SUV pulled to the curb across from the suspected warehouse just as the sun was setting. The sky was ablaze with a phantasmagoria of orange hues enhanced by the ever-present air pollution.

The team spent the next ten minutes observing the warehouse and fine-tuned their tactics accordingly. They spread out on foot and each worked their way into position, adrenaline now masking most of the effects of the disease. The warehouse was set off by itself. It was two stories high and made of concrete and brick. Agents Strickman and Waters took the most direct approach, while Fescue circled around behind. Codi tried to leave Matt in the car, but he was determined to go with them or without them.

Once in position, the three teams checked in with each other. There was no movement at the warehouse. No trucks or lights of any kind. It looked abandoned. "We came all this way, so we might as well check it out," Codi said with a lackluster tone.

"Stay sharp, just in case," Fescue reminded everyone. He was still stinging from his last encounter with these guys. He glimpsed at his hand and noticed it was covered in red spots. He tried desperately to remember what Matt had said, was it red spots and then death or was there another symptom in between?

On Codi's call, the three teams moved forward, careful not to give away their presence too soon. Suddenly, exterior lights flashed on, flooding the area. Joel's right eye in the night vision scope was blinded. Everyone hit the dirt. Up on the roof, Dax lowered the temporary walls that were hiding the helicopter from prying eyes.

"Something's happening on the roof," Fescue broadcasted.

Each team member knew this was it. With the butt of her rifle, Codi popped the lock to the chain-link gate that led to the loading dock. She and Matt stayed low as they made their way to the side of the building. She could see Matt was sweating profusely; his fever was bad and he was trying to suck it up as best he could. She pushed the transmit button on her radio. "Remember, no shooting. We just have to confirm that this is the place and then call it in."

Joel and Agent Waters reached the front door and crouched as they tried to slow their breathing. Joel went to work on the door lock. At the rear of the building, Fescue found an old oil drum and rolled it over and propped it up. By standing on top of it he could just access the back fire escape to the roof. He pulled himself up and started his assent. He keyed his mic. "I'm moving to the roof now; will advise."

The helicopter pilot started his preflight check and the rotors began to rotate. Nial left his final instructions and headed for his place in the copilot seat. Dr. Comstock did a full diagnostics on Skystorm's electronics and gave it his approval. He then loaded the system with as much D3 as it would hold. "Good luck, sir!" The doctor said as he handed the remote to Nial.

The panic that had gripped the world, even the reports of the deaths at the British consulate and the FBI building had not emotionally impacted Doctor Didier Comstock at all. He viewed it in a detached scientific way. He had merely made a few notes on his tablet and felt satisfied at the results. The next task, in his mind, was to improve the efficacy of the weapon. He said to Nial, "I have an idea that might make this technology even more efficient."

Nial sized him up as he climbed into the chopper. "Good to hear. I'll see you in Brussels and we can set something up." Nial closed the door and wondered if he had been premature in ordering the good doctor's death. No, he would sell the weapon and be done with it.

Of the twenty ten-liter petrol cans that had been purchased and filled, only two remained. The rest had been carefully placed throughout the facility, each with a small detonator tied to a signal that worked off Juliette's phone APP. She did a quick diagnostic, locked her phone and placed it in her pocket.

The truck was filled and ready to move out. She had the last two cans of petrol placed in the back of the truck as a back-up—no point in being stuck on the highway for lack of petrol. The stake bed truck was then covered with a drab green canvas and tied down. Two magnetic stickers were affixed to the doors that read Salini Constructtori, complete with a hammer and saw logo. Any cursory inspection would reveal what appeared to be construction equipment of some kind with the canisters well hidden in the mix.

Nial gave Dax a cursory wave as the Eurocopter started to lift off. The flight to London would take ten hours with a planned refueling and layover in Brussels. He then had a short flight to their final meet to make the exchange with the buyer.

Agent Fescue could hear the whine of the helicopter as it started up. He climbed as fast as he could, hoping his five Advil and adrenaline would get him through. As he made it to the top of the roof, the helicopter was just leaving the wash of the floodlights, plunging it into darkness. He saw the man responsible for the deaths of his men watching it lift off. Without hesitation, Fescue fired in the general direction of the departing Eurocopter with a hope and a prayer and then turned his attention to the man he hated. At the same time he called over the radio, "We need to breech now. I say again, *breech now.*"

"Copy that; breeching," Codi said. The gunfire heard from the rooftop galvanized her and without hesitation she fired off four rounds into the lock holding the loading-dock door and pushed it open.

Joel was still fiddling with the door lock when Agent Waters pulled him aside and blasted it to pieces. She kicked the door open and entered, gun first. The two moved quickly through empty offices that made up the front of the warehouse.

"Clear. Clear," could be heard as they tag-teamed room to room. Clues were non-existent, but at one point Joel noticed a printer and pulled some documents out of it. He stuffed them down his shirt and headed for the next room.

Dax dropped to the ground and slipped his AK-12 assault rifle off his shoulder. He and two other men returned fire on the source. The Russian AK-12 is the newest derivative of the soviet AK series. This one had a sixty-round clip and a Trijicon ACOG quick-sight scope.

Agent Fescue's shots were repaid threefold from the men on the roof, each spraying in his direction as they dove for cover. Fescue had nowhere to go but back over the short retaining wall and onto the fire escape. He dropped one man who was trying to get behind an air-conditioning unit. He quickly ducked down as a stream of lead chewed into the retaining wall, showering him with cement chips.

Codi and Matt had made their way into the warehouse but were the next to have bullets fly in their direction. They made it to a row of steel drums and were using them for cover. Bullets were pinging off them like a bad reggae band.

They exchanged fire in alternating movements, each side keeping the other at bay and hoping for a lucky shot. Juliette used her French to bark orders, hoping the FBI intruders wouldn't understand. They kept up a steady rain of bullets as they flanked and closed. A flash of white streaking in her peripheral vision caught Juliette's attention.

Dr. Didier Comstock had decided it was time to quit. He grabbed the briefcase with the cure in it and ran for the nearest exit. Juliette looked up just in time to catch him making for the door. She wasted little time drawing a line of bullets across his torso. Dr. Comstock pitched forward and tumbled into a contortion of arms and legs. The briefcase skittered across the floor. He was a mere two feet from safety. "Cover me," Juliette yelled and ran for the briefcase. She rolled, grabbed the briefcase and was back on her feet and firing in one move.

Codi saw what had happened and did everything in her power to stop Juliette, but a withering volley of 7.62-millimeter rounds tore into the steel barrier that protected her and Matt. She dropped back behind the drums where she spotted a can of gas with a detonator attached to it sitting against the wall behind her. A quick glance confirmed another one thirty feet down the wall. This place was rigged to blow.

Matt dropped down next to her and she pointed out the problem. Maybe they could use it to their advantage, if it didn't kill them first. "See if you can shoot that can across the room. I'm going to try and keep them pinned down."

Once they had secured the offices, Joel and Agent Waters quickly moved to the main warehouse. Lying in a pool of his own blood was a man in a lab coat just a few feet in front of them. A girl with an MP-5 and a briefcase could be seen unloading her weapon at a stack of steel drums across the way.

This is not a drill, Agent Waters thought to herself. She leaned around the doorjamb and opened fire. The girl with the briefcase caught a round and hit the ground hard. The briefcase she was carrying sliding off out of reach. Instinctively, Juliette let her momentum continue and she rolled under the truck to safety. She flipped over and sent bullets back the other way.

Joel had been watching the whole thing unfold and anticipated Juliette's maneuver. He grabbed Agent Waters by the shoulder and flung her back as 9mm projectiles shredded the doorjamb where she had just been crouching. Juliette called for someone to cover her six and spun back around to deal with the two behind the drums, while her men protected her backside. Her shoulder had been hit and she knew it wasn't functioning properly, but for now it would have to do. After all, gunfights rarely lasted more than a minute.

Fescue gritted his teeth. Crouching down put immense stress on the bullet wound in his leg and it was starting to bleed again. He could see two men working their way around to him from different sides, each taking turns firing in his direction. They were keeping him pinned down with well-aimed pop shots. He knew it was only a matter of time. What he needed now was a little luck.

He fired a blind volley to the right as he moved left. Luck was on his side—he was a rewarded with a shriek. He ejected his spent clip and jammed a new one home as something clanged off the steel fire escape next to him. He looked down to see a grenade lying next to him. Instinct took over and without a second thought he jumped. Ten feet down he hooked his arm on a steel cross brace. The sudden stop jarred every bone in his body and his leg hitting against the railing sent an explosion of pain so intense that it caused him to squeal, but the explosion that followed just about killed him.

The blast twisted the platform he had just been standing on and disconnected the top third of the staircase from the building. If Fescue hadn't locked his arm and leg to the structure, he would have flown off to his death.

The concussion had ruptured his eardrums and the intense ringing was matched by the blackness creeping into his vision. Blood oozed from his ears as he frantically tried to blink away the darkness. The sight of ricochets pinging off the steel around him forced him to refocus and concentrate. He shook his head and willed his body to move.

Dax ran to the edge of the roof and looked over. The grenade had landed right where the intruder had been and exploded with a concussive blast. The fire escape looked like some sort of bad metal art as the mangled top portion swayed in the air, partially disconnected from the building. He could see the shooter hanging from the teetering structure a few yards down. He aimed his AK and tried to finish the job, but the man moved to put more steel between them.

Fescue groped for his rifle. It was long gone. He grabbed his pistol and fired a few rounds back up at the rooftop. The silhouette on the roof returned fire. Several fragments ricocheted off the steel and peppered his face, almost causing him to fall a second time. An unmistakable *click* followed. The shooter was out of bullets. This was the lifeline Fescue desperately needed. He moved as quickly as he could back up to the top of the fire escape. He let loose a few shots, but the shooter had backed away and none found their mark.

The fire escape wobbled with every move. Fescue had to be extremely careful. He climbed to what was left of the top platform of the staircase, stood on the shaky platform and looked up just as the man returned. He was holding a long board and they surprised each other.

Agent Fescue twisted and fired too quickly and his bullet went wide. He paused and pulled the trigger again, this time more carefully. His aim was true and the bullet dropped Dax. The board clattered to the ground. Fescue stood all the way up to get a better view, his gun still aimed.

Dax slowly stood back up on wobbly legs. He picked up the two-by-four board he'd been carrying and examined it. A nine-millimeter slug was just poking through the backside of the board. Better to be lucky than good, he thought to himself. The man on the damaged staircase pulled the trigger one more time. *Click.* He, too, was out of bullets.

Fescue cycled his semi-auto one more time to be sure. Yep, he was out of bullets. The man picked up his board and walked to the edge of the roof. Light from below illuminated his face. It was a nasty, crazed look. Fescue said, "Dax Cole, I've been looking for you." The words sounded distant in Fescue's damaged ears.

Dax looked at him with a certain amount of disappointment. The FBI man had stolen his moment, but he quickly regrouped. "Yes, my name is Dax Cole and I am here to kill you."

"That's big talk for a man with no bullets."

The gap between the partially detached fire escape and the building was ten feet. The two titans stared at each other, pure hatred coursing through their veins. The sounds of gunfire were still prevalent in the distance below. Dax rotated the sixteen-foot two-by-four and slid it out over the roof to the staircase. Fescue watched with a curiosity that soon turned to worry.

He pressed it against the steel menagerie and pushed. The metal fire escape groaned as it moved away. He pulled the board back. Agent Fescue had to drop and hang on as the staircase swung back like a pendulum. Dax repeated the process, pushing and releasing, until the whole fire escape was rocking like a crazy see-saw. It was all Fescue could do to hold on.

Fescue said to him, "We know all about your operation. Even if you kill me, there will be no place you can hide."

Dax smiled at the weak verbal threat. He said, "I'm not some fancy FBI agent. I tend to do things one at a time and right now the only thing on my plate is to kill you." He shoved the two-by-four extra hard.

The first retaining bolt sheared off and then the second. The fire escape shuddered and groaned, as the stairs started to completely detach from the building. Dax smiled as he watched the FBI guy realize what was about to happen. Push, release. Push release. The whole thing was rocking intensely.

Fescue moved ever so carefully closer to the edge facing the building. He hung on for all he was worth as the mounting g-force pulled him from this crazy ride. He had one chance and he had to get it right. He considered jumping for the building when the tower rocked in that direction, but his bad leg would make it nearly impossible.

Dax was enjoying the show and loved how such a small amount of effort yielded so much drama. He pushed the fire escape each time it came back his way and as the mounting bolts sheered away, one by one, it was only a matter of time before the whole thing broke free and crashed to the ground.

Fescue knew it was now or never. As the staircase rocked back towards the building, Dax leaned way out to give the two-by-four one more big shove. But instead of the board releasing at the end of its reach it kept pulling. Fescue had grabbed hold of the other end and held on for all he was worth.

The unexpected action caught Dax unaware and yanked him from the rooftop before he could let go of the board. The tower was in the process of swinging back as Dax fell between it and the building. He remembered pushing the board against the tower and then somehow he was falling. How was that possible? His body was slammed between steel and concrete as the pinch point closed.

A crunching sound abruptly slowed the rocking tower, as Dax instantly went from executioner to a smear of blood laced with chunks of meat and bone. Fescue collapsed in a heap on the step. He looked up at the stairs as they swayed back and forth. He was spent.

Matt took aim and missed the gas can across the room for the second time. His fever had spiked and sweat was dripping down his face. Codi had given him this job and he was doing his best. Bullets whizzed by on both sides, making it difficult to aim. He turned and vomited. He was feeling like crap on a stick. Third time's the charm, he thought and fired off another volley. This time he was rewarded as a bullet found it's mark and drilled the gas can. But all that happened was that gas started leaking from the can. This wasn't a Hollywood movie and gas cans don't always blow up from bullets. He needed a spark for ignition.

Codi finally had some luck as a shooter popped his head up a little too high and she caught him just under the chin with a well-placed shot. The man jerked wildly, still holding onto his weapon. Bullets flew in all directions as he dropped to the ground dead but still firing. As the last round left the muzzle it travelled up and to the right, finding a home in one of the overhead sodium vapor lights. The fixture exploded in a shower of sparks that rained down, one of them igniting the gas leaking from the can Matt had shot. He yelled to Codi, "I got it! Take cover!"

She dropped behind the drums as a fireball and explosion rocked the building. It pushed several targets out from behind cover and into a deadly crossfire—Joel and Agent Waters on one side, Codi and Matt on the other. The mercenaries died where they stood, dramatically shifting the odds.

Juliette's survival instinct kicked in. She knew it was time to go and used the distraction to crawl out from under the truck and into the cab. Blood flowed down her arm but she didn't have time to deal with it. She started the truck and slammed it in gear. The tires spun out and pushed the vehicle towards one of the large rollup doors.

Just before the truck slammed into the rollup door, a telling premonition hit hard in her gut. Dax was dead. She knew it as sure as if she had witnessed it herself. The scream that left her mouth as she crashed through the steel door, ripping it off its mountings, would haunt Joel for weeks to come.

Codi yelled across the room, "This place is set to blow! Get out now!"

Matt led the way as each covered the other in an organized retreat. Codi glimpsed a familiar object just before she left the building. The briefcase. The one the woman had been carrying. It was the same one she'd seen back at the fort and it was just twenty feet away from her lying on the floor. "Matt, cover me!" she said and immediately sprinted amid the storm of lead. Matt did what he could to protect her by keeping the other shooters from getting a solid aim at their target.

Special Agent Fescue lifted his head. The fire escape had stopped swinging. He picked himself up and started the decent back to the ground, bloody but alive, for now. He moved as fast as his body would allow, but the disease infecting his body now had full control. It was all he could do to focus on each step, one hand over the other.

Juliette looked back, tears streaming down her face as the truck she was driving hurled away from the warehouse. "No, no, *no!*" she screamed as she reached down with a shaking hand and hit the detonation button on her cellphone.

Codi dove on top of Matt as a ten-story ball of flame blew the roof off the building in an instant. They had gotten just far enough away to feel the heat, but not be taken out by the shrapnel.

Fescue was ten feet from the ground when the blast knocked the fire escape completely off the building. He dove to the right as it fell to the left, narrowly avoiding being crushed. He lay there for a minute trying to catch his breath, not sure whether he had anything left to give. Fortunately, the ground he had landed on was soft. His body pleaded, just stay here for a while.

Joel and Agent Waters faired much worse. The blast caught them just as they were exiting the building and the force of the explosion launched them both through the air. Flames surrounded them, burning their skin and clothes and sucking the oxygen out of their lunges. They landed in a twisted heap some fifty feet away.

Agent Waters lay unmoving. Joel's bad shoulder was shooting with pain as he coughed up smoke. He rolled over to see flames in Agent Waters' hair, but had nothing to put them out with. In desperation, he grabbed some dirt and piled it on the fire, quickly smothering the flames. He lifted her head up to his lap and sat there looking down at her dirt-covered face. He tried to wake her but she was unresponsive.

He started to cry. They had let the helicopter get away, the evidence was blown up, he'd gotten Agent Waters killed and he could see the truck turning down the access road getting away. Worst of all, there was nothing more he could do about any of it.

Codi jumped up off of Matt. "Here, hold onto this." She handed him the briefcase and began to run. She could see the truck turn down the street and start to accelerate away. As soon as Codi cleared the gate, she dropped to a prone position, took aim and willed herself to a calm place. Then she exhaled and pulled the trigger of her AR-15. The rifle barked once and sent a high-velocity round down the barrel and out into the world.

The bullet flew straight and accurate, finding a home in the right front tire. The sudden loss of pressure in the tire caused it to lose all integrity and the rubber disintegrated off the rim. Codi watched as the truck screeched around the corner and disappeared from view. She heard a metal-on-metal crash followed by silence.

She stood up and watched as Matt walked over to her. "This is a mess," he said.

Codi just nodded. "Go check on the others," she told him and jogged off towards the unseen crash to see what was next. An abrupt explosion in the distance amplified her senses and she ran to investigate.

A sudden intake of breath brought Agent Waters back from the dead. She jerked up into a sitting position so fast that Joel let out a little gasp. Her eyes were as big as ping pong balls as she looked around and took stock.

"I thought you were…" Joel said.

"What?"

"Nothing. Are you okay?" he asked.

She blinked her eyes purposefully and said, "I feel like crap."

She had scrapes and dirt all over her and half the hair on her head had been burned. "Something's burning," she said. "What's burning?"

"Nothing, just your hair got a little singed, that's all."

Her left hand reached up to investigate. "Is it bad?"

Joel took a breath and lied. "No, you look great. Especially considering I thought you were dead ten seconds ago."

She smiled and white teeth shone through dirt-brown lips streaked with blood and Joel's tears. He couldn't help himself, he grabbed her and hugged her.

She hugged him back.

"I've been meaning to ask you something," he said.

"Yeah?"

"How do you pronounce your first name? Aseenithe?"

Agent Waters pushed back a little and looked into Joel's eyes. "Asenith, but call me Annie everyone calls me Annie."

Joel smiled and gave her another hug. "Annie Waters, you're really something."

Agent Fescue limped up to the other two agents in mid-hug. "Get a room," he barked at them.

They immediately broke apart, embarrassed.

"Just kidding," Fescue said as he sat next to them. Matt walked over, lugging the briefcase and joined the ragtag group.

"What's in the case?" Joel asked.

"I have no idea, but Codi risked her life to get it." Matt sat down and tried to pry it open. Annie handed him her knife and he pried at the locks.

Codi approached the burning truck with caution. The flames were intense and the driver's compartment was completely engulfed. The smell of burning rubber stung her lungs and eyes. She used the tip of her rifle to flick open the door. Flames shot out in her direction and she had to move back. She could see that the cab was empty. Juliette was gone. Codi stared out into the blackness of the night. Once again they had been left with little or no evidence.

CHAPTER THIRTY-TWO

Codi walked back to the team. She was beginning to wonder if they would ever get a break in this case. She sat down and looked over at Joel, Matt, Agents Fescue and Waters. They were all a mess. Annie had half her hair singed off and seemed to be exhaling smoke every time she breathed. Joel looked more emotionally spent than any of them. Agent Fescue's ears and leg were bleeding and his face was covered in red welts.

The group just stared at each other, grateful to be alive, but for how long, no one knew. Matt finally got the briefcase open and looked inside. "Yahtzee! Is this what I think it is?" Joel and Fescue looked over to see what now. Codi leaned in to get a better look. Sure enough, it was the same briefcase she had seen earlier at the fort. Inside were several syringes and three identical vials all packed in a molded foam cushion.

"It's the vaccine," Codi said.

"How do you know?" said Fescue as he leaned back supporting his weight on his elbows.

"I saw them using this earlier to inoculate themselves." Codi said as Matt picked up one of the vials from the case and examined it. "This is a real spot of luck." He pulled out a syringe and filled it from the vial he was holding. Everyone watched with eager anticipation. He looked around nervously. "Here goes nothing." He injected himself.

Joel waited for Matt to start shaking or morph into a space creature or even to just drop dead, but nothing happened. Fescue slid over and presented Matt with his arm. Matt injected him next, followed by the others. Joel hinged his elbow and rubbed the spot; he hated shots.

Sirens could be heard approaching in the distance. "I think that's for us," Codi said.

"So now what?" Joel asked.

"We need to get this to the authorities," Matt said, holding up the briefcase.

"Yes, but the right authorities," Codi said. "We can't have this to be lost to the Carbinarri or the Italian political system like what happened in France." She reached out and took the briefcase.

Fescue stood uneasily on his good leg. "Time to leave. France is already pissed at us. Let's not add Italy to the list."

"But if Boss finds out we were part of this…" Joel pointed to the destroyed warehouse.

He didn't need to finish the thought. They all headed for the SUV, each a shell of their former selves. "Shotgun," Joel called out.

The SUV pulled past a burning stake bed truck and turned the corner just as a host of Vigili del Fuoco and Carbinarri vehicles flew past, sirens blaring. They watched as the rescue and police vehicles went by, hoping none would turn around for them. Codi didn't care. She punched the SUV and headed back to their hotel.

Annie removed her clothes and stood staring in the mirror. She was still feeling the effects of the impact that had thrown her to the ground and knocked her out. Her normally silky brown hair was matted and much longer on one side. Her olive skin showed a clear demarcation where the dirt and smoke had met her clothing, leaving a paler outline. She looked like a dirt person wearing a tan outfit. The ridiculousness of the reflection made her smile just a bit.

She turned the shower to hot and stepped in. She let the water run on her back for a while and after using the entire bottle of hotel shampoo, she managed to get the dirt out. She stepped out of the shower and toweled off. Taking a breath, she turned to brave the mirror for a second time. When she saw her burned up hair the left side of her mouth pulled up in disgust. She picked up a pair of scissors borrowed from the front desk and began by removing the burnt tips. She thought back to a story her mother used to tell about how, after seeing Mulan for the first time as a child, she had gone into the bathroom and cut her hair like Mulan's.

The next morning, five very hung-over-looking people gathered in the hotel restaurant for breakfast. Nine hours of sleep and the vaccine had made a big difference. The red spots on Fescue's hands were almost gone and his fever was now manageable. But there was no fast way to heal bullet wounds.

Matt and Codi were each down to two Advil every four hours. Annie's hair was styled in an uneven pixie cut that not even a mother could love. Matt could tell she was self-conscious by the way she kept touching it. "You want me to go with you?" he asked her.

Agent Waters looked at him curiously. "What?"

"You know, go with you. To beat up the guy that cut your hair."

"Nice one, Matt," Joel piped in. "Don't be a hater."

"I just unfriended you," Matt said to him.

It had the desired effect and Annie started to smile.

Soon everyone was laughing. Joel had discovered the paper he'd grabbed from the office wadded up in his dirty clothes the night before. He pulled it from his pocket and was in the process of flattening it out on the table so he could read it. The laughter subsided as everyone looked over. Codi tried to focus but her brain was just too spent. Maybe more coffee would help. She rubbed her temples and downed the rest of her cup.

"What's that?" Annie asked as she moved her orange juice to the side to get a better view.

"Something I snatched out of a printer at the warehouse last night. It looks like French."

Codi held her hand out. "Let me take a look." She examined the document.

"You speak French?" Joel asked, continually amazed by her talents.

"Oui." Codi tilted her head as she read to herself. "It's an aeronautical weather forecast for London."

They looked at each other in silence.

"For what day?" Agent Fescue asked.

"Today." The alarm on that unknown clock out there started ringing.

"I think we need to make a few calls and get to the FBI offices in London ASAP," Joel said, handing Codi his cellphone.

"Please tell me that wasn't you in Italy," Boss said, unusually hot under the collar. Codi spent the next ten minutes bringing her up to date. Director Gables couldn't decide if the fact they left the scene of the crime before the Italian authorities arrived was a good thing or not. But evidence of the smallpox contagion was found in the rubble and now Italy was on full alert. All of the rescue teams had been quarantined as a precaution. The fact that her team had acquired a vaccine was the best news so far. But London as a possible target—that was a real predicament.

By pulling a few strings, Director Ruth Anne Gables had her team, as she was now calling them, on the ground in London three hours later. After the incident with the French, Director Calvin Jameson of the FBI had happily loaned out Agents Fescue and Waters to the GSA. To him, they were politically radioactive and best kept at a distance. He could always claim his agents back if things somehow worked out in his favor.

Nial walked into his hotel room like a recently un-caged tiger. Six hours in a helicopter was draining. There had been no word from his warehouse. Dax and his sister had gone dark. He was sure it was a double-cross. And after all he had done for them. He grabbed the remote and flicked on the TV while he tried to get his head around the situation. Surfing from news channel to news channel his pride welled up at seeing how much press was focused on the aggressive smallpox outbreak in France.

Something caught his eye as he passed Al Jezeera. He flicked the channel back to watch. The story was about a warehouse in Italy—his warehouse. It had been destroyed by unknown assailants with no survivors. He slowly dropped to the couch. He absently bit his bottom lip as his mind went into overdrive. First his fort, now his warehouse. Someone was going to pay. Nial picked up his phone and dialed.

Solimon Granger pressed the green button on his phone and answered. "Yes?"

A voice with an Irish lilt cut in. "I am en route and will make the agreed-upon delivery tomorrow as planned." Solimon stood silently, listening.

"Hello? Are you there?"

"I am curious as to why you called me to purvey information I already possess."

"It's called an update."

"Very well. Noon tomorrow." Solimon hung up.

Nial looked at the phone, his face reddening. "Arse hole," he said. For now, he had to deal with the pompous jerk, but in twenty-four hours that would no longer be the case. He still had Skystorm and it could still serve him well. He just needed it for one more job. He grabbed his stuff and headed back to the airport. With Dax and Juliette out of the picture this was going to be a much bigger payoff for him.

CHAPTER THIRTY-THREE

Codi and her group waited as the jet taxied to a hangar in the back part of Heathrow Airport. They were met by a group of some very serious looking agents. The British accents told her they were not FBI. The assault weapons left few options for Codi and her crew. They were escorted to the rear of a black Land Rover Defender 110. They climbed into the back and sat on two bench seats that faced each other. Under a siren escort, they left the airport.

Joel looked out his window at the city he had always wanted to visit. He had a list and London was number one. "Lambeth Bridge. And there's Big Ben."

Codi smiled to herself at her partner's excitement. The cavalcade crossed the unique black and red bridge, took the first roundabout and went west on Millbank. She only hoped they had arrived in time to make a difference. Her mind drifted to her college days when she had missed the train back to school and arrived too late for her final. Her professor, Dr. Bernard, was a total douche and had refused her appeal, saying, you often get only one chance at things in life and some other drivel that she couldn't remember. She'd be damned if the SOB was right this time.

MI5 was a domestic intelligence agency tasked with countering threats to England's national security. It was located in Thames House, a grade II-listed building in Millbank, London. The seven-story stone edifice sat on the north bank of the Thames River adjacent to the

Lambeth Bridge. For all intents and purposes, it was the British version of the FBI.

The black Land Rover pulled to the curb. Codi was the first to step out of the vehicle and attempted to straighten and stretch her body. She could smell the river in the damp air. They were escorted up the stairs and through a huge stone archway that served as the main entrance to MI5. The group entered the left doorway, one of three identical wood entry doors. They passed through security and were taken to the third floor. Codi noticed the looks and whispers coming from employees.

The International Counter-Terrorism unit reports directly to the Joint Terrorism Analysis Centre, or JTAC. It is responsible for intelligence and security as it relates to England's domestic war on terror. It is located on the third floor in the north wing of MI5's offices. There is no sign, just a group of offices with a very specific directive.

Codi sat back in one of the black leather chairs arranged around an oval mahogany conference table. The team had been escorted there and summarily left alone. They sat in silence for a moment, each wondering what would happen next. They had been on a crazy ride for the past week and no one had the energy to go much further. The smallpox symptoms had almost completely subsided, but lack of sleep, bullet holes, explosions and just plain abuse had taken their toll. What they needed was someone to take them seriously so they could pawn this whole mess off and get some much-needed R&R.

Nigel Witherspoon strode confidently through the hallway. He was a rising star in the international counter-terrorism unit and earned his title of intelligence officer with hard work and a smart brain. His boyish good looks fooled many at the agency into not taking him seriously, a mistake they regretted as he was promoted over them. "Sorry for keeping you waiting," he said. Codi looked up at the five-foot-eight sandy-blond man with intense blue eyes parked behind black-rimmed glasses. He said, "Please let me know if there is anything I can do for you."

Everyone started talking at once and for the first time in a long while, Nigel had lost control.

The trip across the channel had taken fifteen minutes. Nial had kept the Eurocopter at a nice steady pace. His eyes lit up as they swooped up over the landmark White Cliffs of Dover and across strikingly green fields. Then it was on into London proper. His plan was to take a full half-hour flying time over the city, travelling to all the most famous sights she had to offer and each time leaving behind a little present.

As they approached Buckingham Palace he flipped on the power to his remote, entered his code and hit the green button. He looked down as they flew past the iconic building. Tourists were filing in and out of the nearby gardens.

"As you may know," Nigel said after regaining control over his charges, "the FBI plays only an advisory role in this country." He was doing his best to pacify the rude Yanks. "If the threat is real, we will need an agency involved that can act." He explained that his superiors, after some debate, had thanked the FBI for their help and dismissed them.

Joel spoke up. "We're not FBI." He pointed to Matt, Codi and himself.

"Yes, well be that as it may, my boss wanted to send you back to the states. However, I convinced him of your value." A long moment of silence followed that made the smile on Nigel's face fade into awkwardness. "So here is what I propose."

Codi interrupted. "I'm not doing anything until I speak with my director."

"Yes, of course, Ruth Anne, I believe her name is, a lovely gal."

After a brief conversation with Boss, Codi put the phone on speaker.

"By the way," she said to Nigel, "you might want to get someone working on this." She slid the briefcase over to him.

He looked up expectantly and said, "The vaccine!"

The meeting continued from there, sharing all the known facts on the case, but Nigel insisted they start at the very beginning.

Matt rolled his eyes at the ridiculousness of the whole thing. He stood up and banged on the table. "You guys are aware that a madman is most likely attacking London today, right?"

Nigel looked at him expectantly.

"We need to do a whole lot less talking and a lot more doing!"

Nigel reasserted himself. "Let me assure you that we have things well in hand."

"What does that mean?" Joel asked.

"That they are well in hand."

Matt sat back down with a frustrated plop.

Nial looked back at the receding Buckingham Palace and all it stood for. With its pomp and circumstance, it had been the perfect place to start his run. He glanced back to the remote control as he released the button. A terminal error message flashed on the screen. He hit the button again and the same message displayed. Nial turned the remote off and then back on again. He waited for it to reboot. It was still not working. *"No!"* He racked his brain for a solution, but none presented itself.

"Take me to my shipyard!" he said to the pilot.

The helicopter banked northeast and left the city. Unknown to Nial, Dr. Comstock's security measure had triggered five hours before. The Skystorm was down and needed the doctor to enter his code before it would work again, but the dead never give up their secrets.

In an effort to get Nigel fully on board they had even mentioned Italy. After a frustrating twenty minutes of backstory they finally got to the part that included London. Nigel suddenly excused himself and ran down the hallway to his boss's office. Ten minutes later emergency response teams were mobilized and put in place.

All law enforcement and military agencies were on high alert. Harrier Jump Jets and Tornado fighter jets blanketed the skies around London. Finally, everyone was looking for Nial and his Eurocopter. The city was effectively locked down and for the first time in a while, Codi relaxed a little.

The Shipwright Repair & Salvage Company was located on the west end of the river Humber in the city of Hull, England, properly known as Kingston-Upon-Hull. Founded in the twelfth century by monks, the city was completely rebuilt after severe damage during World War II and was now one of England's busiest channel side ports. The owner-operator of the shipyard was an old Irish, sea barnacle, by the name of Sean Wright. He spent most of his days doing minor boat repairs and just managed to keep the doors open and the taxman away. The shipyard had a well-aged look that only time near the water could deliver. In the main building was an office and a repair area. It backed up to a dry dock with a short pier that jutted out into the river, a mere eighteen miles to the North Sea.

Sean had a permanent slouch to his posture from too much time bent over a broken engine. He was good with his hands and bad with his hygiene. The local lads were always happy to share a tale or two with him at the pub. What was not known was the side business he ran—importing and exporting illegal goods.

Sean had been duping the local authorities for over twenty years with the help of his owner-partner Nial. They had been in the IRA together and though Sean had put those years behind him, they shared a bond few will ever know.

Sean used his old fishing trawler that he legitimately ran from time to time. He would meet the other party eight miles off the coast to make the exchange of goods. He would then load the contraband into four black plastic drums and seal them. The drums were then placed inside a hidden compartment below deck that ran along the beam of the ship. Once back at his shipyard, the barrels were covertly offloaded onto a custom underwater storage rack beneath the dock. The barrels waited there until the buyer could take delivery.

Their operation had been raided only once and the police with their dogs and electronic devices never found the guns they were certain were on the premises. The dark river under the pier kept the drums hidden and safe. The police never had a clue and with the help of his boss's barrister, Sean had been exonerated and was good with the authorities for now.

Nial jumped out of the copilot seat and watched as workers removed the Skystorm and hauled it inside. Sean jogged over, ducking his head under the rotor wash to greet his boss. Once unloaded, Nial sent the Eurocopter back to its hangar in Brussels for a new paint job and a fresh set of tail numbers.

The old plank floors in the building protested every step as the two walked in. To say the place was run down would be an understatement, but the weathered charm appealed to Sean and the omnipresent history, as he liked to call it, was a comfort. Nial had been rethinking his plan on his way to the old shipyard. There was one name that kept repeating itself in his mind. Once inside the office and away from prying eyes, he picked up his phone and dialed.

On the third ring a voice answered, "Chameleon."

After the briefing with Nigel at MI5, Codi and the group were escorted to a nearby hotel. They were generally happy that they were being taken seriously. After a hot shower and some food, Codi was starting to feel like her old self. The group met at a local pub across the street and claimed a booth in the back corner. The heavy dark wood and checkered tile floor blended with the etched-in ever-present smell of booze and urine. It was going on three PM and there was still no reported attack on London.

"So what do we do now?" Joel asked.

"I think they're just keeping us around in case something new develops," Annie said, adding, "or goes wrong."

Matt lifted his pint. "Here's to scapegoats."

They could all relate and shared a toast and a drop. Matt set his Newcastle down and said, "I can't imagine Nial Brennan is going to get anywhere near this city."

"Check it out," Joel said. "Now everyone is looking for him." The group turned to see what he was talking about. The TV above the bar had Nial Brennan's picture up with some news guy yammering on.

Agent Fescue rubbed the wound on his leg and said, "We can sit around drinking beer waiting for the English to nab this guy, sure. But this is our case. We ran all the leads down, we discovered his plan and we need to finish this." He looked around to judge their faces. "I want this guy and not just because of what he's done so far, but because of what he might still do."

Without hesitation Matt said, "I'm in."

The others slowly nodded their heads. Codi held up her half-empty Fuller's London Pride to concur. She went first. "Pretend I'm Nial. I fly over here in my helicopter and quickly realize the city is too protected. So I take the weapon and do what?"

Joel cleared his throat. "Fly to another city and zap them?"

Matt interrupted. "It's not a zap weapon."

"You know what I mean."

Annie was quick to add, "If I don't hit another city, I, what, go to ground?"

"Especially now." Fescue said, adding, "And I wait or find a different way to accomplish my goal."

"He doesn't strike me as the kind of guy who gives up," said Annie.

"If he strikes another city today, there's not a lot we can do," said Joel.

The brainstorming paused for a moment. Codi knew they were chasing rainbows, but hell, what else were they gonna do? She said, "Let's work under the assumption that he has gone to ground, is overhauling his plan and still wants to hit London."

"Hitting this city would make a hell of a statement," said Agent Fescue.

"And if he does something else, let someone else worry about it," Joel said.

Agent Fescue nodded his head. "Agreed. Let's get to it. Time to dig up everything we can on Nial Brennan." He passed out assignments and each one of the group left to go back to the hotel and get to work. The plan was to meet back at the pub for dinner and an update.

Codi started by updating Boss. Director Gables made it clear they were to do nothing without involving MI5. It was their country and their show now.

Solimon Granger savored the complementary flavors of the lightly smoked white fish and brie. The ringing on his cellphone interrupted the moment. He considered not answering it, but the man on the phone had something he wanted and business was always his first priority. "Yes?"

"There's been a slight delay."

"What is it?"

"We're reworking the power source so you can have an extended firing duration," Nial lied. He'd come up with the lie to get a delivery extension hoping he could somehow get the Skystorm working again in time to sell it and get out.

"How much time do you need?"

"One week."

The request was met with silence. Solimon had learned that control was everything in business. He allowed the man to wait just long enough. "I will give you three days, but after that, we're done. You are too hot right now for me to associate with." Solimon finished the call with a click.

Nial sat down and absently drummed his fingers on the table. He knew Solimon would never agree to a week, but three days was hopefully just enough time. He was so close. What had happened to make Skystorm fail? A million possibilities ran through his mind, none of them very comforting. He felt like a crack addict looking for a fix. His picture was all over the news and every loyal Englishman was looking for him. All he could do now was hide here and wait.

He felt that familiar darkness overcoming him and wrestled to drive it away. He had no time for depression. Nial had bought himself a little time but what he really needed was a way to reset the clock, to strike first. If he could hit London somehow, the authorities would be so busy with the aftermath he could slip away in the chaos. Perhaps that was no longer possible. He began contemplating another city that might have a similar effect.

Nial looked up as Sean escorted an extremely tall gaunt man with stringy long brown hair into the room. He looked as though the sun had never touched his skin. "It's nice to finally meet you," Nial said as he shook hands with the man who called himself Chameleon. They took stock of each other and moved to a plywood table in the middle of the room, illuminated by a single stained-glass skylight. "Can I get you a drink?" Nial asked him.

"Amp," he said.

Nial and Sean looked confused.

"Monster, Red Bull, tea?" the man said.

"That I can do," Sean said and wandered off to brew a pot.

Nial explained his situation. Chameleon required a deposit wired to one of his many accounts before he would start. Nial took a moment and wired the funds. Chameleon double-checked his account and said, "Okay, show me the item."

Nial took him to the supply room and showed him Skystorm's remote control unit. He flicked it on and showed him the error code that started flashing. Chameleon said, "Give me a minute. I'll see what I can do."

Nial left him to do his thing.

Fifteen minutes later Chameleon walked into the room and said, "Done."

Nial looked up in shock. "What?"

"I'm done, as in finished."

Nial couldn't believe his ears. "Show me."

Sean walked out with two cups of tea, but both men ignored him and walked out.

Chameleon flipped the power switch and showed Nial the now working remote. "What was it?" Nial asked.

"Somebody added a rolling sequence code with what I like to call a drop-dead timer. If you don't reset the code every twelve hours, the thing locks up. Pretty basic stuff."

Nial instantly knew the culprit—Dr. Comstock.

"I have reprogramed the remote so it is no longer an issue."

"Astonishing." Nial shook Chameleon's hand vigorously and nearly did a jig. "I always knew you were amazing."

"Until next time," Chameleon said. And just like that, he was gone. It was the fastest hundred thousand he had ever made.

Nial moved to the bathroom and shaved his head but left the beard stubble that was now three days old. He looked at his reflection. The disguise might just work.

Sean walked into the room and sank into the threadbare plaid couch. He watched as Nial paced back and forth nursing his now cold cup of tea. "I've been thinking about your little problem," Sean said.

"Yes?"

"I might just have the perfect solution for you."

Nial stopped and looked over.

"It allows you to get into London and back in time to make the sale."

Nial was all ears. He stopped pacing and came over to sit on the couch.

Sean cleared his throat and said, "Ever heard of a canal boat?"

The pub was packed and the team had to go back to the hotel restaurant to find a table. After a quick meal, Fescue opened the bidding with, "I called a friend in Langley and Nial's helicopter was last reported landing in Brussels."

"He's out of the country?" asked Matt.

"Not necessarily. Satellite imagery showed only the pilot." This brought a moment of contemplation from the group.

Annie raised the anti. "I have two businesses he's tied to here in the UK. The..." she read from her computer, "Shipwright Repair & Salvage Company, a boat repair company in Hull and Flushed Inc., a toilet flushing device manufacturer in Liverpool."

"That's a shitty lead," Matt had to add.

She ignored him and pressed on. "Both have been investigated in the past for smuggling, but no charges were ever filed."

"Hello."

Codi and the team were startled by the intrusion. Nigel Witherspoon stood staring down with a forced smile. "Please continue. I am most interested." He pulled up a chair and sat down.

Codi decided to come clean. She filled him in on their thoughts. He sat for a moment and then said, "First off, I want to say how grateful Her Majesty's Government is for all you have done. There has been no attack on London and I'm sure Nial Brennan has run to ground and at the very least is hiding in or out of the country. However, based on your history, it would be remiss of me not to at least hear you out."

Fescue said, "Ok, Joel you're next."

"I did some deep digging into Nial's past. His mother and sister were killed in a British reprisal in Northern Ireland. He was just seven at the time. He ended up joining the IRA and made quite a name for himself."

Matt added, "I guess he's still pissed about it."

Annie added, "And now he has the means to get his revenge."

Codi snapped her fingers. "That's why he's targeting London. It makes perfect sense."

Nigel puffed up his chest and said, "He cannot get into London by air, sea, or roads. We have everything very tightly controlled right now."

"Plus," said Codi, "the fact that he didn't just pop over to Liverpool or Manchester tells us it's London that matters."

Nigel responded defensively, "As I said, not likely."

But the team took a moment to process the statement Codi made.

Annie said to Nigel, "At the very least, can you have someone check out his two businesses?"

Matt jumped in. "You won't know what to look for without me there."

"He's my charge and he doesn't go anywhere without me," Codi added.

Joel said, "And I'm her partner."

Not wanting to be left behind, Agents Fescue and Waters jinxed, "Me, too."

Nigel put his hands up in surrender. "No one's going anywhere. We have the whole thing well in hand. Why don't you take a couple of days and see the sights? You've earned it. If we need you, I'll come and get you." With that said, Nigel stood. "Again, thank you for your service. I will inform you if we find anything, anything at all." He turned and left.

As soon as he was out of earshot Codi whispered, "Road trip."

Sean briefed Nial on canal boats, explaining that the UK was the first country to implement a canal system. As Britain entered into the industrial age, the canals played a vital role in the transportation of goods throughout the country. After the Second World War, trade on the canal system declined and they were all but forgotten. Recently, a growing leisure industry had popped up and the canals were once again in use. Couples could rent the small but popular houseboats designed to fit the narrow canals and see the countryside as they toured the UK.

Sean had a map of the canal system lying on the table. It looked like a crazy spider web that passed through all the major cities. "That's one of our covers here. We repair canal boats and with a little work, we could disguise one to hold your little toy. You could cruise right down to London and then up and down the Thames with no one the wiser. They are made to go slow, so I'm guessing thirty-six hours to get there, an hour to leave your mark and thirty-six hours back and you'll still have time to make your delivery. Hell, you could probably take the train back since no one is looking for you to leave the city."

Nial pondered the information. The plan had real merit. The last place the authorities would be expecting an attack to come from would be a canal within the country. And the last thing they would consider looking into was a slow-moving vacation houseboat. "Show me the boat," he said.

The average English canal boat, or Narrow Boat, is forty feet long and seven feet wide. The length can vary but the width is fixed if you want to make it through the tight spots. It has a cabin with a flat roof that covers most of the boat. Inside are all the amenities: bedroom, head, galley, living room and even a potbelly stove for heat.

Sean currently had two such boats at his dock. One had a green hull with a red cabin, the other had a dark blue hull with a brown cabin. Sean gave Nial the tour. There was nothing subtle about these boats. They stood out to the point of being almost invisible. Nial nodded at the simple brilliance of the plan. He was convinced. Next step was mounting and hiding the Skystorm on board.

The rented silver Range Rover headed north on the M1. Everyone kept telling them to go on vacation, so they might as well do it. Only Annie and Joel still had their badges and nobody had a weapon. This was certain to be a reconnaissance mission only. Joel guided them to a Debenhams to purchase more clothes, a few burner cellphones, two pairs of binoculars and supplies. Codi and the team had a vague plan in mind. A lot of it hinged on luck.

They dropped the M1 for the M18 in Sheffield and continued east through Doncaster and on into Hull. Joel had done his magic to get them a hotel and had somehow convinced Director Ruth Anne Gables to cover the costs. They were strictly on a fact-finding mission. First to The Shipwright Repair & Salvage Company and then on to Liverpool to the Flushed Inc. manufacturing plant.

The hotel in Hull was musty with the smell of river and mold. Codi opened her room's window to the view of a brick alleyway. The air outside was just as bad. She was drained, maybe a little beat up and generally feeling a bit vulnerable. Her phone rang and she fingered the green button absently. "What are we supposed to do if we find this guy," Matt asked. "Without weapons we have no way of stopping him."

"I'll just run in there and take 'em all out with my bare hands."

"You probably could. I'll bring a couple pencils. I'm sure they're superior to a gun. Besides, what could a bullet do against your determination?"

Codi liked the easy banter; it was just what she needed. "Exactly. Besides, I've been shot before and it didn't slow me down much."

"Seriously?" Matt sounded genuinely surprised.

"Want to see my scar?" Silence filled the phone for a brief second.

"I'm coming over. Bullet scars are definitely sexy."

Codi ran to the bathroom and did a quick fix up. She sprayed some deodorant under her arms and checked with a dip of her nose and a quick sniff to make sure it was working. One last flip of the hair, a breast readjustment and that was as good as it was going to get. The knock on the door put a smile on her face as she swung it open with flare.

Agent Fescue stood in the hallway. "Sorry to bother you. I've been thinking. Can I come in?"

Codi tried to hide her disappointment. "Sure." As he started to walk in, something in his peripheral caught his eye. "Matt, you're here too. Great. Come on in. I'd love to get your take on this as well."

Matt had just put on a clean shirt, ran wet fingers through his hair and practically ran down the hallway to Codi's room.

Codi and Matt shared a what-the-&#@! look. Fescue made himself at home and sat in the one chair in the room. Matt and Codi sat side-by-side at the end of the bed. They couldn't help thinking, here we are together in bed and yet not so much. They shared a quick awkward glance and turned their attention to Fescue.

"I'll make this brief, as we may have a big day ahead of us tomorrow. I've spoken with my FBI counterpart here in London and he has made it abundantly clear that we are not to get involved in any way other than the sharing of information here in England. MI5 is handling the investigation. Period. What we can do is continue our investigation outside of the UK. France has finally put enough of the facts together and they are no longer blaming us. In fact, they might be giving us a medal for what we did there."

Matt was mystified. He said, "Talk about a bi-polar country."

"Exactly."

Fescue continued, looking at Matt as he spoke. "If we get lucky tomorrow and actually find Nial, they're going to need you to identify and deactivate Skystorm."

Codi said, "As long as we stop this guy and put him down or in a cell, I'm good."

Fescue nodded to himself. He wanted to take this guy down too, especially after all that had happened, but orders were orders. He would have to play it their way for now. "Lets all grab a pint," he said. "I'm buying."

Matt and Codi shared a moment of disappointment and followed Agent Fescue out the door.

The Skystorm looked like a storage hatch on the top of The Lady Rose. It had been painted the same color red and decorated with gold *fleur-de-lis* to match the rest of the craft. She was a forty-foot canal boat and her insides had been quickly converted to house the extra power generator for Skystorm. Sean walked over to Nial. "I've got a couple of lads I want to send with you. They're Former British SAS."

Nial looked a bit shocked by the suggestion.

"Don't worry. They're good Irish lads. We *take* from the Brits, not give and what they took was a first-rate education and some of the best commando training in the world."

Nial liked that idea.

"They can run the boat and ward off anyone of a curious nature," said Sean.

Shamus and Grant shook hands with Nial and got to work. They were both physical specimens and seemed genuinely excited at the chance to strike a blow to the British. These were Nial's kind of people. The last touches were put in place, like a removable top panel to further disguise the weapon.

They loaded enough bullets and food to last the trip and then some. Nial looked up at what now seemed to be part of the boat, not a deadly weapon, perched on top. This was going to work, he thought to himself. He went down into the cabin and checked the remote twice to make sure it was still working, satisfied that everything was ready.

Before dawn, the bright red boat with the green hull left the dock and started its southern journey to London. At an average speed of five miles-per-hour in the canals, it would take the full thirty-six hours to get there. Nial and his two crewmen had brainstormed what they thought would be the perfect cover—three obviously gay men on a river vacation.

To help sell it, they'd each brought flamboyant clothing. Any passerby would get a quick snapshot of the situation. They played the role in their mannerisms and dress, effectively making them just another fun loving group of vacationers, completely invisible as a threat.

Neatgangs Lane dead-ends at the shore of the river Humber in Hull. The river is a mile and a quarter across and the constant activity of ships and boats make it one of the busiest waterways in England. The team walked down by the water's edge, careful not to get stuck in the ever-present mud. They set up shop by some abandoned pilings with a few large stones as cover.

Codi focused her binoculars on the other side of the river.

"What is that smell?" Joel asked, making a face in protest.

"It should be the building two over from that big crane," Annie said as she looked at her laptop. Codi panned the binoculars left to the two structures.

Fescue's nose located the source of the smell. "Looks like a dead seal," he said, pointing at a puffed-up, half-eaten seal-like carcass on the bank nearby.

"Argh. That explains it," Joel said.

"Guys, can we focus?" Codi said.

Joel forgot about the smell for a second.

Codi breathed through her mouth as she adjusted the focus on the binoculars. A dilapidated single-story warehouse with a small dry dock and a single pier jutting out into the river came into view. Everything looked either corroded or weathered. What was once bright red was now grey and rust. "Doesn't look like much," she said. "What do they do there?"

"I think I'm going to be sick."

"Joel, forget about the seal."

"Oh, crap," she said.

"What?" A police boat came steaming up the river. It stopped right in front of the warehouse and was met by several police and unmarked vehicles that converged upon the facility in unison.

The team watched in surprise as authorities surrounded and swarmed the place.

"That's how we do things in England."

Joel jumped at the sudden intrusion. Nigel was standing a few feet away with his hands on his hips.

"Damn it, will you stop doing that," Joel said.

"Agent Witherspoon," Fescue said. "I thought I smelled something."

"Funny, Agent Fescue."

"You really don't trust us, do you?" Codi said.

"You are my responsibility and I take my job very seriously." He looked at the group and saw that none of them were buying in. "You might as well come with me."

The team followed Nigel back to their car where a red Vauxhall Corsa was idling.

The Shipwright Repair & Salvage Company was teeming with activity. They had one man in custody, handcuffed and sitting in the back a of a police vehicle, while a horde of officers sifted through the building. Codi and Matt were instructed by Nigel to find some piece of equipment that could link the place to Skystorm. The others were not allowed to enter the alleged crime scene.

"There's nothing here that couldn't be part of a dozen other uses," Matt said as he put down the spanner on the workbench he was looking over.

"Like repairing boats?" Nigel asked.

"Exactly," Matt said.

It was a dead end. "This place is definitely not it," Matt said.

"Or, he was tipped," Codi said as she pointed to the man in the back of the police car. The police cruiser holding Sean Wright backed out. They were taking him in for questioning, but it didn't look promising. As they left, Sean glanced down at the pier making sure the incriminating evidence was still hidden in the drums under the water. Once again Nial's contact had paid off.

Nigel escorted Codi and Matt back across the police line to the others. "So this is how you choose to spend your vacation?" he asked.

Codi shrugged.

"My Director has informed me that you are no longer needed on this case here in England. So unless you are going to actually vacation, I would ask that you leave the country forthwith."

Codi stared Nigel down. "You know there is very likely a maniac here trying to unleash holy terror on your country."

"Agent Sanders, I appreciate your concern." He gestured around. "But as I have stated, as far as England goes, this is no longer your concern. Perhaps you can aid in the investigation back in France." He paused before proceeding. "Please don't take this wrong, but bugger off to somewhere else. I'm tired of babysitting."

Codi got it. If the shoe was on the other foot she would hate being in charge of a bunch of uncooperative Brits back in DC. Their time could be better spent elsewhere. The group shuffled back to their Range Rover and left for the hotel. The trip back was marked with silence and a heavy dose of introspective what's next.

CHAPTER THIRTY-FOUR

That night, the team shared a solemn meal at a local Italian restaurant. The food and beer was good enough to elicit a few laughs, mostly aimed in Nigel's direction. Codi had checked in with Boss and they were being ordered back to the states. This case was over for them. They had come so close. Not that they hadn't made a difference; they just felt hollow for not finishing. Dessert was passed up for one last round and finally everyone went his or her own way. Matt and Fescue found a local pub, The Bonny Boat, while the rest of the group headed back to the hotel in hopes of a good night's sleep. It had been a long ride. Maybe it was time to give it a rest.

The sound of pounding on her hotel room door woke Codi in an instant. She slipped out of bed ready to fight. As her brain processed the information, she realized it was two drunken guys banging on her door. She tried to decide between calling the manager or taking the matter into her own hands and releasing some frustration in the process. "Go away," she said.

"Codi." The name came muffed and slurred through the door. She paused at the sound of her name and the slightly familiar voice. She opened her door a crack, leaving the chain in place. Through the gap she saw Matt and Fescue. They gazed back, swaying on unsteady legs.

"How much did you have to drink?" she asked them.

"Four," Matt said, holding up five fingers.

"Go sleep it off."

"*No!*"

"Shhhhh."

"We gotta talk to you."

"Shhhh!"

"We have a pheory." Fescue looked confused as he tried to process and correct his word. "Theory."

Codi reluctantly let the two into her room, mostly to keep them from waking everyone else in the hotel. She had dealt with drunks before. "Sit," she commanded. Matt and Fescue sat on the end of her bed while she remained standing. "Okay, what?"

Fescue went first. "I was thinking–"

Matt interrupted. *"We* was thinking."

"We was thinking."

Codi was losing patience but played along. "What were you two thinking?"

"You know how the cops only let you and Matt look at the equipment and they wouldn't let any of us go through the evidence?"

"Yes."

Matt and Fescue shared a look. "What if the cops are in on it?"

Codi held her hands up to calm Agent Fescue. "Guys, seriously?"

"Codi, we need to go back there and see everything for ourselves."

"Slow down, Speed Racer," she said and then stopped and thought for a second. She had considered the exact same thing. What if? It was a big risk. They had been ordered back. But what if? She let the thought hang in her brain for a second. "You know, most drunks come up with really good ideas until they sober up and realize how stupid they really are."

Matt and Fescue shared a guilty look. "But in your case... I don't know. It just might be worth a look." Fescue smacked Matt on the arm in an I-told-you-so way. Both of them sat there with a stupid grin. "Go get dressed," Codi said. "I'll wake the others. We'll meet in the parking lot in fifteen and get some coffee into you."

By the time they approached the shipwright building Matt and

Fescue had sobered up just enough to at least keep quiet. Codi picked the lock and they all slipped inside.

Agent Fescue, playing the role of Captain Obvious, said, "Remember, we are looking for anything that might get us closer to Nial or Skystorm."

Codi shook her head and tried not to laugh. She said, "A quick look around and then we're out of here. No one can know we did this."

The team picked through everything and after thirty minutes it was looking bleak. "Guys, what does this look like to you?" Codi said.

Matt had curled up on an old couch. He forced an eye open and walked over to where she was standing.

One section of the wall was extra thick. Matt looked at it for several seconds. He tilted his head left and then right. He tapped it and it rang hollow. He then reached out and pressed on a section of worn molding and the wall clicked and opened up a crack. He walked back to his couch and went back to sleep. Everyone just stared in wonder at what had just transpired.

Inside the wall was a hidden storage compartment. There were three guns: two Glock nineteen's, an L1A1 rifle and ammunition. Codi didn't hesitate to arm herself. Joel was the first to speak up. "You are aware of the ramifications of carrying a firearm in the UK, right?"

"I am really tired of being shot at."

Agent Fescue grabbed the other pistol and Annie grabbed the assault rifle. Joel was left holding air.

Ten minutes later, Annie called from across the room. "I think I got something." She'd been going through a stack of invoices. "There are two open work orders for canal boats, but there's only one canal boat on the pier."

"There's a missing boat?"

"Yes and the work order has the original pick-up date crossed out with next Tuesday's date handwritten in."

"What's a canal boat?" Codi asked.

Matt called out from his couch, "It's a skinny houseboat used by hundreds of vacationers every year to cruise the extensive canal system in the UK." He sat up and stretched, no longer able to sleep.

"Joel," said Codi, "Grab your computer. Let's take a look at this canal system."

Joel ran out to the car and grabbed his laptop. When he came back, the group gathered around him as he set it on a plywood table and powered up. He linked it to his cellphone's hot spot and went to work.

"England's canal system is very extensive," he said. The map looked like a child had drawn it, with squiggly lines all over the country and all intersecting. "It was the original way goods were shipped across the country. Now it's just a forgotten path used by sightseers."

Matt yawned as he came over to look at the screen.

Codi ran her finger along a canal path that went from Hull almost straight to London. She snapped her fingers. "That's it."

"What's the hull identification number?" Fescue asked.

Annie checked the work order. "I don't see a number, but the name on the stern is The Lady Rose."

"It makes sense," Codi said. "With the authorities watching all the roads, ocean ports and airports, nobody is watching a seldom-used canal with a slow moving houseboat. He'll be able to slip right in and out and no one will be the wiser." She was pacing and getting more agitated with every word. Everything suddenly became very clear. Nial was backdooring his weapon into London through the canal system.

"Now what?" Joel asked. "We're armed, pissed off and know where to look. Who else do we tell about this?"

Joel's words hung in the air for a minute. No one was willing to answer.

The English countryside is normally an impossible collection of every shade of green, but at night green becomes a very black color. Nial stood on the bow of The Lady Rose as the wind rushed around his face. It was going to be an unusually nice sunrise in a rare cloudless sky still filled with stars. Shamus and Grant had pushed the boat just over the allowed limit all through the night and with dawn approaching, had backed off to exactly the speed limit.

They were halfway to their objective and all was well. Nial climbed back into the cabin and closed the hatch. Once the sun came up, he could no longer afford to show his face.

Nigel Witherspoon looked like he had just eaten an extra-strength sourball. "What's all this?" he whined as he entered the office. Codi and her team had taken the liberty to set up shop in the shipyard, no longer feeling the need for secrecy. They took turns updating Nigel. He looked at them incredulously. The one thing they left out were the weapons they had found. No sense in getting Nigel all wound up. "Who else is in on this?" Nigel asked.

"Just us," Codi said. "We thought we would get your advice before contacting our agency."

"That is appreciated."

Nigel scratched his ear as he processed the information. "I say we bring the house down on Nial and his plans, but I have a boss and things work a certain way here in jolly old England. I'll make a call, get us more agents and we'll all make the arrest together. Once I have a plan in place, together we'll call your people and give them the details." He smiled at the group and they smiled back. Finally, he was letting them in on the case. This was what they'd wanted all along. Nigel stepped out of the office as he dialed.

Joel pulled up the canal system and overlaid it on a highway map. There were several points of contact but mostly the canal system moved through the rural countryside. "We need more throughput. Two laptops using one phone's hot spot is too damn slow."

Annie stopped typing and stood up. "My phone's in the car. Be right back." She left the office. The air was cool and thick with moisture. She could just make out a crescent moon reflection rippling on the river. It would be morning soon. She popped the lock and grabbed her cell from her purse. As she walked back from the car she heard a soft voice. Nigel was talking in a whisper off to the side of the building. She paused. It seemed odd. She moved in to investigate.

"I'm sure you can," she heard Nigel say. "But there is no way I'm making that play for the same fee." Nigel paused for a second before saying, "Okay, deal. Wire the funds and consider your American problem over." There was another pause. "Don't worry, I'll stay out of London for a few days."

The light suddenly went on for Annie. That's why they'd been thwarted at every step in the UK. She started to back up. The team needed this information and they needed it now.

Her foot caught on a discarded lanyard and she tripped. The sound alerted Nigel to her presence. He was on her in a flash. His Sig P226 was drawn and menacing. Annie looked up at the man she had once trusted. "You pull that trigger and everyone will be out here in a flash."

"Yes, but you'll be dead and I have the gun."

"You think that will stop them, one little pistol? Besides, they're armed."

"I don't believe you. I have been watching your every move."

Annie stared up at him with hatred in her eyes.

Nigel cocked his head slightly, inspecting his catch. "I want you to dial Joel and tell him you need help opening the car."

"Not a chance."

"Do it or I'll kill you where you lie." Nigel reinforced his point by jabbing the gun in her direction.

Annie slowly dialed. "Hey. Can you help me with the car? No, just you. Thanks. Love you."

Nigel watched very carefully. The moment she hung up, he slammed his pistol into the side of her head and she collapsed.

Joel couldn't believe what he had just heard. His head was spinning.

"Love you." No sweeter words were ever spoken. He hurried outside to help, but as he stepped outside, there was no sign of Annie anywhere.

"Agent Strickman, come here, I need help. Agent Waters is hurt."

Joel turned to the voice to find Nigel standing over a prone body. A shot of adrenaline coursed through his body as he ran to her side. *Nooo!* "What happened?"

"I don't know. I was on the phone and I saw her fall." Joel knelt down and coddled Annie's head in his arms. He marveled at how beautiful she was even with her crazy pixie cut. He tried to triage her injuries, but a sudden impact on the back of his skull turned his world upside down and everything went black.

Officer Nigel Witherspoon looked down at the two bodies that lay before him. This was too easy. He took out his spring-assist Microtech 142-4 combat knife and flicked it open. He contemplated the best way to silently dispatch them without getting blood all over his shoes. He'd follow with a quick drop in the river and then on to the unsuspecting fools inside the building.

A shooting impact to his shins sent him toppling over. Annie had kicked him as hard as she could. She tried to stand but her vision spun. She tried to call out but only a soft squeak escaped her lips. The blow to the back of her head was serious. She had opened her eyes to see Nigel moving a knife to unconscious Joel's throat and had used her rage to pull her from the depths of blackness and into action.

Nigel hit the ground hard and his gun skittered away. He re-gripped his knife and slashed out at Annie. She barely pulled back in time to avoid the blade. Agent Witherspoon moved to his feet. Annie was pushing hard to regain full consciousness. Her reactions were slow and her equilibrium was still off, but she managed to get to one knee before Nigel quickly closed and slashed out with the knife again. She raised her forearm and blocked the blade, but not before it sliced through meat and tendon before coming to rest in bone. The maneuver had saved her, but the force and incredible pain knocked her back down.

She tried to use her feet to keep Nigel back but he lunged and pinned them down. Annie punched, scratched and clawed at her attacker. Nigel fended her off and brought the business end of the blade to bear. Annie had to use both her hands and all her strength to keep the steel from penetrating her torso. Nigel leaned in with all his weight, pushing the knife down. Annie countered with all she had, but gravity was winning. The blade inched closer and Nigel could smell victory.

Time was running out for Annie. She tried to buck him off but was unsuccessful. Finally she had the strength to scream and took a breath to let it loose. "Hel–"

It was stopped short with a hand to her mouth. She tried to bite the hand but a sudden sharp pain in her chest took her breath away.

Joel's head lolled to the side as his brain tried to reboot. He opened his eyes and instinctively reached for the back of his head. He tried to make sense of what he was seeing. Annie was lying on the ground with Nigel on top of her. He was holding something—a knife!

Instantly, Joel sat up. The world spun and he closed his eyes and forced it away. He opened them back up and looked around. The closest thing within reach was a rigging block with a metal hook and chain. He grabbed it and with all the strength he could muster, screamed and swung for Nigel's head.

Nigel's head was no match for the twenty-pound chunk of wood and steel. It snapped his head sideways and Nigel fell off Annie and rolled across the decking and into the black water of the Humber. He lay face down, unmoving, as he slowly drifted away and started to sink.

Joel scuttled over to Annie. She was breathing shallowly, a knife completely embedded in her chest. Joel took her hand. "It's going to be alright," he lied. "Annie, don't die, I..."

Annie's eyes fluttered closed. The last thing she remembered was the two words she had spoken to Joel over the phone—love you. She smiled and then she was gone.

Joel tried to tell her how he felt. "I love you, Annie Waters," he said but it was too late. He took her in his arms and hugged her. He had

missed his chance. He had failed to save her. He was to blame. If only...
It hit him with such power. He started to weep.

The shout came from outside the office and in an instant Agent
Fescue, Matt and Codi grabbed their hidden firearms and flew out the
door. They found Joel crying, holding Annie in his arms. There was no
sign of Nigel.

Matt ran over to his side while Codi and Fescue checked the area
for possible threats.

"Oh my God!" Matt said. He kneeled down and reached out to
check Annie.

"Don't touch her! She's just sleeping," Joel protested between sobs.
Matt glanced over at Codi and shook his head; he could tell she was
gone.

"We got a body in the water!" Fescue called out at seeing Nigel's
corpse floating away.

"Let him rot," Joel blubbered. "He was a traitor. He killed Annie
and he tried to kill me, all of us."

The unexpected information hit Codi like an uppercut, leaving her
with more questions than answers. How had she not seen this coming
and was there any way she could have prevented it?

Chapter Thirty-Five

The call from his man inside MI5 had been expected, but the fact that it was about the same American agents who had disrupted his plans twice before was almost too much to take. Nial had cut a deal with Nigel and didn't hesitate to wire the extra funds. Having the meddlesome agents out of the way was worth it. He would finally be rid of them.

The slow-moving houseboat was perfect cover for his operation. But should they be discovered they'd be like a fly in a honey jar. With top speeds slower than a bicycle, there would be no escape. It was an all risk/all reward scenario.

Nial munched on a protein bar and glanced out the window—daylight and more green pastures with a stone farmhouse off in the distance. They were just four hours away from London. He would be enjoying the trip more except for the fact that he hadn't heard back from Nigel or Sean. Had something gone wrong? It was time to build a better back-up plan. He had one last trusted associate in the country. He picked up his phone and dialed.

"Flushed Inc. Toilet Devices, this is Carson."

The team was shell-shocked. They finally got Joel to let go and carried Annie's body into the office where they laid it down on the couch. Joel came over and carefully covered her with a blanket. He said a few words over her and turned away. Each member grieved in his or her own way and each now had an additional reason for wanting and needing Nial strung up, drawn and quartered.

Agent Fescue pulled the focus back to the matter at hand. "Joel, you gonna be okay?" he asked.

Joel wiped the snot running from his nose and looked up with vacant eyes. Codi sat next to him and said, "Joel, I'm so sorry, but we can grieve after we get this guy. I need you now. We need you."

Joel nodded slowly, clenched his fists and said, "Let's finish this thing."

Codi couldn't have been more proud of her partner. She placed a hand on his shoulder and said, "Yeah, let's."

Codi started pacing back and forth. "As I see it," she said, "We're on our own." Everyone looked at her. "MI5 can't be trusted, our own government has ordered us back home and nobody is doing anything to stop what is about to happen. Joel, send an email and update Director Gables on everything."

"Email?"

"I don't want to call her. We might not like what she has to say."

The group nodded in understanding.

"It's up to us," Codi said. "Failure is not an option. There are hundreds of lives at stake, so if you get a chance to put Nial Brennan in the ground, you do it."

Joel and Fescue crawled up along the concrete dock where it met the entry gate. An eighteen-foot rigid-hull inflatable floated nearby. It was white with brown interior. It had two outboards and a cockpit covered by a small rigid roof that was supported by black steel tubing. Joel tested the lock on the gate, only to discover that it had failed to function some years ago.

They slipped onto the dock and padded over to the craft. Joel inspected the fuel tanks. "We're full here," he said and replaced the gas cap, while Fescue twisted the ignition wires together and touched the starter wire to the hot lead. The two Evinrude E-Tec 250 4-stroke outboards fired up. Joel released the bow and stern lines from their cleats and within a minute they were steering across the river at flank speed, heading for the canal system that led to London.

Codi stomped the pedal on the Range Rover, turned onto the M1 and headed southbound. They had left a man behind and it made her stomach churn, but time was critical. If any of them survived the next twenty-four hours, they would come back for Annie. Codi and Matt were aiming for Luton where Joel had calculated they would be able to intercept Nial and The Lady Rose along the Grand Union Canal. They had about 150 miles to go and the clock was ticking.

Codi reconsidered calling Boss to bring her up to speed. She was now the only one they knew who could be trusted and frankly, she could use the help. But based on their luck so far, she decided to keep things to themselves for now. This forced her to drive only slightly over the speed limit, as they could not afford the attention or a delay any authorities might cause. Codi had never been so determined to finish something. There was no ringing the bell to say I give. This guy had been one step ahead at every turn and it was time to change that. Time to dig deep and find a way, any way, to stop him.

Agent Fescue had no such concerns about the authorities. He hit the canal entrance at thirty knots, sending a wave of water over the sides of the normally four-knot-limit canal route. His catch-me-if-you-can attitude left little interpretation as to his desire. He knew the cost of failure and if they couldn't stop Nial, their careers would be over anyway. Caution was a luxury none of them could afford.

The Range Rover leaned as Codi turned on Beech Hill and drove east to Lilly Bottom Road. The two-lane blacktop meandered with the countryside. Codi and Matt continued south as the road slowly narrowed into a one-lane affair. They crossed the canal just before Whitewell. The arched stone bridge was straight out of the medieval period and was just wide enough to accommodate one car at a time. Codi turned off the road and parked the vehicle in the cover of a large bush. Once she turned off the engine, they were hit broadside with a silence that only the countryside can provide. Peaceful and calm, broken only occasionally by an insect or bird. Codi grabbed her cell and dialed.

Joel answered on the second ring. Static from the wind blowing across his microphone made it hard to hear. There had been no sign of The Lady Rose yet. "Only some very pissed off house boaters who we nearly capsized as we blew past them," he said. According to Joel's information, they were about an hour behind and closing fast. Codi decided to wait.

Over the next twenty minutes, four houseboats passed. Each was painted in bright colors and looked to be a throwback to a bygone era. None of them however, were Nial's. Codi was getting impatient and worried that he may already be ahead of them.

"I see a red one coming," Matt said as he handed the binoculars over to Codi.

She took a look. Two very chummy grown men were chatting from the rear rudder position. One had his shirt off and the other was wearing a pink wife–beater. His hand was on the shoulder of the driver and they were laughing about something. She lowered the glasses. "Just another couple on vacation."

"Patience, we'll get 'em." Matt rolled on his back and looked up at the sky. It was a blue canvas with puffy cotton clouds rolling in. They were nestled on a grassy knoll surrounded by wolfsbane, its distinctive indigo flowers reaching for the sun. They had a good view of the canal but were still well hidden from all but the keenest eyes. "Come over here."

"Oh yeah?" Codi played hard to get for a moment, but eventually moved next to Matt. He gently caressed her cheek and pulled her towards him. Lips touched lips in a gentle dance that grew in fervor.

Codi pressed up against him and then paused to look in his eyes. He was the real deal. They'd both been waiting for this and finally it was here. Codi pulled him towards her in an embrace that led to a second passionate kiss. She pulled back slightly. But the timing was rotten. His body felt good against hers—too good. She tried to focus on the mission. Matt pushed a lock of hair from her face and ran his hand tentatively down her back ending on her firm ass. Codi rolled up on top of Matt in a move that surprised and excited him at the same time.

"Tell me what you're thinking?" Matt asked.

Codi paused. "I'm thinking..." She glanced away to find the words. "The Lady Rose!"

"What?"

"The Lady Rose! She's getting away." Codi pushed off Matt, jumped to her feet and ran for the car.

Matt sat up, confused. "Come back over here, we still have time." He looked again at the houseboat with the two guys cruising away down the canal. On the stern was clearly painted the words The Lady Rose. A couple expletives flew as he jumped up and ran after her.

Matt pulled up a map and tried to find the next place the road crossed the canal. Codi had left the last bridge in a cloud of dust. The rover protested the reckless speed over the underused dirt road. She called Joel. "We got 'em," she said. "They're two clicks south of the..." She looked over to Matt for the name.

He squinted at the map, but the bouncing vehicle made it almost impossible to read. "Mimram Bridge." The roads rarely intercepted the canal and they had to take the long way around to get in front of the houseboat. "Take a right up ahead," he said to Codi.

The cell signal was weak and she had to repeat their location to Joel several times. She then waited for a reply.

Joel double-checked the map. "We're about thirty-five minutes behind."

"Good. We're going to try to intercept at..." she looked at Matt.

"The lock at Water Hall Farm," he said. "They'll have to stop and we'll be waiting."

"Be careful," said Joel.

"Always am," Codi lied in response as she disconnected the call. The last of the blue sky left as English rain moved in.

The Canal System in the UK utilizes a variety of locks to maintain proper water levels throughout the country and allow for changes in elevation. Some are automatic but most are hand-operated. A crew-member must go out and open the gate to allow the boat to enter. The gate is closed behind the boat and a lock paddle is used to raise or lower the level of the water inside the lock. Once the water has equalized with the canal water on the other side of the lock, the second gate can be opened and the boat continues on its way.

Nial peeked out of the window of The Lady Rose. Bullet-sized rain-drops pelted the glass. He could just make out the lock they were approaching up ahead. He could tell they were getting close to London, as he saw the occasional person jogging along the sides of the canal. In typical British fashion the ever-present rain did little to dissuade outdoor activities. By his calculations, they were about ninety minutes away from using Skystorm. Soon London would suffer her most tragic affront since the war.

Codi and Matt had found cover behind a small retaining wall made of stacked stones that paralleled the canal. They were soaked to the bone. They spotted The Lady Rose as she entered the lock, the sound of its diesel engine puttering along. She reminded herself that this could still be a wild goose chase. Just because the houseboat was not at the repair shop didn't mean that the occupants were terrorists. The guy she'd seen steering the boat before closed the first gate behind the houseboat. They watched as he moved forward to the lock paddle to open the flow of water and lower the boat down to the next canal's level. She quickly picked up on his determined gait. This man moved with purpose; there was no mistaking it.

While the man was focused on turning the paddle, Codi sprinted from behind the wall. She had her 9mm Glock out and aimed at his spine. The raindrops and the rain slicker he wore made her approach all but silent. "Special agent!" she announced. "Get down on the ground now!" The man looked genuinely startled, like this had never happened to him before, but Codi caught the look in his eye. She knew it well from her days with Special Forces. This was no tourist; this man was a trained killer.

He pretended to drop to a knee feigning innocence as he covertly reached for his gun hidden inside his yellow rain slicker. Codi didn't hesitate. She put two rounds in his head and dropped him where he stood, his weapon falling to the ground. The sound of the shots carried to the stern of the boat. Shamus reacted immediately. He sent full auto rounds back in Codi's direction.

Gunfire from the rear cockpit of the boat galvanized Matt into action. He returned fire from his hide, trying to keep the single shooter from hitting Codi. She had dropped behind the lock paddle and used the twelve-inch wide steel base as cover. Bullets ricocheted off the metal and nipped at her skin. She returned fire blindly as an approaching jogger turned and ran for his life.

Matt kept his aim focused on the guy with the assault weapon trying to kill Codi, forcing him to split targets. He hoped that would allow Codi to find better cover. He tried to remember what Codi had told him about conserving ammunition, but was amazed by how fast two clips full of bullets disappeared in a gun battle.

From the other side of the bow, a rifle appeared at the forward hatch. It was twenty feet away and had an angle on Codi the other shooter did not. He couldn't miss. "Agent Sanders," the man called out. "Drop your weapon or I will drop you."

Codi turned to see the barrel of an assault rifle aimed her way. She lowered her Glock.

"Kick it in the water. Now!" Codi complied with the demand. "Okay, very slowly, come aboard." With her hands open and at her sides Codi climbed onto the bow of the houseboat.

Matt hid behind the stone wall. He had fired his last round and was trying to see what was going on without getting his head blown off. The man on the stern of the boat had his rifle pointed his way, but wasn't firing. A second man who looked like Nial but without hair, was pointing a gun at Codi. He yelled out, "Doctor Campbell! I'll be taking Agent Sanders here for a little ride. If anyone, Bobbies or otherwise, gets within fifty feet of this boat, I'll kill her. Answer if you heard me."

"I heard you."

The man at the stern jumped off the boat. He kept his gun pointed in Matt's direction while he opened the second gate to release the now raised boat. He then pulled out a heavy-duty paddle lock and locked the gate in place. No other boat would be able to follow without the key.

Matt watched helplessly as The Lady Rose powered away into the rain. He dropped a few expletives and ran to the Range Rover. Locked. Codi had the keys and the phone. He was stranded, soaked and pissed.

CHAPTER THIRTY-SIX

Inside the houseboat, Nial had Codi lie face down on the floor with her hands behind her back. He was taking no chances. "Time to play a little game of truth or dare," he said. "You tell me the truth and I'll dare not to shoot you."

"That's not how the game is played, asshole," Codi said.

Nial fired off a shot that just missed her head.

"Let's try again. Who else knows what's going on here?"

"After we killed your mole in MI5 we alerted Scotland Yard and our FBI offices. They're setting up a trap for you down river as we speak." Nial fired a shot into Codi's thigh. She went rigid, trying to suck up the pain. "I was right," she said. "You really are an asshole."

"I warned you about lying to me. There's no way you and the doctor would have tried to stop us here if there is a large force waiting to do so down the canal. Don't play me for a fool, Agent Sanders, it will be a very costly mistake on your part."

With that, Shamus, who had entered during the questioning kicked Codi in the side of the head. Darkness narrowed her vision, threatening to overtake her. She heard a muffled, "That's for Grant." After another sudden impact to her head, Codi was gone.

Shamus stood over Codi ready to beat her to death. He was visibly angry and had lost control.

"Shamus!" said Nial. "We don't need her healthy, but I do need her alive, for now. When that time has passed, you can do with her as you will."

Shamus kicked her one more time and spit on the now unmoving body. He headed back to the rain-swept cockpit.

Matt turned and ran to the Range Rover. The hi-tech vehicle was locked and this was no movie, without a key there would be no moving the car short of a tow truck, or what ever they called that in England. He let of a string of obscenities—it seemed to help.

The houseboat was gone from sight. Matt had stopped pacing and was sitting by the side of the canal next to the dead terrorist. He had the man's gun and a spare magazine but there was nothing to shoot at.. He had failed. The sound of an approaching honeybee gave way to a buzz that grew in volume. Matt stood up and squinted through the heavy rain. A spec grew in size until he could see Fescue and Joel flying through the canal at a reckless speed. Matt ran to them waving his hands.

Once the boat stopped, Matt brought them up to speed on what had happened. Fescue tried a few bullets on the paddle lock and determined there was no way they could get it to open. But he had not come all this way to be thwarted. He took off running in the direction of London. "Come On!"

Joel dialed Boss while running after Fescue. It was time to ask for help from someone they trusted.

In between breaths, he tried to fill Director Gables in on the details and most importantly, tell her what they needed now in order to stop the threat. Unfortunately, the news on her end was not so good. Agent Witherspoon's body had been found and there was evidence linking them to his murder.

"Of course there's evidence. I killed him," Joel said. Matt and Fescue glanced back at Joel with real concern on their faces.

There was silence on the other end of the phone for a second, the only sound was Joel's ragged breaths as he ran. He re-gathered himself and told Director Gables about Agent Waters.

She said, "You have the MI5 and Scotland Yard both looking for you and they are not happy."

Joel nearly tripped on the uneven ground and dropped the phone, but he recovered and tried to keep pace with the others.

"Screw them," he said to Director Gables. "Matt identified the man on the houseboat as Nial Brennan. You can either help us or stay out of our way."

"Joel," she said, "that's not how this works. We have no authority to—"

Joel hung up the phone. A fire inside him started to rage. He had reached his limit. He flung the phone down on the ground with all his might and yelled in frustration.

Matt and Fescue both stopped and looked back. Fescue said, "Did you just hang up on Director Gables?"

Joel stood there in the rain clasping and unclasping his hands.

Fescue smiled. "Good for you. Now come on."

Director Gables looked at her phone in disbelief. She tried calling back but there was nothing. She drummed her fingers on her desk for a moment. Right now MI5 and FBI relations were at an all time low and to top things off, Director Jameson of the FBI would not return her calls. It seemed they were afraid to go down with the ship.

Ruth Anne sighed, grabbed her purse and left the office.

"Here!" Agent Fescue said as he turned right and disappeared from the path. A minute gap in the greenery led to a small farm. The two-story cottage was straight out of a Thomas Kinkade painting, but the beauty of the idyllic setting was missed by all three men as they ran past a blooming rose garden.

Matt pounded on the cottage door while trying to catch his breath. Fescue ran to the barn to see what he could find. After a minute of banging Matt turned back. "Nobody's home," he said.

Joel walked past him and fired three rounds into the door lock and kicked the door open. Matt jumped and said, "Jeez! You could warn a guy before you go postal."

They quickly checked the house but nothing useful presented itself.

Fescue pulled the tarp off an old Land Rover Defender 90 sitting in front of the barn. It was faded blue with a tan canvas top. The four-cylinder diesel engine turned over after a few attempts and Fescue managed to find first gear. He pulled up next to the front of the house and honked.

It was all they could do to keep the vehicle on the road. The old shocks had no life left in them and the vehicle hadn't gone faster than 80 kph in over ten years. The dirt road, now a mud road, finally turned into blacktop and soon they found a two-lane motorway heading south to London. At 86 kph the old diesel was maxed out, but it would have to do. The gears whined with every mile.

The rain was letting up which was a blessing as the windshield wipers were useless. Fescue leaned out and used an old rag Joel had found in the back to wipe the windscreen every few minutes.

The first thing Nial saw was the London Eye peeking up in the distance. The giant Ferris wheel on the south bank of the River Thames was a popular tourist attraction. The houseboat left the Grand Union Canal and steered left onto the main river. Shamus shoved the throttle to its stops and the boat slowly picked up speed. It hit the limit at just over ten knots as it made its way up the Thames to London proper.

Nial pulled the remote down from the cubby in the galley, placed it on the table and sat down. He heard a soft moan from the female on the floor. He glanced down and watched as Codi regained consciousness. She tried to get up but her hands were tied behind her back. When she rolled over, he said, "Still with us, I see." He looked disappointed.

Codi felt weak. She glanced down at her leg and saw that the flow of blood from the bullet she'd taken had slowed but had not stopped. Her life was literally draining away.

Nial looked at the growing pool of blood on the floor. He estimated that, if not treated, she would last maybe another half-hour. But it was no concern of his. She was nothing but leverage and that need was just about over.

He grabbed a walky-talky and told Seamus to start the generator. A few moments later the rumble of Skystorm's power source came to life.

Codi could just make out what Nial was up to. She needed to stop him and was looking for the chance. Nial glanced out the window and realized they were nearly in position. Codi used his distraction to try to make a move. She sat up but her head spun so hard she almost vomited. Nial sensed the motion, grabbed his pistol and aimed with true intent to kill her. "Try it," he said.

She stopped trying to get up and lowered herself back down to the floor, the wash of nausea slowly dissipating. Nial walked over to her brandishing his gun. "That was foolish, you are no match for the speed of a bullet. I personally would prefer to keep you around for a little while, just in case I have to remind someone to keep their distance. But I'd be just as happy to kill you right now if you wish."

He walked back to the table and powered up his remote. He estimated they had about twenty minutes worth of D3 in their possession. That meant ten minutes up one shore and ten back the other shore. He was hoping to start in the sweet spot of downtown London. He would fire the weapon starting with Westminster Abby and continue up to London Bridge and then head back down the other shore to Archbishop's Park. No one would be the wiser until London had a massive health crisis on its hands.

A police patrol boat with the signature blue hull and fluorescent yellow and teal checkerboard cabin pressed in their direction. Seamus placed his weapon under the seat cushion and radioed Nial the warning. He then sat back and casually waved as they approached. The armed man on the deck looked him over carefully and waved back. Nial had his pistol sighted on Codi's head. She wanted to call out but it would have meant certain death. Patience. She would get her chance. The police boat sped off to continue their patrol, alert to anything suspicious. The message was clear to Nial—they were still incognito.

After years of looking for the right way to avenge his family's death at the hands of the calloused Brits, Nial now had the means. It was right in front of him and only a button push away. "Time to make history," he said and used his radio to call Seamus. "Remove the cover."

Seamus locked off the rudder so the boat would continue on a straight course. He climbed up to the roof of the houseboat and unlocked the faux roof panel.

Steam was starting to spew out of an overworked radiator, as the Defender 90 came to an abrupt stop. A line of cars close to a kilometer in length plugged the expressway. Fescue, without much thought pulled to the shoulder and kept going. Up ahead was a roadblock. The police were checking every car in a carefully orchestrated plan to keep London safe.

"We don't have time for this shit," Matt said.

Fescue knew he was right, but getting shot while trying to break through a roadblock seemed idiotic.

As they approached, several policemen took notice of the Defender driving on the shoulder and prepared to repel all boarders. Guns aimed and men fell into position to make short work of the approaching vehicle. Fescue waved frantically out the window, trying to look less threatening, but a police vehicle blocked the path and he hit the brakes.

The Defender was quickly surrounded and pandemonium followed, each party yelling at the other. Fescue desperately tried to plead his case. In the end Matt, Fescue and Joel all ended up face down on the ground, handcuffed.

One of the officers approached and said, "You are wanted in

connection with a murder of a government official. I recommend you save your statements until later."

"That was me!" Matt cried out. "These men were taking me to the police station."

Joel and Fescue looked over at Matt like he was crazy.

"They're with the FBI," Matt said, "and have been tasked with helping MI5 stop the threat to London."

Fescue was catching on. A slim glimmer of hope had appeared in the form of Matt playing the role of sacrificial lamb. "That's why we skipped the line of cars so we could get to you," Fescue said.

The officer paused.

"Call it in and see for yourself," Fescue said. "We're only minutes behind the madman and his planned attack and we need your help."

"Help them up and put them in the wagon. I'll call it in. You come with me." He pointed to Agent Fescue and walked over to his car radio.

Matt and Joel were escorted into the back of a police station wagon. It had a metal cage separating the front from the back. They were unceremoniously thrown inside and the door locked behind them.

Fescue knew he had about one minute before the officer learned the truth and they were all on their way to prison. The officer said, "Tell me what I need to know and I'll call this in."

Fescue gave the man his name, badge number and a contact. The officer seemed appeased for the moment and reached in to grab his radio. Rookie mistake, Fescue thought, as he reached his shackled hands around to his side and grabbed the man's gun. He whispered just loud enough for the man to hear. "Do anything stupid and I'll end you right here and now."

The officer's eyes widened in surprise and he made a very subtle nod. Agent Fescue kept his body against the car to block the view of the gun he was now holding. He also adapted a very casual body profile, one leg crossed over the other.

"Keep one hand on the radio and pass me your handcuff keys."

The officer complied.

Fescue removed one of his cuffs while still keeping the gun covertly pointed at his hostage. "Now hang up the radio mic and tell the other officers that we check out and that you're going to escort us into MI5 headquarters. Remember, if you try anything at all, you'll be the first to die. Nod one more time if you got it."

The officer nodded.

After a short speech, the officer and Fescue walked over to the police wagon. Just to be safe, Fescue had the officer enter on the passenger side and slide across to the driver's side. He followed behind with the pistol concealed in his shirt and aimed at the officer.

They drove off in a cloud of dust as the other officers pondered the strange event that had just taken place. They discussed it amongst themselves for a minute until one of them spoke the words they were all thinking: "Something's not right." He ran to his car and grabbed the radio.

"What's your name?" Fescue asked, as he passed the handcuff key through the mesh to Joel and Matt. They just looked at it, perplexed. They were both handcuffed with their hands behind their back. Fescue paid them no attention. He kept his focus on the driver.

Matt was the first to come up with a solution. He took the key with his lips, bent over and dropped the key into Joel's waiting hands.

"Officer Tommy Cromwell," the man said.

"Like in Oliver Cromwell?"

The man nodded.

"Exit up here." Fescue pointed to the Hendon Way ramp approaching on the left. "Be advised, possible police hostage situation..." The voice on the police radio left no doubts as to the severity of their situation.

"Tommy," Fescue said, "we are not going to kill you, so you can relax. But we are going to drop you off right here. Pull over and thanks for your help."

They dropped him off and the police wagon sped down Hendon Way, leaving Officer Cromwell in its wake. Fescue pushed the vehicle as hard as he could. The time for stealth was gone, each man knowing that any further delay guaranteed certain failure.

"Joel, I need your help," Fescue said. "Where are we and where are we going?"

Matt called out from the back seat, "We need to get to Grosvenor Road. It parallels the Thames along the north shore. It's our best chance to get eyes on the boat."

Joel, out of pure frustration said, "I'm sorry; I no longer have my phone or my computer."

"You mean the phone you smashed back there on the trail?" Matt said.

Joel looked even more miserable.

Fescue's phone wouldn't fit through the metal mesh, so he rolled down his window and handed it back to Joel, saying, "This is our last one, so try not to break it."

"My window won't roll down."

"Damn it!" Fescue looked over the buttons in the car and flicked one. Just then, a car pulled out in front of them and he had to swerve left and then make a sudden right to avoid it. "Try opening your door," Fescue said.

The unlock button did the trick and Joel opened the door and leaned out to grab the phone. Suddenly, the door of a parked car opened and Joel got back inside just before his door impacted with the other door. There was a sudden violent smash as Joel's door ripped loose. It dragged along the pavement, creating a shower of golden sparks that shot out behind them. Then it completely disconnected and was gone. Joel put his seatbelt back on and tightened it.

The closer they got to Grosvenor Road, the more traffic became a problem. Fescue flicked on the siren and one stubborn man finally pulled over. Joel was using Fescue's phone from the back to navigate. "At A202, turn right!" he called out to Fescue.

"Back seat driver," Fescue said as he turned the squealing vehicle down the new course.

But luck was in short supply and soon they had a tail. "Two police cruisers closing fast," Matt called out while looking over his shoulder.

"Great." Fescue said. "This day just keeps getting better and better."

Fescue swerved into oncoming cars to facilitate a possible delay for his new pursuers. The panicked drivers spun out in all directions, leaving a pile of cars for the chasing cops to navigate around. Matt watched their six o'clock. "That should buy us about ninety seconds," he said.

Joel kept up his stream of directions. "Grosvenor Road, two hundred meters." As Fescue turned left, Joel pointed. "There she is!"

Coming down the river was The Lady Rose. She was about fifty feet from shore and running at about ten knots. A sudden impact spun the vehicle around and into the curb. The police wagon sputtered and died.

Joel lifted his head and looked around. The front passenger section of the wagon was collapsed. Matt was on his lap, moaning, with blood in his hair. Broken glass was everywhere. Up front, Fescue was trying to kick his door open. Joel unbuckled his seatbelt and slid out of the wagon. He turned his attention to The Lady Rose, wondering if the pistol Fescue had would do any damage.

The door to the driver's side finally burst opened and Fescue crawled out.

Joel said, "They're getting–"

"I see it; come on." Fescue grabbed Joel's shirt and pulled him over to the van that had crashed into them. They helped the dazed man out of the driver's seat and placed him on the sidewalk.

Fescue reversed the grey Austin J2 van out of the crash. Steam shot from the radiator and one of the front wheels was bent. He jammed it into first gear, popped the clutch and immediately hit the brakes. Matt, still groggy, stood in the street right in front of them with one hand up. Joel scampered out of the van and pulled him inside. They quickly left the scene. A second later, multiple police cruisers appeared, guns drawn on the man lying on the sidewalk trying to remember what had happened.

Agent Fescue floored the old van, pushing it to the limit. He weaved in and out of several cars, trying to close the gap. They could see a man on the roof lowering a panel from what looked like a storage bin. Matt recognized it immediately. "They're getting ready to fire Skystorm!" he shouted.

Fescue slammed his fist on the steering wheel. They were out of time. He looked around frantically for a way to stop them. One pistol fired from the shore would have little or no effect.

"We need a boat," Joel said.

Fescue found what he was looking for, a chance at revenge and redemption all at once. "There's one right here. Get out!" He slammed the brakes and pointed to several skiffs tied along the water's edge. "Get out now!"

Joel and Matt exited the van armed with one pistol and a truckload of determination. Fescue smashed the pedal down on the van and sped off as fast as the old clunker would go. It took a couple of seconds for Matt and Joel to process his plan.

"Move it!" Joel said as he ran down to the shore to pick a boat.

Matt was close on his heels and nursing a massive headache.

Fescue tried to figure out his timing. There was an old dock that ran out about forty feet into the river. The tide was down and the dock was about ten feet out of the water. The Lady Rose would cross its path in about forty seconds. He jerked the wheel to the left and crashed through a pile of crab cages and onto the rickety dock. He held the accelerator to the floor and prayed. It was going to be close.

Rubber tires bit on loose wooden planks. Some gave way, others held in place. The dock's support poles groaned at the added weight of the vehicle. Fescue could feel the old dock shuddering, but somehow she held. The man on the roof had his back to the shore as he removed the shroud concealing Skystorm. Fescue leaned forward as if to will the van to move faster.

Over the years, the old dock had sunk slightly in the middle, making the last twenty feet act as a ramp. The man on the houseboat turned to see the speeding vehicle coming his way. It took a beat for him to realize what was happening. Agent Fescue gripped the steering wheel and let loose a wild battle cry as he flew off the end of the pier and went airborne.

Codi was desperate to make a move, any move. Her leg burned like crazy and she could feel how light-headed she'd become from blood loss. The worst of it was being forced to lie on her stomach. Any kind of quick attack was impossible. Nial would see it coming a long way off. She peeked over her shoulder and watched as he laid down his pistol next to a remote of some sort.

Seamus' voice came over the radio. "We are good to go."

Nial glanced down at Codi to be sure she was still just where he needed her. He flicked the safety switch off and pressed the green button to fire Skystorm. He looked out the window at the crowded skyline. This was it.

Codi didn't hesitate. She rolled under the table and onto her back. She used her legs like a catapult and launched the table up into the air. Nial's gun and the remote went flying.

He quickly responded and threw the table off to the side as he lashed out at Codi who was still on the floor. She started to get up but Nial pounced, body impacting body. They wrestled and fought in an ugly way. Nial used his knee to inflict more pain in Codi's bullet wound and Codi used her elbows to keep Nial off balance, each one trying to gain advantage over the other, until, finally, Codi managed to get one of her knees up under Nial. He stabbed his thumb deep into her wounded leg. She grimaced at the pain but managed to thrust him back and away.

The van angled up slightly as it left the dock, wheels still spinning looking for purchase that would never come. It then angled nose-down as it made contact with the side of The Lady Rose. Metal and wood parted and shredded in every direction. Everything moved in slow motion for Fescue. The man on the roof disappeared, as did a large chunk of the roof. The steering wheel flew towards his forehead, or was it the other way around? Everything went black.

Seamus had just finished removing the last panel attached to the roof of the houseboat. Skystorm was ready to fire. He had called down to Nial to see if he had heard his radio message when a strange sound caught his attention. He turned to see a mass of steel and aluminum soaring through the air right at him. By the time he took action, everything he once was, was gone.

After Codi pushed him, Nial landed on his feet like a cat. A loud crunching noise followed as the damaged front grill of a grey Austin J2 van entered the room, catching Nial just above the shoulders on its journey to the other side of the cabin and into the river. Nial had no time to react or think. His head simply removed itself from his body and flew out of the cabin with the van.

The impact on The Lady Rose slammed Codi against the bulkhead. It was so violent that the hull of the ship broke apart and the ship began to sink. Codi lay in a contorted heap as the world around her began to ripple. She felt her body slip beneath the void. No struggle, no fight, just a peaceful embrace and a short trip to the other side.

Matt and Joel scrambled over the bank and down to the collection of small craft. Joel jumped into the nearest skiff, connected the fuel line and pulled the cord to start her up. The old wooden skiff's fifteen-horsepower outboard coughed a bluish-grey smoke and turned over. He backed it out while Matt loosed the lines and jumped aboard. They turned and headed for The Lady Rose with one pistol and a single mindset—kill or be killed.

The wreck site was a mess of flotsam and jetsam. Matt had one thing on his mind and she was nowhere to be found. A sliver of a reflection from the dark water caught his attention. Without a second thought, he dove in.

The water was cold and strived to pull the air from his lungs, but Matt held tight, pushing himself deeper into the abyss. He was chasing a ghost, a reflection. As he moved deeper, that reflection materialized into an unmoving Agent Codi Sanders. He kicked a little more and grabbed an arm that was drifting upwards. He turned and pushed himself to the surface. His lungs bucked with an intense desire to breathe in. Matt fought it, but he was losing the battle as sparks and darkness flashed in his periphery.

His body moved mechanically, towing Codi upward to salvation. He could sense more than see the surface as his body started to fail him. It was shutting down, but he continued upward solely on muscle reflex. Three feet from breaking the surface, it was over. He involuntarily opened his mouth and the water poured in. The cold liquid filled his lungs and caused him to spasm twice. A white hand reaching out for him glowed in the distance and then darkness enveloped him.

Matt was dragged to the surface. Joel had a firm grip on him and somehow Matt still held onto Codi. Joel pulled them into the boat and started resuscitation on Codi while Matt lay on the deck coughing up a lung-full of water.

When his lungs were finally clear, Matt took in his surroundings.

Joel was not stopping his mouth-to-mouth on Codi, no matter what. Several seconds passed with no results and then a minute. Joel kept checking for a heartbeat. It was still perceptible, but fading. The two-minute mark came and went, still nothing.

"Come on, you stubborn bitch—*breathe!*" Matt yelled at her.

The cough that followed was the sweetest sound either man had ever heard. Joel turned Codi on her side as she coughed and vomited her way back to life. Afterward, she sat up on the side of the boat and looked around, a bit confused. She was a mess. Her hair was matted against her head. Her face and skin was as pale as snow. Joel and Matt just sat staring back at her with the biggest smiles ever.

"Where's Fescue?" she asked in a raspy voice. There was no sign of The Lady Rose or the Skystorm.

"Crap!" They'd forgotten all about him. Matt and Joel looked around. About three hundred yards downriver was a semi-submerged grey Austin J2 van floating with the tide.

The three jumped into the skiff. Matt hit the gas and motored alongside the van. Inside, the driver was rubbing his bloody forehead trying to orient himself. "Need a lift?" Matt asked him.

Agent Fescue looked at the waterlogged trio and started to laugh. But his head throbbed so badly he had to stop. "Any thoughts on how we're going to explain our way out of a British prison?" he asked as he climbed out the window and into the boat.

Matt turned the craft and returned to shore. "No," he said. "But if you think I'm going to be your bunkmate, forget it."

"Don't worry. I'm sure you and Bubba will get along just fine."

CHAPTER THIRTY-SEVEN

Parked along the Albert embankment next to the St. Thomas Hospital, Carson of Flush, Inc. Toilet Devices waited for a man that would never arrive. Nial had arranged for him to wait there to pick him up. But there was no sign of him and he was not answering his phone. After waiting three hours past their meeting time, Carson put his cargo van in gear and returned to Liverpool.

Solimon Granger had arrived at the appointed time, but Nial was no-where to be found. He sent for Sean Wright to join him on the yacht and Sean did his best to appease the buyer. But Solimon was not a patient man and after a host of unacceptable excuses from the operator of the Shipwright Repair & Salvage Company, Solimon gave a barely imperceptible nod. His assistant pulled a silenced Walther PPK from behind his back and shot Sean in the face. The luxury yacht turned and left Hull, steaming back across the channel to Rotterdam. A weighted body would be discreetly dropped over the side on the trip back.

"Let me see if I have this right," Director Ruth Anne Gables read from a very official-looking document as she paced the small conference room at MI5. "Wanton destruction of public property, stolen property, kidnapping a fellow officer, exceeding the speed limit multiple times on land and over water." She looked over at them and said, "Too bad you didn't have a plane, you could have gone for the trifecta."

Codi, Joel and Agent Fescue sat at the table as she summarized their "escapades," as she called them.

"Threatening citizens with guns," she continued.

Joel tried to remember when they had done that, "Oh yeah," he said.

"Destruction of property, both government and civil, multiple murders, attempted murder." Director Gables let out a heavy sigh and put the document down. "Need I go on?"

"What about saving the lives of thousands of people?" Codi asked.

The group had been met at the river's edge by a host of guns and MI5 agents. They were temporarily patched up and taken to the basement of MI5 headquarters where they were locked in the small room with a few bottles of water and a cold pizza. Matt, being a civilian, was taken to another room.

Joel inspected the pizza and said, "Last meal, anyone?"

Fescue's entire head was wrapped in gauze. Codi had her leg patched up and was wearing MI5 sweatpants.

Director Gables was torn. She wanted to believe her team, but the evidence against them was overwhelming. "You have to see things from their perspective," she said. "A group of rogue agents sent the authorities chasing their tails for two days at the cost of over a million dollars. For what? There has been no attack and *no* evidence of any weapon or Nial Brennan." She lowered her head at the next thought. "They are beginning to think you made everything up to save your asses back in France."

Agent Fescue attempted to explain. "Director, we–"

"No! You don't get to speak yet. I have backed your play because I believe what you have told me. But right now, very few others do. So what I want is one hundred percent cooperation until we get this mess sorted out. Is that clear?"

Subtle head nods followed.

There was a brief knock on the door followed by a man wearing a custom tailored Andersen & Sheppard suit entering the room. He cleared his throat and spoke in a hushed tone to the Director. She nodded and stepped aside. The man cleared his throat. "I am Jonathan Stanberry, Director General here at MI5." He hemmed and hawed a bit and then, in a softer voice said, "It appears we owe you an apology."

"Guinness all around," Matt ordered.

Codi and the team were at a large table in the back of the Bleeding Heart Yard, a famous French restaurant in the heart of London. The authorities, with the help of divers, had managed to salvage what was left of Skystorm and a couple of the canisters of the hybrid smallpox virus. They had also recovered the headless body of Nial Brennan. The coroner made a positive ID and the group suddenly looked like heroes instead of suspects. This was what prompted the turnaround from the Director General himself.

Director Ruth Anne Gables had insisted on taking everyone out to dinner to celebrate on the GSA's dime. She couldn't have been more pleased with her team. In spite of the loss of a key team member and the hell they had all endured, not one of them had given up. They had come through and done whatever it took to save lives and solve the case.

The group, on the other hand, had only one desire—find a bed and sleep for the next five days. Two of them had only <u>one</u> bed in mind.

EPILOGUE

DC was thick with traffic as Joel made his way to the cemetery. The sky was heavy with clouds and the air was chilly. The funeral of Special Agent Annie Waters was an affair the FBI took very seriously. A twenty-one-gun salute and even the Director, James T. Morrison, gave a speech. His black Burberry trench coat was a perfect match to his jet-black hair. Joel and Codi stood next to Agent Fescue among a group of other government agents. Joel had already come to terms with Annie's death, but seeing her coffin lowered into the ground brought back a host of emotions. The cost was heavy.

The following day, Joel's trip to the office was made in silence rather than with the radio chatter that filled his usual commutes. He held his coffee cup in one hand as he turned into the parking structure with the other. Two weeks off had healed his physical wounds, but the events he endured were still fresh in his mind. He was ready to get back at it. More than anything, he needed the distraction.

As he walked past the glass wall that separated the conference room from the rest of the offices, a raised hand motioned him in. Inside, his boss, Director Ruth Anne Gables, was meeting with Codi and Agent Fescue. Joel took a seat and a sip from his coffee.

"Good morning, sunshine." Codi smiled.

"How are you feeling?" asked Director Gables.

"I actually feel pretty good."

"Good, because we have some business to attend to and you're part of it."

Director Gables sat down. "First off, to bring you all up to date since your little vacation."

Codi's mind flashed back to the time she and Matt had spent at the little coastal cottage in Ireland. The Director General of MI5 had personally set it up. In fact, he had set up each member with a two-week all-expenses-paid leave to rest and recuperate, compliments of Her Majesty's government.

Agent Fescue had his wife Leila and their four-year-old son Tristan, meet him in Bermuda where they stayed at the Rosedon Hotel on Hamilton Harbor.

Joel finally got to see London as a real tourist, though the pain in his heart dimmed his enthusiasm. He kept himself busy enough and tried not to let the what-ifs get to him. They put him up in The Langham London on Bond Street. His bed was a dream to behold and the suite was first rate. He could easily access all the popular sights and the selfie he took with the unflinching palace guard would have a place of prominence on his desktop.

The Irish coast is littered with green cliffs and sandy beaches. Matt and Codi's cottage had a traditional thatched roof and whitewashed rock façade. The two-bedroom home was steps away from the sand where it slipped into a beautiful blue-tinged sea, too cold to swim in. Matt built a fire in the fireplace to chase away the ever-present chill.

Codi used her crutches to maneuver to the couch. Her wounded leg set limits, but her long slender body, full breasts and longing look had Matt's mouth watering and his mind racing. He stepped over to the couch and paused for a second before bending over and taking her into his arms. He picked her up and carried her into a quaint bedroom with natural hand-hewn wood ceiling beams. The simple modern furnishings contrasted nicely with the white walls. The royal blue hand-quilted comforter was the only pop of color in the room. He laid her on the quilt taking extra care of her leg. "Ouch!"

Codi grimaced as she slid back onto the bed to get more comfortable. Matt followed, crawling up beside his beautiful prize, hoping.

"I can see you're out of commission for a while," he said. "Pain is to be expected, but a life without passion is one I'll skip" she said as she grabbed Matt and pulled him down on top of her. The pain was excruciating, but she had more important things on her mind. She drew his lips to hers and finally relaxed. This time, they felt like they had all the time in the world. Matt was gently aggressive and took his time. Soon they found a position that worked for both.

"Agent Sanders?"

Codi snapped out of her trance at the sound of her name. "Huh?" she said.

"I asked, how's the leg?" Director Gables said.

"As you can see, no crutches," Codi answered. "But I won't be winning any races anytime soon."

"Good to know." Director Gables continued. "A quick update. The vaccine that you gave Agent Witherspoon never made it into the hands of MI5. But luckily, a group out of South Africa has discovered one and is shipping it out as fast as they can manufacture it."

"We should have bought stock," a jaded Agent Fescue added.

"The death toll stands at thirty eight. We're lucky it wasn't in the thousands or more. No additional deaths have been reported in the last week. Honestly, a large part of the credit goes to everyone here today. MI5 tracked multiple calls on Agent Witherspoon's phone to a burner found on the body of Nial Brennan. Doctor Campbell is in a military lab somewhere rebuilding Skystorm, this time with the utmost security. Basically, the threat is over. Good work by all."

"On another note," Director Gables continued, "I am being transferred to a new position."

Codi suddenly perked up.

"I will be director of special projects, a division within the FBI."

They were happy for their boss and congratulated her.

"But I took the job on one condition." Director Gables paused to make sure she had their attention. "I want you three to come and work with me."

The silence in the room was palpable. Then, one by one, they started to get excited. For Codi, this was a dream come true. She had always felt like she had more to offer and this was exactly how she could do it.

"One more thing," Director Gables said. "It seems there are a few people that have requested your presence for a personal thank you." Director Gables picked up a document and read. "The President of France, the Prime Minister of England and the President of the United States all want to meet you."

Codi and Agent Fescue were shell-shocked, but not Joel, who said, "Prime Minister? I was hoping to meet the Queen."

Everyone broke out in laughter except Joel.

"What?"

THANKS

Thank you for taking the time to read this book. As the author, there is nothing better than for others to enjoy reading as much as I enjoyed writing this book. If you liked it please let others know and please post a positive review. It is the single best way to promote what I am doing and critical to the continuation of the characters.

Interesting Facts

For more details go to my website and see as well
as read these details. brentladdbooks.com

Cat Island War Dog Reception and Training Center

During World War II, Cat Island was the location of the Cat Island
War Dog Reception and Training Center. Americans sent family dogs
to be trained by the US Army Signal Corps for military service. An attempt was made to train them to sniff out Japanese Americans with the
belief that they had a distinct odor. After much time and money the center was closed as this particular experiment was totally unsuccessful.

SS Dagger

The SS Ehrendolch (SS honor dagger or SS dagger) was considered
an honor weapon of the SS in the Third Reich. Heinrich Himmler
personally designed the awarding ceremony conducted according to
a strict set of rules. The SS dagger was introduced in December, 1933.
Production of these honor daggers was suspended in 1940.

Welrod

The Welrod was a British bolt-action magazine-fed suppressed pistol. It was devised during World War II at the Inter-Services Research
Bureau (later Station 9). It was designed for use by irregular forces and

resistance groups. It used baffles in the barrel to slow the 9mm round down to subsonic speed. Approximately 2,800 were made.

WWII Black Soldiers With Gas Masks

World War II experiments with poisonous gas were done in secret and weren't recorded on the test subjects' official military records. Most soldiers did not have proof of what they went through. African-American soldiers were the most common guinea pigs. They received no follow-up health care or monitoring of any kind. Some were sworn to secrecy about the tests under threat of dishonorable discharge and military prison time.

X Gas rationing Sticker

The "X" sticker was issued in special instances of high-mileage jobs such as traveling salesmen that needed be able to purchase gasoline in unlimited quantities. Many of the wealthy and politicians also received these stickers. But the average American had to severely limit their driving. Gas rationing wasn't their primary objective. The main purpose was to conserve tires. Japanese armies had cut off the US from its chief supply of rubber.

Ball lightning

Ball lightning is an unexplained atmospheric electrical phenomenon. The term refers to reports of luminous, spherical objects, which vary in diameter. It is usually associated with thunderstorms but lasts considerably longer than the split-second flash of a lightning bolt. Many early reports said that the ball eventually explodes, sometimes with fatal consequences. Laboratory experiments can produce effects that are visually similar to ball lightning.

Quonset Hut

A Quonset hut is a lightweight prefabricated structure of corrugated galvanized steel. It has a semicircular cross-section. The Q-hut was developed in the United States, but the design was based on the Nissen hut introduced by the British during World War I. Hundreds of thousands were produced during World War II and many were sold to the public as military surplus.

Fort Boyard

Fort Boyard is a fort located in the Pertuis D' Antioche Straits on the west coast of France. In the 1800s under Napoleon Bonaparte, work began. Fort Boyard is oval-shaped, 223ft long and 102ft wide. The walls were built 66ft high. At the center is a courtyard and the ground floor provided stores and quarters for the men and officers. The fortifications were completed in 1857. However, by the time of its completion, the range of cannons had significantly increased, making the fort unnecessary for national defense. After 1871, Fort Boyard served briefly as a military prison before being abandoned at the beginning of the 20th century. It still stands today and is an imposing sight.

Canal Boat

A narrowboat or canal boat is a boat of a distinctive design, made to fit the narrow canals of the United Kingdom. These boats were built as early as the 18th century and were used to carry and transport goods throughout he country. The canals are now used only for recreation and hundreds of Canal Boats filled with vacationers ply the countryside every year.

ACKNOWLEDGEMENTS

With deep appreciation to all those who encouraged me to write and especially those who didn't. I wanted to thank the following editors for their efforts to keep my punctuation honest. First my editors Cathy Hull and Jordan Kaiser. A host of family and friends who suffered through early drafts and were kind enough to share their oppinions. Jeff Klem, who came up with the book's title, Dodie Merrill, Debbi Stephenson, Jeff Loefke and my lovely wife Leesa. Also to Raymond Obstfeld who has been an encouraging force to me and many other writers. As many concepts as possible are based on actual or historical details. Special thanks to the original action hero—my dad, Dr. Paul Loefke. Also writers live and die by their reviews – So if you liked my book PLEASE review it!

ABOUT THE AUTHOR

Writer Director Brent Ladd has been a part of the Hollywood scene for almost three decades. His work has garnered awards and accolades all over the globe. Brent has been involved in the creation and completion of hundreds of commercials for clients large and small. He is an avid beach volleyball player and an adventurer at heart. He currently resides in Irvine, CA with his wife and children.

Brent found his way into novel writing when his son, Brady showed little interest in reading. He wrote his first book making Brady the main character – *The Adventures of Brady Ladd*. Enjoying that experience, Brent went on to concept and complete his 1st novel, *Terminal Pulse, A Codi Sanders Thriller* - The first in a series.

Brent is a fan of a plot driven story with strong intelligent characters. So if you're looking for a fast paced escape, check out the Codi Sanders series. You can also find out more on his next book and when it will be available, please visit his website – BrentLaddBooks.com

Printed in the United States
By Bookmasters